Going
HOME

Going HOME

BRIDES OF WEBSTER COUNTY I

WANDA E. BRUNSTETTER

BARBOUR BOOKS
An Imprint of Barbour Publishing, Inc.

© 2007 by Wanda E. Brunstetter

Print ISBN 978-1-63058-712-3

eBook Editions:
Adobe Digital Edition (.epub) 978-1-63409-233-3
Kindle and MobiPocket Edition (.prc) 978-1-63409-234-0

All scripture quotations are taken from the King James Version of the Bible.

All Pennsylvania Dutch words are taken from the *Revised Pennsylvania German Dictionary* found in Lancaster County, Pennsylvania.

This book is a work of fiction. Names, characters, places, and incidents are either products of the author's imagination or used fictitiously. Any similarity to actual people, organizations, and/or events is purely coincidental.

Published by Barbour Books, an imprint of Barbour Publishing, Inc., P.O. Box 719, Uhrichsville, Ohio 44683, www.barbourbooks.com

Our mission is to publish and distribute inspirational products offering exceptional value and biblical encouragement to the masses.

Member of the
Evangelical Christian
Publishers Association

Printed in the United States of America.

Dedication/Acknowledgments

To my in-laws in Pennsylvania who make
"going home" a joyful experience.
And to all my Amish friends who make me
feel at home whenever I come to visit.

Without faith it is impossible to please him:
for he that cometh to God must believe
that he is, and that he is a rewarder
of them that diligently seek him.
Hebrews 11:6

Chapter 1

Faith Andrews stared out the bus window, hoping to focus on something other than her immediate need. She feasted her eyes on rocky hills, scattered trees, and a June sky so blue she felt she could swim in it. Faith had always loved this stretch of road in her home state of Missouri. She'd traveled it plenty of times over the last ten years, going from Branson to Springfield and back again, making numerous stage appearances in both towns. She had also been in Tennessee, Arkansas, and several other southern states, but her favorite place to entertain was Branson, where the shows were family-oriented, lively, and fun.

Not like some nightclubs where her husband, who had also doubled as her agent, had booked her during the early days of her career. Faith hated those gigs, with leering men who sometimes shouted obscene remarks and people who asked dumb questions about the getup Greg insisted she wear for a time.

"You need to wear your Amish garb," he had told her. "It can be your trademark."

Faith shook her head at the memory. *I'm glad I finally convinced him to let me go with the hillbilly look instead. Wearing Amish clothes only reminded me of the past and made me feel homesick.*

Whenever Faith was onstage, the past, present, and future disappeared like trees hidden in the forest on a foggy day. When she entertained, her focus was on only one thing: telling jokes and yodeling her heart out for an appreciative audience—something she had wanted since she was a child.

Faith closed her eyes, relishing the vision of a performance she had given six months ago at a small theater in the older part of Branson. Her jokes had brought down the house. She liked it when she could make people laugh. Too bad it was a talent that had never been valued until she'd become a professional entertainer. Her family had made it clear that they didn't care for humor—at least not hers. Maybe she wouldn't have felt the need to run away if they'd been more accepting of her silliness.

Faith's thoughts took her back to the stage as she remembered receiving a standing ovation and basking in the warmth of it long after the theater was empty. How could she have known her world would be turned upside down in a single moment following the performance that night? When Faith took her final bow, she had no idea she would be burying her husband of seven years a few days later or that she would be sitting on a bus right now, heading for home.

Going back to her birthplace outside the town of Seymour, Missouri, was something Faith had been afraid to do. So near yet so far away, she'd been these last ten years, and never once had she returned for a visit. She feared that she wouldn't have been welcomed, for she'd been a rebellious teenager, refusing baptism and membership into the Amish church and running off to do her own thing.

During the first few years of Faith's absence, she had sent a couple of notes to her childhood companion Barbara Raber, but that was the only contact she'd had with anyone from home. If not for the necessity of finding a stable environment for Melinda, Faith wouldn't be going home now.

She turned away from the window, and her gaze came to rest on the sleeping child beside her. Her six-year-old daughter's cheeks had turned rosy as her eyelids had closed in slumber soon after they'd boarded the bus in Branson.

Faith smiled at the memory of Melinda bouncing around while they waited in the bus station. "Mama," the little girl had said, "I can't wait to get on the bus and go see where you used to live."

"I hope you like what you see, my precious little girl," Faith murmured as she studied her daughter. The little girl's head lolled against Faith's arm, and her breathing was sweet and even. Melinda had been sullen since her father's death. Maybe the change of scenery and a slower-paced, simpler lifestyle would be what she needed.

Faith pushed a wayward strand of golden hair away from Melinda's face. She looked a lot like Faith had as a little girl—same blond hair and clear blue eyes, only Melinda wore her hair hanging down her back or in a ponytail. In the Amish community, she would be expected to wear it pulled into a tight bun at the back of her head, then covered with a stiff white *kapp*, the way Faith had done for so many years.

Will Mama and Papa accept my baby girl, even though they might not take kindly to me? Will Melinda adjust to her new surroundings, so plain and devoid of all the worldly things she's been used to? When I'm gone, will she feel as though I've abandoned her, even though I'll promise to come and visit as often as I can?

As Faith took hold of her daughter's small hand, she felt a familiar burning in the back of her throat. She relished the warmth and familiarity of Melinda's soft skin and could hardly fathom what it would be like for the two of them once they were separated. Yet she would do anything for her child, and she was convinced it would be better for Melinda to live with her grandparents than to be hauled all over the countryside with only one parent. She'd been doing that ever since Greg had died six months ago, and things hadn't gone so well.

Besides the fact that Faith still hadn't secured another agent to book her shows, she'd had a terrible time coming up with a babysitter for Melinda. At times, she'd had to take the child with her to rehearsals and even some shows. Melinda sat offstage and one of the other performers looked after her as Faith did her routine, but that arrangement was anything but ideal. Faith had finished up her contract at a theater in Branson last night, and this morning, she and Melinda had boarded the bus. Faith wouldn't go back to entertaining until she felt free to do so, which meant she had to know Melinda was in good hands and had adjusted to her new surroundings.

Faith had left her name with a couple of talent agencies in Memphis and Nashville and had said she would call them soon to check on the possibility of getting an agent. She hoped Melinda would have time to adapt before Faith had to leave her.

Faith gripped the armrest as she thought about her other options. When Greg's parents had come to Branson for his funeral, they'd offered their assistance. "Remember now, Faith," Elsie had said, "if you need anything, just give us a call."

Faith figured the offer was made purely out of obligation, for Jared and Elsie Andrews were too self-centered to care about anyone but themselves. She wasn't about to ask if Melinda could live with Greg's parents. That would be the worst thing possible, even if his folks were willing to take on the responsibility of raising their granddaughter.

Elsie and Jared lived in Los Angeles, and Jared was an alcoholic. Faith had met her husband's parents only once before his death. That was shortly after she'd married Greg. She and Greg had stayed with the Andrewses for one week while they visited Disneyland, Knott's Berry Farm, and some other sights in the area. It hadn't taken Faith long to realize that Greg's parents weren't fit to raise any child. Elsie Andrews was a woman who seemed to care only about her own needs. During their visit, the woman had talked endlessly about her elite circle of friends and when she was scheduled for her next facial or hair appointment. Greg's father always seemed to have a drink in his hand, and he'd used language so foul Faith had cringed every time he opened his mouth. Melinda would be better off in Webster County with her Plain relatives than she would with grandparents who thought more about alcohol and mudpacks than about having a relationship with their only son and his wife.

Faith let her eyelids close once more, allowing herself to travel back to when she was a teenager. She saw herself in her father's barn, sitting on a bale of hay, yodeling and telling jokes to her private audience of two buggy horses and a cat named Boots. . . .

"Faith Stutzman, what do you think you're doing?"

Faith whirled around at the sound of her father's deep voice. His face was a mask of anger, his dark eyebrows drawn together so they almost met in the middle.

"I was entertaining the animals," she said, feeling her defenses rising. *"I don't see any harm in doing that, Papa."*

He scowled at her. *"Is that a fact? What about the chores you were sent out here to do? Have you finished those yet?"*

She shook her head. *"No, but I'm aimin' to get them done real soon."*

Papa nudged her arm with his knuckles. *"Then you'd better get up and do 'em! And no more of that silly squawkin' and howlin'. You sound like a frog with a sore throat, trying to do that silly yodeling stuff."* He started for the barn door but turned back around. *"You've always been a bit of a rebel, and it isn't getting any better now that you've reached your teen years."* He shook his finger at Faith. *"You'd better start spending more time reading the scriptures and praying and less time in town soaking up all kinds of worldly stuff on the sly. You'll surely die in your sins if you don't get yourself under control and prepare for baptism soon."*

When the barn door slammed shut, Faith stuck out her tongue, feeling more defiant than ever. *"I should be allowed to tell jokes and yodel whenever I choose,"* she grumbled to Barney, one of their driving horses. *"And I shouldn't have to put up with my* daed's *outbursts or his mean, controlling ways, either."* She plucked a piece of hay from the bale on which she sat and snapped off the end. *"I'll show you, Papa. I'll show everyone in this family that I don't need a single one of you. I'll find someone who appreciates my talents and doesn't criticize me for everything I do."*

As Faith's thoughts returned to the present, she tried to focus her attention on the scenery whizzing past. She couldn't. Her mind was a jumble of confusion. Was returning to Webster County the right thing?

I'm doing what I have to do. Melinda needs a secure home, and this is the best way to make that happen. Faith thought about Greg and how, even though he wasn't the ideal husband, he had secured plenty of engagements for her.

Never mind that he'd kept a good deal of the money she'd made to support his drinking and gambling habits. Never mind that Greg had been harsh with her at times.

It's sad, she mused. *Greg's been gone six months, yet I grieved for him only a short time. Even then, it wasn't really my husband I missed. It was my agent and the fact that he took care of our daughter while I was working. If he hadn't lined up several shows for me, I probably would have returned to Webster County sooner.*

Faith popped a couple of her knuckles. It was a bad habit—her parents had said so often enough—but it helped relieve some of her tension. *I'll never marry again—that's for certain sure. It would be hard to trust another man.* She drew in a deep breath and tried to relax. She'd be home in a few hours and would know whether she had made the right decision. If her folks accepted Melinda, the grandchild they knew nothing about, Faith could be fairly certain things would work out. If they rejected her, then Faith would need to come up with another plan.

❦

Noah Hertzler wiped his floury hands on a dish towel and smiled. He was alone in the kitchen and had created another cake he was sure would tempt even the most finicky person. Being the youngest of ten boys, with no sisters in the family, Noah had been the only son who had eagerly helped Mom in the kitchen from the time he was a small boy. In Noah's mind, his ability to cook was a God-given talent— one he enjoyed sharing with others through the breads, cookies, cakes, and pies he often made to give away. If he heard of someone who was emotionally down or physically under the weather, he set right to work baking a scrumptious dessert for that person. He always attached a note that included one of his favorite scripture verses. "Food for the stomach and nourishment for the soul"—that's what Mom called Noah's gifts to others.

Noah stared out the kitchen window into the backyard where he had played as a child. Growing up, he'd been shy, unable to express his thoughts or feelings the way most children usually did. When his friends or brothers gathered to play, Noah had spent time either alone in the barn or with his mother in the kitchen. Even now, at age twenty-four, he was somewhat reserved and spoke only when he felt something needed to be said. Noah thought that was why he hadn't married yet. The truth was, he'd been too shy to pursue a woman, although he had never found anyone he wanted to court.

Noah figured another reason for his single status was because he wasn't so good-looking. Not that he was ugly, for Mom had often said his thick, mahogany-colored hair was real nice and that his dark brown eyes reminded her of a box of sweet chocolates. Of course, all mothers thought their offspring were cute and sweet; it was the way of a good mother's heart to see the best in her flesh-and-blood children.

Instinctively, Noah touched his nose. It was too big and had a small hump in the middle of it. He'd taken a lot of ribbing from his friends during childhood over that beak. He could still hear his schoolmates chanting, "Noah! Noah! Nobody knows of anything bigger than Noah's huge nose!"

Forcing his thoughts to return to the present, Noah's gaze came to rest on the old glider, which sat under the red-leafed maple tree in their backyard. He had seen many of his brothers share that swing with their sweethearts, but Noah had never known the pleasure. Since his teen years, he'd shown an interest in only a few girls, and those relationships didn't involve more than a ride home in Noah's open buggy after a young people's singing on a Sunday night. He had never taken it any further because the girls hadn't shown much interest in him.

Most everyone in the community thought Noah was a confirmed bachelor; some had said so right to his face. But he didn't care what others thought. Noah was content to work five days a week for Hank Osborn, a local English man who raised Christmas trees. In the evenings and on weekends, Noah helped his mother at home. Mom was sixty-two years old and had been diagnosed with type 2 diabetes several years ago. As careful as she was about her diet, her health was beginning to fail so she needed Noah's help more than ever—especially since he was the only son still living at home. All nine of Noah's brothers were married with families of their own. Pop, at age sixty-four, still kept busy with farm chores and raising his fat hogs. He surely didn't have time to help his wife with household chores or cooking. Not that he would have anyway. Noah's father disliked indoor chores, even hauling firewood into the kitchen, which had been Noah's job since he was old enough to hold a chunk of wood in his chubby little hands.

Bringing his reflections to a halt, Noah began to mix up the batter for two tasty lemon sponge cakes in separate bowls. He would make one of the cakes using a sugar substitute, for him and his folks. The other cake would be given away as soon as he found someone who had a need. Noah had already decided to use Hebrews 11:6 with the cake: "But without faith it is impossible to please him: for he that cometh to God must believe that he is, and that he is a rewarder of them that diligently seek him."

"Is someone in the community struggling with a lack of faith?" Noah murmured. "Do they need a reminder that will encourage their heart and help strengthen their trust in God?" He felt confident that the Lord would direct him to the right person. He could hardly wait to see who it might be.

When Faith and Melinda got off the bus at Lazy Lee's Gas Station in Seymour, Faith picked up their two suitcases and herded Melinda toward the building. The unmistakable aroma of cow manure from a nearby farm assaulted her. She was almost home, and there was no turning back. She had come this far and would go the rest of the way as soon as she found them a ride.

Faith didn't recognize the balding, middle-aged man working inside the gas station, but she introduced herself and asked him about hiring someone to drive them to her folks' place. He said his name was Ed Moore and mentioned that he'd only been living in Seymour a couple of years.

"My wife, Doris, is coming in for some gas soon, and since we live just off Highway C, she plans to stop by an Amish farm out that way and buy some fresh eggs," Ed said. "I'm sure she'd be more than happy to give you a lift."

Faith wondered which Amish family from her community was selling eggs. Could it be Mama or one of her sisters? "If your wife is willing to give us a ride, it would be most appreciated," she said.

"Don't think it'll be a problem. Nope, not a problem at all." Ed grinned at her, revealing a set of badly stained, crooked teeth. "You can wait here inside the store if you want to."

"It might be best if we waited outside," Faith replied. "I wouldn't want to miss your wife."

"Suit yourself."

Faith led Melinda outside, and they took a seat on the bench near the front door. "You'll be meeting your grandpa and grandma Stutzman soon," she said, smiling at Melinda, whose eyes darted back and forth as she sat stiffly on the bench.

Melinda's nose twitched. "Somethin' smells funny. I don't know if I'm gonna like it here."

"That's the way farms smell, Melinda. We're in the country now."

Melinda folded her arms but said nothing more.

A short time later, a red station wagon pulled up to the pumps, and Ed came out of the building and proceeded to fill the tank with gas. When he was done, he said something to the dark-haired, middle-aged woman sitting in the vehicle. After a few minutes, he motioned for Faith and Melinda to come over. "This here's my wife, Doris, and she's agreed to give you a ride." Before Faith could respond, Ed opened the back of the station wagon and deposited their suitcases inside.

"I appreciate this, and I'll be happy to pay

you," Faith said to Doris as she and Melinda climbed into the backseat of the vehicle.

"No need for that," Doris said with a wave of her hand. "Ed and I live out that way anyhow."

"Thank you." Faith tucked her daughter's white cotton blouse under the band of her blue jeans; then she buckled the child's seat belt just as Doris pulled her vehicle out of the parking lot.

Melinda pressed her nose to the window as the station wagon headed down Highway C. "Look at all the farms. There's so many animals!"

"Yep, lots of critters around here," Doris chimed in.

Faith reached over and patted Melinda's knee. "Your grandma and grandpa have all kinds of animals you'll soon get to know."

Melinda made no comment, and Faith wondered what her little girl was thinking. Would her daughter find joy in the things on the farm, or would she become restless and bored, the way Faith had? She hoped Melinda would adjust to the new surroundings and respond well to her grandparents and other family members.

Closing her eyes, Faith leaned into the seat and tried to relax. She would deal first with seeing her folks and then worry about how well Melinda would adjust. She only had the strength to work through one problem at a time.

Twenty minutes later, they pulled into the gravel driveway of her parents' farm. Faith opened the car door and stepped out. Letting her gaze travel around the yard, she was amazed at how little it had changed. Everything looked nearly the same as the day she'd left home. The house was still painted white. The front porch sagged on one end, the way it had for as long as Faith could remember. Dark shades hung at each of the windows.

A wagonload of steel milk cans was parked out by the garden, and two open buggies sat near the barn. Her folks' mode of transportation was obviously the same as it always had been. Even as a child, Faith had never understood why their district drove only open buggies. Traveling in such a way could be downright miserable when the weather turned cold and snowy. She'd heard it said that the Webster County Amish were one of the strictest in their beliefs of the Plain communities in America. Seeing her parents' simple home again made her believe this statement must be true.

Faith noticed something else. A dark gray, closed-in buggy was parked on one side of the house. How strange it looked. Her mind whirled with unanswered questions. *I wonder whose it could be. Unless the rules around here have changed, it surely doesn't belong to Papa.*

"Is this the place?" Melinda asked, tugging on Faith's hand.

She looked down at her daughter, so innocent and wide-eyed. "Yes, Melinda. This is where I grew up. Shall we go see if anyone's home?"

Melinda nodded, although her dubious expression left little doubt of the child's concerns.

Once more, Faith offered to pay Doris, but the smiling woman waved her away. "No need for that. I was heading this way anyhow. So I'll be off to get my eggs over at the Troyers' place."

Faith thanked Doris, grabbed their suitcases, and gulped in another breath of air. It was time to face the music.

Chapter 2

Faith had only made it to the first saggy step of the front porch when the door swung open. Her mother, Wilma Stutzman, stepped out, and a little girl not much older than Melinda followed. In some ways, Mama looked the same as when Faith had left home, yet she was different. Hair that used to be blond like spun gold was now dingy and graying. Skin that had once been smooth and soft showed signs of wrinkles and dryness. Mama's face looked tired and drawn, and her blue eyes, offset by metal-framed glasses, held no sparkle as they once had.

"Can I help you with something?" her mother asked, looking at Faith as though she were a stranger.

Faith stepped all the way onto the porch, bringing Melinda with her. "Mama, it's me."

The older woman eyed Faith up and down, and her mouth dropped open. Then her gaze came to rest on Melinda, who was clinging to Faith's hand as though her young life hung in the balance.

"Faith?" Mama squeaked. "After all these years, is—is it really you?"

Faith nodded as tears stung the backs of her eyes. It was good to see her mother again. She hoped Mama felt the same.

When Mama stepped forward and gave Faith a hug, Faith nearly broke down in tears. Despite the resentment she'd carried in her heart for the last ten years, she had missed seeing her family.

"This is my daughter, Mama. Melinda's six years old." Faith gave the child's hand a gentle squeeze. "Say hello to your grandma Stutzman."

"Hello, Grandma." Melinda's voice was barely above a whisper.

Mama's pale eyebrows lifted in obvious surprise, but she offered Melinda a brief smile. Her brows drew together as she looked back at Faith. "I didn't even know you were married, much less had a child. Where have you been these last ten years, daughter?"

Faith swallowed hard as she formulated her response. "I followed my dream, Mama."

"What dream? You ran off the day you

turned eighteen, leaving only a note on the kitchen table saying you were going to become part of the English world."

"My dream was to use my yodeling skills and joke telling to entertain folks. My husband, Greg, made that happen, and I've been on the road entertaining for quite a spell now."

Mama's eyes glistened with unshed tears. "It broke your daed's and my heart when you left home, Faith. Don't you know that?"

"I—I did what I felt was right for me at the time." Faith dropped her gaze to the slanting porch. "Greg was killed six months ago when a car hit him." No point telling Mama that her husband had been drinking when he'd stepped in front of the oncoming vehicle. Mama would probably think Faith also drank liquor and then give a stern lecture on the evils of strong drink. Faith had endured enough reprimands during her teen years, even being blamed for some things she hadn't done.

"I'm sorry about your husband." Mama's voice sounded sincere. Maybe she did care a little bit.

Feeling the need to change the subject, Faith nodded at the gray, closed-in buggy sitting out in the yard. "Mind if I ask who that belongs to?"

"Vernon Miller, the buggy maker. He's out in the barn with your daed."

"Does that mean the Webster County Amish

are allowed to drive closed-in buggies now?"

Mama shook her head. "Vernon built the Lancaster-style carriage for an English man who lives out in Oregon. The fellow owns a gift shop where he sells Amish-made items. Guess he decided having a real buggy in front of his place would be good for business." She lifted her shoulders in a brief shrug. "Vernon wanted to test-drive it before he completed the order and had it sent off."

"I see."

Faith was going to say more, but the young girl with light brown hair and dark eyes who stood beside Mama spoke up. "Do I know these people, *Mamm*?"

Mamm? Faith felt a jolt of electricity zip through her body. Was the child hanging on to Mama's long blue dress Faith's sister? Had Mama given birth to a baby sometime after Faith left home? Did that mean Faith had three sisters now instead of two? She could even have more than four brothers and not know it.

"Susie, this is your big sister," Mama said to the girl. "And her daughter's your niece."

Susie stood gaping at Faith as though she had done something horribly wrong. Was it her worldly attire of blue jeans and a pink T-shirt that bothered the girl? Could it have been the long French braid Faith wore down her back? Or was the child as surprised as Faith was over the news that each of them had a sister they knew nothing about?

"So what are you doing here?" Mama asked, nodding at Faith.

"I—I was wondering if Melinda and I could stay with you." Faith held her breath and awaited her mother's answer. Would she and Melinda be welcomed or turned away?

"Here? With us?" Mama's voice had raised at least an octave, and her eyes, peering through her glasses, were as huge as saucers.

Faith nodded.

"As English or Amish?"

Her mother's direct question went straight to Faith's heart. If she told the truth—that she wanted her daughter to be Amish and she would pretend to be until she was ready to leave—the door would probably be slammed in her face.

Faith nibbled on her lower lip as she considered her response. She had to be careful. It wouldn't be good to reveal her true plans until the time was right. "I. . .uh. . .am willing to return to the Amish way of life."

"And you'll speak to Bishop Jacob Martin before you attend church with us in the morning?"

Faith gulped. She hadn't expected to speak with the bishop on her first day home. She'd probably be subjected to a long lecture about worldliness or maybe told that she must be baptized into the church before she would be fully accepted.

Melinda tugged her hand. "Are we gonna stay here, Mama?"

"I—I hope so." They couldn't be turned away. They had no place to go but back on the road, and Faith was through dragging Melinda all over creation. It wasn't good for a child to live out of a suitcase, never knowing from week to week where she would lay her head at night. Melinda should attend school in the fall, and she needed a stable environment.

"Will you speak with Jacob Martin or not?" Mama asked again.

Faith gritted her teeth and gave one quick nod. She would keep up the pretense that she planned to stay for as long as it was necessary.

Mama stepped aside and held the screen door open. "Come inside then."

⁂

Wilma's legs felt like two sticks of rubber as she motioned Faith and her daughter to follow her into the kitchen. As each year had passed without a word from her oldest daughter, she'd become more convinced that she would never see Faith again. But now Faith was home and had brought her daughter with her—a grandchild Wilma had known nothing about. Did Faith plan to stay, or would she be off and running again as soon as she felt the least bit discontent?

"Who was at the door, Mama?" Grace Ann,

Wilma's seventeen-year-old daughter, asked as they stepped into the kitchen.

Wilma motioned first to Faith and then to the child who clung to her mother's hand with a wide-eyed expression. "Your big sister's come home, and this is her daughter, Melinda."

Grace Ann's mouth opened wide, and she nearly dropped the plates she held in her hands. "Faith?"

Faith nodded, but before she could say anything, fourteen-year-old Esther, who had been placing silverware on the table, spoke. "Mama, is this the disobedient sister you told us about who ran off to the English world so she could yodel and tell silly jokes whenever she wanted?"

Wilma could only nod in response. When Faith had left home at the tender age of eighteen, Grace Ann had been seven, and Esther had just turned four. If not for Wilma telling the girls about Faith and her desire to be an entertainer, she was sure they wouldn't even have remembered that they'd had an older sister.

Esther eyed Faith up and down. "Did you come here for a visit, or are you home to stay?"

Faith shifted from one foot to another, looking like a bird that had been trapped between the paws of a hungry cat. "I brought Melinda home and"—she paused and moistened her lips with the tip of her tongue—"we're. . .uh. . .here for more than just a visit."

Grace Ann set the plates on the table and scurried across the room. "It's good to have you home, sister," she said, giving Faith a hug. "Papa and the others will sure be surprised." She patted Melinda on her head. "How old are you?"

"I'm six," the child replied.

"Just a year younger than Susie." Grace Ann glanced around the room. "Where is our little sister, anyway?"

Wilma's brows knitted together as she turned to look behind her. She thought Susie had been with them when they'd headed for the kitchen. "Esther, would you run upstairs and see if Susie went to her room?"

Esther hesitated as she looked over at Faith.

"She'll still be here when you get back," Wilma said with a wave of her hand.

"Okay." Esther scampered out of the room.

Faith smiled, although it appeared to be forced. Wasn't she happy to be home and seeing her family again?

Wilma motioned to the table. "If you'd like to have a seat, we can visit while I finish getting supper on."

"Isn't there something I can do to help?" Faith asked.

"Grace Ann and Esther have the table almost set, and the stew I'm making is nearly done." Wilma released a soft grunt. "You can start helping tomorrow with breakfast."

Faith pulled out a chair. Once she was seated, she hoisted her daughter into her lap, and the child snuggled against Faith's chest. "How are my brothers doing?" Faith asked. "I imagine they're pretty big by now."

Before Wilma could reply, Grace Ann spoke up. "John's courting a woman named Phoebe." She chuckled and waved her hand like she was swatting at a fly. " 'Course, he's been kind of sneaky about it, and I'm sure he thinks we don't know what's up."

"I remember when John was a boy he always kept things to himself." Faith glanced over at Wilma. "And how is Brian now?"

"He says he's still looking for the right woman." Wilma moved over to the stove and lifted the lid on the pot of stew. A curl of steam rushed up, and she drew in a deep breath, savoring the delicious, sagelike aroma. "Your older brothers, James and Philip, are both married. They each have four *kinner* of their own, and they've recently moved their families up north near Jamesport."

"How come?" Faith asked.

"Neither one likes to farm, and there's more work available for them."

Faith released a sigh. "I can't believe how much has changed since I left home."

Wilma resisted the temptation to tell Faith that if she had stayed home the way she should have and not run after a worldly dream, she would have been part of that change and things wouldn't seem so strange to her.

Several minutes later, Esther returned to the kitchen without her little sister. "Susie wasn't in her room, Mama. I don't know where she could be."

"Maybe she went outside," Grace Ann suggested.

Wilma was about to tell Esther to go out and check, when the back door swung open and Susie rushed into the room, followed by Wilma's husband, Menno, and their two youngest sons.

"Susie said Faith has come home." Menno's face was red, and he huffed as if he'd been running and was out of breath. "Is it true?"

Faith set her daughter on the floor and stood. "Yes, Papa, I'm here." She motioned to the child. "This is my daughter, Melinda—your granddaughter."

Menno looked down at Melinda, and his forehead creased, but he didn't comment. He just stood there, staring at the child.

"Susie told us that your husband died and that's why you and your daughter have come here to live." John stepped forward. "It's good to see you, sister. Welcome home."

"*Jah,*" Brian said with a nod. "We've missed you all these years."

"I–I've missed you, too."

Menno cleared his throat loudly. "Where have you been all this time, Faith, and what have you been doing?"

"She's been yodeling and telling jokes for English folks in places like Branson," John said before Faith could respond. "Not long ago, I saw her picture in one of them flyers advertising shows at Branson." He glanced over at his father. "Remember when I told you and Mama about it?"

Menno mumbled something Wilma couldn't quite understand as he ambled across the room toward the sink. She waited until he had washed and dried his hands, then she motioned to the table and said, "Supper's ready now, so why don't we all find our places? While we're eating, Faith can answer everyone's questions."

Chapter 3

Faith cringed as her family joined her and Melinda at the table. She didn't want to answer anyone's questions. Truth be told, she didn't really want to be here, but bringing Melinda to live with her folks was the only way she knew to give her daughter a stable home.

You had a stable home once, and you left it, a little voice niggled at the back of Faith's mind. She shook her head, trying to clear away the disturbing thoughts. She had to stay focused on her goal for Melinda.

Faith glanced over at her father, a tall, muscular man with a good crop of cinnamon brown hair and a beard that was peppered with gray. He cleared his throat loudly, the way he'd always done whenever it was time to bow their heads for silent prayer. Faith leaned close to Melinda, who sat in the seat beside her. "Close your eyes now; we're going to pray."

Melinda's forehead wrinkled, and Faith realized that the child didn't understand. How could she? Faith had quit praying a long time ago, and she hadn't taught her daughter how to pray, either. "Shut your eyes," she whispered in Melinda's ear.

Melinda did as she was told, and everyone else did the same. Several seconds later, Papa cleared his throat again, and all eyes opened. Everyone's but Melinda's. Faith squeezed her hand, and when Melinda still didn't open her eyes, she quietly said, "You can open your eyes now."

Melinda blinked and looked around the table. "But nobody said nothing. When I watched *Little House on the Prairie* on TV, Laura's pa always said the prayer out loud."

Mama opened her mouth as if to say something, but Brian spoke first. "We offer silent prayers here."

"But if it's silent, how does God know what you want?"

"We pray in our minds," Grace Ann said. "God hears what we think same as when we speak."

Melinda seemed to accept that explanation, for she gave one quick nod, grabbed the glass of milk sitting before her, and took a drink.

She smacked her lips as she set the glass down. "Umm. . .that's sure tasty."

"It's fresh milk taken from one of our best milking cows early this morning," John said, smiling over at Melinda.

"Can I milk a cow?" she asked with a look of expectation. "Laura helps her pa milk their cow on *Little House*, and it looks like a lot of fun."

"Milking cows is hard work, but I'd be happy to show you how," Faith's father said. It was the first time since he'd come into the room that Faith had seen him smile. Maybe he was glad to have her home. At least he seemed pleasant enough with Melinda. To Faith, he hadn't said more than a few words, and those were spoken with disdain. Well, it didn't matter. Faith would be leaving in a few weeks or months—however long it took for Melinda to become used to her new surroundings. The only thing that really mattered was Melinda developing a good relationship with her grandparents, aunts, and uncles. Everyone in the family could give Faith the cold shoulder for the rest of her life, and it wouldn't matter.

She looked around the table at the somber faces of her family. She couldn't allow herself the luxury of caring about these people or worrying about whether they accepted her. Her life was on the stage, yodeling and cracking funny jokes for English folks who paid money to enjoy the entertainment she offered. It wasn't here in

Webster County, where everything she did was under scrutiny.

"I wanna learn about all the animals on this farm." Melinda nearly knocked over her glass of milk as she wiggled around in her seat.

"Be careful now, or you'll spill something," Faith admonished.

"She's just excited about seeing the animals," Mama said, smiling at Melinda.

Susie, who sat on the other side of Melinda, reached over and touched Melinda's hand. "If you'd like, we can go to the barn after we're done eating, and I can show you the kittens that were born last week."

Melinda's head bobbed up and down. "I'd like that."

Faith remained silent throughout most of the meal, only responding when she was asked a question or Melinda requested more to eat. Susie made up for Faith's lack of conversation, as she chattered nonstop, offering to show Melinda all sorts of interesting things in her father's barn and telling her how much fun it was going to be to have someone close to her age living with her.

Melinda, too, seemed eager, and it was almost as if the girls had known each other all their lives. It made Faith feel guilty for not having brought Melinda to meet her family sooner. *Well, better late than never,* she thought as she poured another glass of milk for Melinda.

Besides, we might not have been welcomed before.

They had just finished supper and the women were clearing away the dishes, when a knock sounded on the back door. "John, would you get that?" Papa asked before he drank some coffee from the cup Mama had placed in front of him moments ago.

John slid his chair away from the table and left the room. A few seconds later, he was back with Bishop Martin at his side. Except for his hair and beard turning mostly gray, the portly man looked almost the same as he had when Faith had left home ten years ago.

"Come in. Have a cup of coffee," Papa said, motioning for the bishop to take a seat at the table.

The bishop smiled and shook his head. "I can't stay. Just dropped by to let you know that tomorrow's church service, which was going to be held at Henry Yoder's home, will be held at Isaac Troyer's place."

Papa's eyebrows rose. "Oh? Why's that?"

"Henry's mother, who lives in Kentucky, is real sick, and Henry and his family had to hire a driver to take them there."

"That's too bad. Sorry to hear of it."

Mama moved from her place in front of the sink and gave Faith a little nudge with her elbow. "Since the bishop is here now, don't you think this would be a good time for you to tell him what's on your mind?" Before Faith could respond, Mama looked over at the bishop and said, "Our daughter Faith's come home, and she wants to join the church."

Faith swallowed hard and nearly choked. She hadn't expected to see the bishop quite so soon. She needed more time to prepare for this—to think through what she wanted to say.

"Is that so?" Bishop Martin eyed Faith curiously as he tipped his head. "Where have you been all these years?"

"She's been on the road, yodeling and telling jokes in the English world," Papa spoke up before Faith could formulate a response. He motioned toward Melinda. "Right out of the blue, she and her daughter showed up on our doorstep a little while ago."

The bishop opened his mouth as if to say something, but Faith spoke first. "My husband died a few months ago, and I decided it would be best for Melinda if we came here."

"I see." He gave Faith a quick nod. "Since you weren't a member of the church when you left, you won't be expected to offer any kind of confession to the church, but I think, given the circumstances of your leaving home in the first place, it would be good for you to give yourself some time to readjust to things before you take instruction to join the church."

A huge sense of relief settled over Faith as she nodded. "Yes, I think that would be best." This would give her a chance to get her daughter settled in, and no one would suspect that her real plans were to leave Melinda here and be on the road again.

❀

"I still can't believe our daughter's come home," Wilma said to Menno as the two of them got ready for bed that night.

He pulled the covers to the foot of bed. "Jah, well, it sure seems odd to me that she would return home after this much time. It makes no sense at all."

"You heard what she said, Menno. Faith's come home because her husband is dead and she wants a stable home to raise her daughter in."

"You think she's telling the truth?"

Wilma took a seat on the edge of the bed and pulled the pins from the bun at the back of her head. "What reason would she have to lie about her husband dying?"

"That's not what I meant. If she says her husband's dead, then I'm sure it's true." Menno flopped onto his side of the bed and punched the pillow a couple of times. He had a hunch there was more to the story than Faith was telling. Unless their daughter had changed a lot from when she was a girl, it was quite likely that she had something more up her sleeve than just looking for a stable home for Melinda.

"I sure hope she stays for good this time," Wilma said as she began to brush her waist-length hair. "I don't think I could stand losing her again."

"I'd like to believe she will stay, but she's been living in the world these last ten years." He reclined on the bed and raised his arms up over his head as he rested against the pillow. "Do you really think she can give up all the modern things she's become accustomed to having?"

"Well, I don't know, but I'm hoping—"

"I don't trust her, Wilma. I think Faith is probably down on her luck and can't find a job now that her husband's gone, so she needs a place to stay for a while." He frowned. "Mark my words. In a couple of weeks, Faith and her daughter will be on the road, and we'll probably never hear from them again."

Wilma's eyes widened, and her chin quivered slightly. "Oh, I hope that's not the case." She reached over to touch the Bible on the nightstand beside their bed. "Proverbs 22:6 says, 'Train up a child in the way he should go: and when he is old, he will not depart from it.' We did our best to teach Faith and the rest of our kinner about God's laws and His ways, so now we must trust that she has come back to those teachings."

"Jah, that's all we can do. Trust and pray," he mumbled as his eyes drifted shut.

<hr>

As Faith helped Melinda get ready for bed that night, her head pounded like a blacksmith's anvil at work. It had been all she could do to keep from telling her folks and the bishop what her true intentions were, but she knew Melinda would never adapt to the Amish way of life unless Faith stayed for a while and helped her fit in. It would be too traumatic for both of them if Faith left the child with strangers. No, the best thing was for her to pretend she was home to stay until she felt the time was right for her to leave. She just hoped she wouldn't be pressured to join the church, because that would be impossible if she planned to leave.

"How come everyone in your family kept starin' at me during supper?" Melinda asked from where she sat on the bed. "And how come they dress different than us?"

"They were probably staring because you're so cute and they were happy to meet you." Faith tweaked her daughter's turned-up nose. "And they dress different than we do because they're Amish and they believe God wants them to wear simple, plain clothes, not fancy things like so many other people like to wear."

Melinda's forehead wrinkled. "Maybe some were happy to see me, but not Grandma Stutzman. She frowned when you told her who I was."

"That's because she was so surprised." Faith sat on the edge of the bed and took hold of the child's hand. "As I told you before we left Branson, I hadn't seen any of my family for ten years, and they didn't know I had a daughter."

Melinda sat with a sober expression, as though she were mulling over what Faith had said. Then her face broke into a smile. "Susie's real nice, and I think she likes me."

Faith nodded. "I'm sure she does. I believe you and my little sister will become good friends in no time at all."

"When we went out to the barn after supper, she let me pet the baby kitties and even a couple of the horses." Melinda crawled under the covers and snuggled against her pillow. "I'd better go to sleep now so I can get up early and help Grandpa Stutzman milk his cows."

Faith smiled and bent to give her daughter a kiss. It was seriously doubtful that Melinda would be awake early enough to milk any cows, but it made Faith feel hopeful about things, knowing her father had shown an interest in Melinda. Too bad he hadn't taken much interest in Faith when she was a child.

As Melinda drifted off to sleep, Faith lay on her side of the bed, wondering how she would handle being separated from her daughter when the time came for her to leave. Would she be welcome to return for visits? How long would she need to stay here in order for Melinda to fully adjust?

Chapter 4

Noah looked forward to going to church at his friend Isaac Troyer's place. Isaac and his wife, Ellen, had been married four years and already had two small children. Noah enjoyed spending time with other people's children. He figured that was a good thing, since it wasn't likely he'd ever have any of his own.

"Got to be married to have kinner," Noah muttered as he scrambled a batch of eggs for breakfast.

"Couldn't quite make out what you were saying, but I'm guessing you were talking to yourself again, jah?"

Noah turned at the sound of his mother's voice. He hadn't realized she had come into the kitchen. "I guess I was," he admitted, feeling a sense of warmth cover his cheeks.

"You've got to quit doing that, son." Mom's hazel-colored eyes looked perky this morning, and Noah was glad she seemed to be feeling better. Yesterday she'd looked tired and acted kind of shakylike.

His mother shuffled over to their gas-operated refrigerator, withdrew a slab of bacon, and handed it to Noah. "Some of your daed's best."

He chuckled. "All of Pop's hogs are the best. At least he thinks so."

Mom's head bobbed up and down, and a few brown hairs sprinkled with gray peeked out from the bun she wore under her small, white head covering. "My Levi would sure enough say so."

"You're right about that. Pop gets up early every morning, rain or shine, and heads out to feed his pigs. Truth is, I think he enjoys talking to the old sows more than he does me."

Mom's forehead wrinkled as she set three plates on the table. "Now don't start with that, Noah. It's not your daed's fault that you don't share his interest in raising hogs."

"That's not the problem, Mom, and you know it." Noah grabbed a butcher knife from the wooden block on the cupboard and cut several slices of bacon; then he slapped them into the frying pan. The trouble between him and Pop went back to when Noah was a young boy. He was pretty sure his father thought he was a sissy because he liked to cook and help Mom with some of the inside chores. That was really dumb, as far as Noah was concerned. Would a sissy work up a sweat planting a bunch of trees? Would a sissy wear calluses on his hands from pruning, shaping, and cutting the Christmas pines English people in the area bought every December?

Mom took out a container of fresh goat's milk from the refrigerator. "Let's talk about something else, shall we? Your daed will be in soon from doing his chores, and I don't want you all riled up when he gets here."

Noah grunted and flipped the sizzling bacon. "I'm not riled, Mom. Just stating facts as I see 'em."

"Jah, well, you have a right to your opinion."

"Glad you think so. Now if you want to hear more about what I think—"

"Your daed loves you, Noah, and that's the truth of it."

Noah nodded. "I know, and I love him, too. I also realize that Pop doesn't like it because I'd rather be in the kitchen than out slopping hogs with him, so I'm trying to accept things as they are."

Mom sighed. "None of my boys ever enjoyed the pigs the way that husband of mine does."

Noah realized it was past time for a change of subject. "I baked a couple of lemon sponge cakes while you and Pop went to town yesterday. One with sugar and one without."

"Are you planning to give one away or set both out on the table at the meal after our preaching service?"

Noah pushed the bacon around in the pan, trying to get it to brown up evenly. "The cake I made with a sugar substitute is for us to have here at home. I figured I would give the one made with sugar to someone who might need a special touch today."

"Guess God will show you who when the time is right."

"Jah. That's how it usually goes."

"I just hope you don't develop baker's asthma from working around flour so much."

Noah snickered. "I don't think you have to worry none. That usually only happens to those who work in bakeries and such. One would have to be around flour a lot more than me to develop baker's asthma."

Pop entered the kitchen just as Noah was dishing up the bacon and scrambled eggs. Noah's father had dark brown hair, with close-set eyes that matched his hair color, but his beard had been nearly gray since his late fifties. Now Pop was starting to show his age in other areas, too. His summer-tanned face was creased with wrinkles, he had several dark splotches on his hands and arms, and he walked with a slower gait these days.

"Something smells mighty good this morning," Pop said, sniffing the air. "Must have made some bacon."

Noah's mother pointed to the platter full of bacon and eggs. "Our son has outdone himself again, Levi. He made sticky buns, too." She nodded toward the plate in the center of the table, piled high with rolls. Noah had learned to make many sweet treats using a sugar substitute so Mom could enjoy them without affecting her diabetes, and he knew how much she appreciated it.

"You taking the leftover sticky buns to church?" his father asked after he'd washed his hands at the sink.

"Guess I could." Noah smiled. "I also made a sugar-free lemon sponge cake." Noah made no mention of the cake that he planned to give away. Pop liked lemon so well, he might want that one, too.

Pop smacked his lips. "Sounds good to me."

Noah smiled to himself. His dad might not like him spending so much time in the kitchen, but he sure did enjoy the fruits of Noah's labor. And Pop hadn't said one word about Noah not helping out with the hogs. Maybe it was a good sign. This might be the beginning of a great day.

"I can't believe how much our two boys are growing," Barbara Zook said to her husband,

David, as they headed down the road in his open buggy toward Isaac and Ellen Troyer's home. She glanced over her shoulder at their two young sons. "I made a pair of trousers for Aaron but two months ago, and already they're too short for his long legs."

David smiled and nodded. "Jah, it won't be long and both our boys will be grown, married, and on their own. Someday we'll be retired, and Aaron can take over the harness shop."

She reached across the seat and gently pinched his arm. "Don't you be saying such things. I want to keep our kinner little for as long as I can."

He shook his head. "Now, Barbara, you know that's not possible, so you may as well accept the changes as they come."

She released a sigh. "I can accept some changes, but others aren't so easy."

"Are you thinking of anything in particular?"

"Jah. I was thinking about my old friend Faith. This morning as I was looking through the bottom drawer of my dresser, I came across a handkerchief Faith had given me on my twelfth birthday. The sight of it made me feel kind of sad." Barbara blinked a couple of times as the remembrance of her friend saying good-bye washed over her like a harsh, stinging rain. "I haven't heard from Faith in a good many years, but I still remember to pray for her every day."

David reached for Barbara's hand and gave her fingers a gentle squeeze. "Prayer is the key to each new day and the lock for every night, jah?"

"That's right, and I'll keep praying for my friend whether I hear from her again or not."

David smiled. "I feel blessed to have married someone as caring as you."

Barbara leaned her head on his shoulder. "I'm the one who's been blessed, husband."

Faith felt as fidgety as a bumblebee on a hot summer day. She hadn't been this nervous since the first time she had performed one of her comedy routines in front of a bunch of strangers. She and Melinda sat in the back of her parents' open buggy, along with young Susie. Faith's sisters, Grace Ann and Esther, had ridden to church with their brothers John and Brian.

Faith reached up and touched her head covering to be sure it was firmly in place. She'd been in such a hurry this morning, having to get herself dressed in one of Grace Ann's plain dresses and Melinda in one of Susie's, that she hadn't taken the time to do up her hair properly. Rather than being parted down the middle, twisted, and pulled back in a bun, she'd brushed her hair straight back and quickly secured it in a bun, then hurried downstairs to help with breakfast. She would be meeting others in their congregation today, not to mention facing Bishop Martin again.

Thinking about the bishop caused Faith to reflect on her conversation with him. She'd left the bishop, as well as her family, with the impression that she had come home to stay and had given no hint that she planned to go back to her life as an entertainer.

You won't have your daughter with you, her conscience reminded. *Can you ever be truly happy without Melinda?* Faith shook her head as though the action might clear away the troubling thoughts. She wouldn't think about that now. She would deal with leaving Melinda when the time came. For now, Faith's only need was to make everyone in her Amish community believe she had come home to stay.

Soon they were pulling into the Troyers' yard, and Faith looked around in amazement. Isaac Troyer's house and barn were enormous, and a huge herd of dairy cows grazed in the pasture nearby. Papa had mentioned something about the Troyers' dairy farm doing well, but she'd had no idea it would be so big.

Faith let her mind wander back to the days when she had attended the one-room schoolhouse not far down the road. Isaac Troyer, her brother John, and Noah Hertzler had all been friends. She remembered Noah as being the shy one of the group. Faith could still see his face turning as red as a radish over something one of the scholars at school had said. He'd hardly spoken more than a few words, and then it was only if someone talked to him first. Noah hadn't been outspoken or full of wisecracks the way Faith had always been, that was for sure. She would have to watch her mouth now that she was back at home. Her jokes and fooling around wouldn't be appreciated.

I wonder if Noah's still around, and if so, is the poor man as shy as he used to be?

"You getting out or what?"

Faith jerked her head at the sound of her father's deep voice. He leaned against the buggy, his dark eyes looking ever so serious. He was a hard worker, and he could be equally hard when it came to his family. As a little girl, Faith had always been a bit afraid of him. She wasn't sure if it was his booming voice or his penetrating eyes. One thing for sure, Faith knew Papa would take no guff from any of his children. The way he looked at her right now made her wonder if he could tell what was on her mind. Did he know how much she dreaded going to church?

Faith stepped down from the buggy and turned to help Melinda and Susie out. Chattering like magpies, the little girls ran toward the Troyers' house. Faith was left to walk alone, and as she headed toward the Troyers' house, she shuddered, overcome by the feeling that she was marching into a den of hungry lions. What if she and Melinda weren't accepted? What if either one of them said or did something wrong today?

Faith drew in a deep breath and glanced down at her unadorned, dark green dress. It felt strange to be wearing Plain clothes again, and she wondered if she looked as phony on the outside as she was on the inside. Melinda hadn't seemed to mind putting on one of her aunt Susie's simple dresses. She'd even made some comment about it being fun to play dress-up.

Oh, to be young again. I hope Melinda keeps her cheerful attitude in the days ahead. Faith kept her gaze downward, being mindful of the uneven ground and sharp stones in the Troyers' driveway. She had taken only a few steps when she bumped into someone. Lifting her head, Faith found herself staring into a pair of brown eyes that were so dark they almost looked black. She shifted her body quickly to the right, but the man with thick chestnut-brown hair moved to his left at the same time. With a nervous laugh, she swung to the left, just as he transferred his body to the right.

"Sorry. We seem to be going the same way," he mumbled. There was a small scar in the middle of his chin, and for a moment, Faith thought she recognized him. Noah Hertzler had been left with that kind of a scar from a fall on the school playground many years ago. But this mature-looking man couldn't be the same scrawny boy who had fallen from the swings.

"I—I don't believe we've met," the man said. "My name's Noah Hertzler."

"I'm Faith Andrews...used to be Stutzman."

Noah's jaw dropped open, and at the same time, Faith felt as if the air had been sucked from her lungs. The man who stood before her was no longer the red-faced kid afraid of his own shadow, but a tall, muscular fellow who was looking at her in a most peculiar way.

"Faith Andrews, the comedian who can yodel?" he asked, lifting his dark eyebrows in obvious surprise.

She nodded and tucked a stray hair behind one ear. "One and the same."

Chapter 5

Noah could hardly believe Faith Stutzman, rebellious Amish teenager turned comedian, was standing in front of him dressed like all the other Plain women who had come to church this morning. Only Faith was different. Not only had her last name changed, but she didn't have the same humble, submissive appearance most Amish women had. Her eyes were the clearest blue, like fresh water flowing from a mountain stream. There was something about the way those eyes flashed—the way she held her head. She seemed proud and maybe a bit defiant.

"What are you doing here?"

"You know about me being a comedian?"

They'd spoken at the same time, and Noah

chuckled, feeling the heat of embarrassment flood his cheeks. He hated how easily he blushed. "You go first."

She lifted her chin. "No, you."

Noah acceded to her request. "I—I'm surprised to see you. How long have you been home?"

"We arrived yesterday afternoon."

"We?" Noah glanced around, thinking maybe Faith had a husband who had accompanied her.

"My daughter, Melinda, is with me," Faith explained. "My husband died six months ago."

Noah sucked in his breath as he allowed himself to feel her pain. "I'm sorry for your loss."

She stared down at her black shoes. "Thank you."

He wouldn't press her for details. Maybe another time—when they got to know each other better. "It's your turn now," he said quietly.

Her head came up. "Huh?"

"You started to ask a question a few minutes ago. About me knowing you were a comedian."

"Oh yeah. I'm surprised you knew. I obviously didn't become a professional entertainer while I was still Amish." Faith pursed her perfectly shaped lips, and he forced himself not to stare at them. "I didn't figure you would know about my new profession."

"My boss is an English man. He often plays tapes, or we listen to his portable radio while we work, and I heard an interview you did on the air once." Noah paused. "You yodeled a bit and told a few jokes, too."

She tipped her head to one side. "And you lived to tell about it?"

He nodded. "As I remember, the jokes you told were real funny."

"You really think so?"

"Sure. When I was a boy and came over to your place to spend time with John, your silliness and joke telling used to crack me up."

Faith stared up at him. "Really? You never said anything."

He kicked at the small stones beneath his feet. "I was kind of shy and awkward back then, and I guess I still am sometimes."

"Do you really believe I have a talent to make people laugh?" she asked, making no comment about his shyness.

"Jah, sure." He shifted his weight from one foot to the other. "So. . .uh. . .what brought you back to Webster County?"

She stood straighter, pushing her shoulders back. "I've returned to my birthplace so my daughter can have a real home."

"Not because you missed your family and friends?"

She shrugged. "Sure, that, too."

Noah had a feeling Faith wasn't being completely honest with him. Her tone of voice told him she might be hiding something. He didn't think now was the time or place to be asking her a bunch of personal questions, though. Maybe he would have that chance later on. He glanced around and noticed his friend Isaac watching him from near the barn. Noah figured Isaac would probably expect him to give a full account of all he and Faith had said to each other.

"I'd better go since church will be starting soon. It's. . .uh. . .nice to see you again," Noah said. "I hope it works out for you and your daughter."

"Things are a little strained for us right now. It's going to be a difficult adjustment, I'm sure."

"Soon it will go better."

"I hope so."

Faith walked off toward the house, and Noah headed over to see Isaac. He knew if he didn't, the nosy fellow would most likely seek him out.

"Who was that woman you were talking to?" Isaac asked as soon as Noah stepped up beside him. "You two looked pretty cozylike, but I didn't recognize her."

"It was Faith Stutzman, and we weren't being cozy."

Isaac's dark eyebrows shot up. "Faith Stutzman? Menno and Wilma's wayward daughter?"

"Jah. Her husband died awhile ago, and she and her daughter have moved back home. Her last name's Andrews now."

Isaac reached up to scratch the back of his head. In the process, he nearly knocked his black felt hat to the ground, but he righted it in time. "So how'd you happen to strike up a conversation with her?"

"We sort of bumped into each other."

"Did you get all tongue-tied and turn red in the face?"

Noah clenched his teeth. "To tell you the truth, I didn't feel quite as nervous or shy in Faith's presence as I usually do when I'm talking to a young, single woman."

"Right. And pigs can fly," Isaac said with a snicker. He motioned toward the house, where several people were filing in through the open doorway. "Guess we'd better get in there now."

As Noah and his friend moved toward the house, Noah made a decision. He knew now who should get that lemon sponge cake he had brought today. The scripture verse he'd attached was about having faith in God, so it seemed appropriate to give it to a woman whose name was Faith. It would be like a welcome-home gift to someone who reminded him of the prodigal son in the Bible.

❧

As Wilma approached a group of women who had gathered outside the Troyers' home to visit, she glanced across the yard and noticed

Faith standing under a leafy maple tree by herself. Faith's arms were folded, her shoulders were slumped, and she stared at the ground as though she might be looking at something.

There's no mistaking it, Wilma thought ruefully. *My daughter isn't happy about being here today. Is it because she doesn't want to be home, or could she be feeling nervous about seeing all the people from our community and having to explain why she's come back to Webster County with her daughter?*

"I hear your oldest daughter has come home," Annie Yoder, one of the minister's wives, said as she stepped up to Wilma.

Wilma nodded, realizing how fast the news of Faith's arrival must have traveled. Maybe Bishop Martin had spread the news as he'd gone from house to house last night, letting everyone know about the change in plans concerning where church would be held today. "Yesterday evening, Faith arrived home with her daughter, Melinda," Wilma said, trying to make her voice sound casual.

"Is she here for a visit, or is she planning to stay?"

"Her husband recently died, and she says she's home for good." Even as the words slipped from Wilma's tongue, she wondered if they were true. Did Faith plan to give up her modern ways and join the Amish church, or would she soon tire of things and head back on the road?

No matter how hard Faith tried, she couldn't find a comfortable position. She'd forgotten how hard the backless wooden benches the people sat on during church could be. She glanced at Melinda, who sat on a bench beside Susie and some other young girls about their age. How well would her daughter manage during the long service, most of which was spoken in a language she couldn't understand? Faith was glad she had thought to bring a basket filled with some snack foods along, in case her daughter got hungry.

As the service continued, Faith's mind began to wander, taking her back in time, back to when she was a little girl trying not to fidget during one of the bishop's long sermons, and she found herself becoming more restless. Every few minutes she glanced out the living-room window, wishing for the freedom to be outside where she could enjoy the pleasant summer day. She knew they would be going outdoors for their noon meal after the service, but that was still a ways off. Besides, she would be expected to help serve the men before she could relax and enjoy her meal.

Faith's thoughts drove her on, down a not-so-pleasant memory lane. She had struggled on her own the first years after she'd left home and had ended up waiting tables and performing on a makeshift stage for a time. Then Greg had come along and swept Faith off her feet. He'd said she was talented and could go far in the world of entertainment. Greg's whispered honeyed words and promises had been like music to her ears, and it hadn't taken her long to succumb to his charms.

During the early years of their marriage, Faith had thought she was in love with Greg, and she'd believed the feeling was returned. Maybe it had been at first, but then Greg began to use her to gain riches. The more successful she became as an entertainer, the more of her money he spent on alcohol and gambling. She suspected he thought she didn't know what he was up to, but Faith was no dummy. She knew exactly why Greg often sank into depression or became hostile toward her. Never Melinda, though. Thankfully, Greg had always been kind to their child.

Of course, he might not have remained docile toward Melinda if he had lived and kept on drinking the way he was, Faith reminded herself. *If he could smack me around, then what's to say he wouldn't have eventually taken his frustrations out on our daughter?*

"As many of you may already know, one of our own who has lived among the English for the last several years returned home yesterday. We welcome Faith Stutzman Andrews and her daughter, Melinda, to our worship service this morning."

Faith sat up a bit straighter as Bishop Martin's comment drove her thoughts aside. She glanced around the room, feeling an urgency to escape but knowing she couldn't. All eyes seemed to be focused on her. Many nodded their heads, some smiled, and others merely looked at her with curious stares. What were they thinking? Did everyone see her as a wayward woman who had come crawling home because she had no other place to go? Well, it was true in a sense. She had nowhere else to go. At least no place she wanted to take Melinda. If she had kept the child on the road with her, it would have been only a matter of time before her innocent daughter fell prey to some gold digger like her father had been. Faith desired better things for her little girl. She wanted Melinda to know that when she woke up every morning, there would be food on the table and a warm fire to greet her. She needed her precious child to go to bed at night feeling a sense of belonging and knowing she was nurtured and loved.

You had all those things when you were growing up, but you left them, the voice in her head reminded. Faith shook the thoughts aside as she forced herself to concentrate on the bishop's closing prayer. Better to focus on his words than to think of all she'd given up when she left home. She hadn't really wanted to leave, but she'd done it to prove to herself and to her family that she was her own person and had been blessed with a talent for yodeling and joke telling.

A rustle of skirts and the murmur of voices made Faith realize the service was over. She glanced around. Everyone was exiting the room.

Faith saw to it that Melinda was in Esther's care, since she was also overseeing Susie. Then Faith excused herself to go to the kitchen, where several women and teenage girls scurried about, trying to get the meal served as quickly as possible.

"What can I do to help?" she asked her mother, who stood at the cupboard piling slices of bread onto a plate.

Before Mama could respond, Ellen Troyer spoke up. "Why don't you help David Zook's wife serve coffee to the menfolk out in the barn, where tables have been set up?" She handed Faith a pot of coffee. "It's good to have you back among the people. You've been missed."

Nodding at Ellen, Faith accepted the coffeepot and turned and headed out the back door.

When Faith entered the barn a few minutes later, she noticed a dark-haired woman serving coffee at one of the tables. *That must be David Zook's wife.*

She approached the woman, whose back was to her, and asked, "Which tables are yet to be served?"

The woman turned around, and a slow smile spread across her face. "*Ach,* Faith! It was a surprise to see you in church, and I'm so glad you're back home."

Faith squinted as she looked more closely at the woman. "Barbara? Barbara Raber?"

"Jah, only it's Zook now. I've been married to David for close to five years." Barbara smiled, revealing two deep dimples in her round cheeks. "Remember David? He was a year ahead of us in school."

Faith wasn't sure what to say. She and Barbara had been friends while growing up, but the truth was, she barely remembered a fellow named David Zook.

"It—it's nice to see you again." Faith's voice sounded formal and strained. She couldn't help it; she felt formal and strained around everyone here today. Everyone except for Noah Hertzler. She'd actually enjoyed their brief conversation and had felt more at ease with him than she felt with Barbara right now. It made no sense. She hadn't known Noah all that well when they were growing up, as he was four years younger than her. Noah had been John's friend, not hers. He'd also been so shy back then that he hadn't said more than a few words to anyone in their family except John. Today, however, Noah seemed easy to talk to, and there had only been a hint of shyness on his part.

"Faith? Did you hear what I said?"

Barbara's soft-spoken voice and gentle nudge drove Faith's thoughts aside.

"What was that?"

"I said I'm glad you've come home."

Faith nodded.

"Now about the tables needing to be served—you can take those four." Barbara motioned to the ones on her left.

"Okay." Faith moved away, thinking how much her friend had changed. Barbara Raber had been as slender as a reed when they were teenagers. Barbara Zook was slightly plump, especially around the middle. The mischief that could be seen in young Barbara's eyes had been replaced with a look of peace and contentment. For that, Faith felt a twinge of envy. In all her twenty-eight years, she'd never known true peace or contentment. She had always wanted something she couldn't have. Something more—something better.

Faith avoided eye contact as she served the men, but as she poured coffee into the last cup at the table, she felt gentle but calloused fingers touch her arm. *"Danki."*

"You're welcome," she murmured, daring to seek out the man's face. It was Noah Hertzler, and his tender expression was nearly her undoing.

"I have something for you," he said quietly. "It's in the Troyers' house."

She tipped her head in question. *Why would Noah have anything for me? He hardly knows me, and I'm sure he didn't know I would be here today.*

"Will you be heading back to the kitchen soon?" he asked.

She nodded.

"Okay. I'll meet you there in a few minutes."

Faith nodded mutely and moved away. She walked back to the house a few minutes later, feeling like a marionette with no control over its movements.

Relief swept over Faith when she stepped into the kitchen and realized that no one else was there. She figured the other women must have gone to the barn to eat their meal after the men were done.

Faith pulled out one of the mismatched wooden chairs and sat down. When she placed her hands on the table, she noticed that they were shaking. *What's wrong with me? I've faced tougher crowds than the one here today and didn't feel half as intimidated. I used to make an audience howl and beg for more, even when I was dying on the inside because of the way things were with Greg and me. Yet here, among my own people, I can barely crack a smile.*

Faith squeezed her eyes shut, wishing she remembered how to pray. If she could, she would ask God to calm her spirit.

When the back door creaked open, Faith jumped. She turned her head to the right.

Noah stood in the doorway with an easy-going grin on his face.

She swallowed hard. What did he have for her? What did he want in return?

Noah closed the door and strolled over to the cupboard across the room. He opened one of the doors and took out a cake carrier, which he set on the table in front of Faith. "This is for you."

"You're giving me a whole cake?"

Noah nodded. "It's a lemon sponge cake, and I made it with the idea of giving it away today."

"Why me?"

His face flooded with color. "Just call it a welcome-home gift." He pushed the plastic container toward her. "Sure hope you like lemon."

She nodded. "It's one of my favorite flavors."

"That's good. I hope you'll enjoy every bite, as well as the verse of scripture," he said.

Verse of scripture? Faith's gaze went to the little card attached to the side of the pan, and her heart clenched. She would take the cake, but she had no desire to read the scripture.

Chapter 6

"What have you got there?" Mama asked as Faith climbed down from the buggy behind Melinda and Susie.

Faith looked down at the cake Noah had given her, hoping it hadn't spoiled. She had placed a small bag of ice she'd found in the Troyers' refrigerator on top of the plastic container, taken it out to the buggy earlier, and slipped it under the backseat. She still wondered why Noah had chosen her to be the recipient of his luscious-looking dessert.

"Faith? Did you hear what I asked?"

Clutching the cake in her hands, she faced her mother. "Uh. . .it's a lemon sponge cake."

Mama's eyebrows arched upward. "Where'd you get it?"

Faith drew in a deep breath. She may as well get the inquisition over with, because she was sure her mother wouldn't be satisfied until she'd heard all the details. "Noah Hertzler gave it to me."

Mama chuckled softly. "I thought as much. That young fellow is always handing out his baked goods to someone in our community. Ida Hertzler is one lucky mamm to have him for a son; he's right handy in the kitchen."

"Is that so?"

"Jah. From what Ida's told me, Noah's been helping out with the cooking and baking ever since he was a kinner."

Faith hadn't known that. The only thing she knew about Noah was that he used to be shy and seemed to be kind of awkward.

"Noah's not married, you know," Mama said as they headed for the house.

Faith figured as much since she hadn't seen him with a woman and he wasn't wearing a beard, which meant he wasn't married. It didn't concern her, however, so she made no response to her mother's comment.

"Maybe after you've settled in here and have joined the church, you and Noah might hit it off."

Faith whirled around to face her mother. "Mama, Greg's only been dead a short while. It wouldn't be proper for me to think about another man right now, in case that's what you're insinuating." She sniffed. "Besides, I'm not planning to remarry—ever."

Mama gave her a curious look, but Faith hurried to the house before the confused-looking woman could say anything more. She didn't want to talk about her disastrous marriage to Greg or the plans she had for the future.

Barbara Zook collapsed onto the sofa in her living room with a sigh. She'd just put her boys to bed and needed a little time to herself.

"Mind if I join you?" her husband asked, as he stepped into the room.

She patted the cushion beside her and smiled. "Not at all. I'd be happy for the company of someone old enough to carry on adult conversation."

David grinned as he seated himself on the sofa and scooted close to her. "You visited with some of the women from church today. Wasn't that adult conversation?"

Barbara nodded. "Jah, but that was some time ago. I've spent the last couple of hours feeding our boys, listening to their endless chatter, and getting them ready for bed." She took hold of his hand. "Now I'm ready for some quiet time."

"You just said you wanted some adult conversation. If you need quiet time, then maybe I'd better sit here and keep my mouth shut."

She chuckled and squeezed his fingers. "I'm sure you know what I meant."

"Jah." David leaned his headful of thick, dark hair on her shoulder and closed his eyes. "This does feel good."

They sat in companionable silence until Barbara decided to ask him a question. "What did you think when you saw Faith at church today?"

David lifted his head and opened his eyes. "It was a surprise to me, as I'm sure it was to most. She's been gone a long time, and I didn't figure she would ever come back. How about you? What were your thoughts about seeing your old friend again?"

Barbara frowned. "It was strange, David. . .very strange."

"In what way?"

"Faith was dressed in Amish clothes, so she looked sort of the same, but her personality has changed."

"How so?"

She released a groan. "Faith isn't the same person I used to know. Even after only a few minutes of talking with her, I could tell that she's unhappy."

"Well, of course she would be. Her husband died recently, isn't that what you heard?"

"That's true," Barbara said with a nod, "but I have a feeling that Faith's unhappiness goes much deeper. Truth be told, I think Faith's misery goes back to her childhood. I suspect she carried that sadness and sense of bitterness along with her when she left home ten years ago."

"You think it's because her folks disapproved of her yodeling and joke telling?"

"Not the yodeling, exactly—or the joke telling, either. There are others in our community who like to yodel and tell funny stories."

"That's true," he said with a nod. *"Mer yodel laut, awwer net gut."*

She nodded. "We do yodel loudly but not well. But I think what the Stutzmans disapproved of was Faith cutting up all the time when she should have been getting her chores done."

Deep lines etched David's forehead. "I can't imagine what it must have been like for her to get up onstage in front of a bunch of people and put on an act. It goes against everything we've been taught to show off like that."

"I don't believe Faith saw it as showing off, David. I think she only ran away and became an entertainer because she didn't feel what she enjoyed doing the most was accepted at home."

"Sure hope none of our kinner ever feels that way. I don't know what I'd do if one of them were to up and leave home."

"Sell kann ich mir gaar net eibilde." She patted his hand and repeated, "I can't conceive

of that at all. I'm sure neither of our boys will do something like that as long as they know we appreciate their abilities and God-given talents."

David leaned over and kissed Barbara's cheek. "You're a *schmaert* woman, you know that?"

She nodded and stroked his bristly, dark beard. "I had to be smart to find a good husband like you."

※

"Church was good today, jah?" Noah's mother asked as she handed Noah and his father each a cup of coffee, then took a seat at the table across from Noah.

Noah nodded. "It's always good."

"Seemed a little strange to see Faith Stutzman back and with a little girl she said was her daughter, no less," Noah's father put in from his seat at the head of the table.

Mom smiled. "It's nice that she's come home and wants to be Amish again."

Noah stared into his cup of coffee as he pondered things. After his short visit with Faith this morning before church and then again after church was over, he wasn't sure she wanted to be Amish. He had a hunch the only reason Faith had come home was to find a place for her daughter to live, and if that meant Faith having to give up her life as an entertainer, then she would do it. It was obvious by the look he'd seen on Faith's face when she spoke of her child that she loved Melinda and would do most anything for her. He just wished she hadn't looked so disinterested when he'd given her the cake with the scripture verse attached. Hopefully, she would take the time to read and absorb what it said.

"You're looking kind of thoughtful there, son," Mom said, breaking into Noah's thoughts. "Is everything all right?"

"Jah, sure." He picked up his cup and took a drink of coffee. "I was just thinking is all."

"So, Noah, who'd you give the cake you made to?" Pop asked.

"Gave it to Faith, figuring she might need some encouragement today."

"That makes sense to me," Mom put in. "Faith's a nice-looking woman, wouldn't you say?"

Noah shrugged. "I suppose she does look pretty good in the face."

"So do some of my baby pigs, but looks ain't everything." Pop thumped his chest a few times. "It's what's in here that counts, and I have a hunch that wayward woman isn't as pretty on the inside as she is on the outside." He grunted. "Let's hope she's learned her lesson about chasing after the things of the world and has come home to stay."

Noah could hardly believe his father would compare Faith's beauty to one of his pigs, but the thing that really riled him was Pop's comment about Faith not being pretty inside.

He sat there a moment, trying to decide how best to say what was on his mind. Pop could be stubborn and rather opinionated at times, and Noah wasn't looking for an argument. Still, he felt the need to defend Faith.

"I think we need to pray for Faith, don't you? Pray that she'll find peace and contentment here in Webster County, and that her relationship with God will be strengthened by her friends and family."

Pop's forehead wrinkled, and he opened his mouth as if to reply, but Mom spoke first. "Noah's right. What Faith needs is encouragement and prayer." She smiled at Noah and patted his arm. "I'm glad you gave her that cake, and I'm sure she'll enjoy eating it as much as we do whenever you bake something for us."

Noah chuckled. "Was that a hint that I should do more baking soon?"

She nodded and took a bite of the sugar-free cake Noah had made especially for her.

"I'll probably do more baking after I get home from work tomorrow evening," Noah said.

Pop snorted. "You ought to quit that foolish job at the tree farm and come back to work for me."

Noah shook his head. "No thanks. I had enough dealings with smelly hogs when I was a boy and we were raising them to put food on our own table. You're better off having Abel Yoder working for you. Ever since he and his family moved here from Pennsylvania, he's been most happy to help with your hogs."

"That's because raising hogs is good, honest work, and Abel knows it." Pop leveled Noah with an icy stare, making Noah wish he'd kept his comments to himself.

"What Noah does for a living is honest work, too," Mom defended.

"Jah, well, it may be honest, but Christmas trees aren't part of the Amish way, and if Noah's not careful, he might be led astray by working with that English fellow who likes to listen to country music all the time."

Noah's mouth dropped open. He'd never said anything to either of his folks about Hank playing country music, and he couldn't figure out how Pop knew about it.

"News travels fast in these parts," Pop said before Noah could voice the question. "You'd better be careful what you say and do."

"I'm sure our son hasn't gotten caught up in the world's music," Mom was quick to say. "And just because his boss chooses to listen to country music, that doesn't make him a bad person."

Noah smiled. He couldn't have said it better himself.

Pop set his cup down so hard on the table that some of the coffee spilled out. "Jah, well, just don't let anything Hank says or does that's worldly rub off on you, Noah."

"Like I would," Noah mumbled as he turned away. Why was it that Pop always looked for the negative in things—especially when it came to Noah?

Chapter 7

In the days that followed, Faith and Melinda settled into a routine. Faith got up early every morning to help with breakfast, milk the cows, and feed the chickens. She labored from sunup to sunset, taking time out only for meals and to help Melinda learn the traditional Pennsylvania Dutch language of the Amish.

The child had also been assigned several chores to do, and even though she seemed all right with the idea of wearing her aunt Susie's Plain clothes, she wasn't used to having so many responsibilities placed on her shoulders. Nor was she accustomed to being taught a foreign language. Amish children grew up speaking their native tongue and learning English when they entered school in the first grade. Since

Melinda would be starting school in the fall and already spoke English, her task was to learn Pennsylvania Dutch.

"I don't like it here, Mama," Melinda said one morning as she handed Faith a freshly laundered towel to be hung on the clothesline next to the house. "When can we go home?"

Faith flinched. Home? They really had no home. Hotels and motels in whatever city Faith was performing in—those were the only homes Melinda had ever known.

She clipped the towel in place and patted the top of her daughter's head. "This is your home now, sweet girl."

"You mean, *our* home, don't you, Mama?"

"Oh yes," Faith said quickly. "And soon you'll get used to the way things are."

Melinda lifted her chin and frowned. "Grandma Stutzman makes me work hard."

Faith wasn't used to manual labor either, and every muscle in her body ached. In the past few weeks, she had pulled so many weeds from the garden that her fingers felt stiff and unyielding. Heaps of clothes had been washed and ironed, and she'd helped with the cooking and cleaning and done numerous other chores she was no longer accustomed to doing. It wasn't the hard work that bothered Faith, though. It was the suffocating feeling that she couldn't be herself. She desperately wanted to sit on the porch in the evenings and yodel to her heart's content. She would enjoy telling some jokes or humorous stories and have her family appreciate them, but that was impossible.

"Mama, are you thinking about what I said?"

Melinda's question caught Faith's attention. "Everyone in the family has a job to do," she said patiently. "In time you'll get used to it."

Faith could see by the child's scowl that she wasn't happy.

"How would you like to eat lunch down by the pond today?" Faith asked, hoping to cheer up Melinda.

Melinda's blue eyes seemed to light right up. "Can Aunt Susie come, too?"

"If Grandma says it's all right."

"Can we bring our dolls along?"

"If you want to."

As Melinda handed Faith a pair of Grandpa Stutzman's trousers to hang on the line, she asked, "How come only the men wear pants here?"

"Grandpa and Grandma belong to the Amish faith, and the church believes only men and boys should wear pants."

Melinda's forehead wrinkled. "Does that mean I ain't never gonna wear jeans again?"

"I'm not ever," Faith corrected.

Melinda nodded soberly. "You and me ain't never gonna wear jeans."

Faith bit back a chuckle as she knelt on the

grass and touched the hem of Melinda's plain blue cotton dress. "I thought you liked wearing dresses."

"I do, but I also like to wear jeans."

"You'll get used to wearing only dresses." Even as the words slipped off her tongue, Faith wondered if her prediction would come true. Melinda had worn fancy dresses, blue jeans, and shorts ever since she'd been a baby, and wearing Plain dresses all the time would be a difficult transition.

"Here's the last towel, Mama. Now can I go swing?"

"Maybe after lunch." Faith was relieved that Melinda had quickly changed the subject. Maybe the child would adjust after all. She seemed to enjoy many things on the farm—spending time with Aunt Susie, playing with the barn cats, helping Grandpa milk the cows, swinging on the same wooden swing Faith had used when she was a little girl. In time, she hoped Melinda would learn to be content with everything about her new life as an Amish girl. In the meantime, Faith would try to make her daughter feel as secure as possible and show her some of the good things about being Plain.

Faith was determined to make this work for Melinda and equally determined to get back on the road as soon as possible. Mama was already pressing her about taking classes so she could be baptized and join the church. Faith didn't know how much longer she could put it off, but for now she had convinced her mother that she needed more time to adjust to the Amish way of life. She'd been gone a long time and couldn't be expected to change overnight. Not that she planned to change. Whenever Faith had a few moments alone, she practiced her yodeling skills and told a few jokes to whatever animal she might be feeding. Soon she would be onstage again, wearing her hillbilly costume and entertaining an approving audience. Around here, no one seemed to appreciate anything that wasn't related to hard work.

Faith hung the last article of clothing on the line, picked up the wicker basket, and took hold of Melinda's hand. As much as Faith wanted to go back on the road, she had to stay awhile longer—to be sure Melinda was accepted and had adjusted well enough to her new surroundings. Besides, despite several phone calls Faith had managed to make from town, she hadn't found an agent to represent her yet. Without an agent, her career would go nowhere. On her own, all Faith could hope for were one-night stands and programs in small theaters that didn't pay nearly as well as the bigger ones.

"Let's go to the kitchen and see what we can make for our picnic lunch, shall we?" Faith suggested to Melinda, knowing she needed to get her mind on something else.

The child nodded eagerly, and the soft *ma–a–a* of a nearby goat caused them both to laugh as they skipped along the path leading to the house. On the way, they tromped through a mud puddle made by the rain that had fallen during the night. Faith felt the grimy mud ooze between her bare toes. She'd almost forgotten what it was like to go barefoot every summer. It wasn't such a bad thing, really. Especially on the grass, so soft and cushy. It was good to laugh and spend time with her daughter like this. No telling how many more weeks she would have with Melinda.

When Faith and Melinda entered the kitchen a few minutes later, they were greeted with a look of disapproval from Faith's mother. "Ach, my! Your feet are all muddy. Can't you see that I just cleaned the floor?"

Faith looked down at the grubby footprints they had created. "Sorry, Mama. We'll go back outside and clean the dirt off our feet." She grabbed a towel from the counter, took Melinda's hand, and scooted her out the door.

"Grandma Stutzman's mean," Melinda said tearfully. "She's always hollering about something or other."

"It might seem so, but Grandma just wants to keep her kitchen clean." Faith led her daughter over to the pump. She washed their feet and dried them.

"Can we still take our lunch down by the pond?" Melinda questioned.

"Sure we can."

"And Susie can come, too?"

"If Grandma says it's all right."

Melinda's lower lip protruded. "She'll probably say no 'cause she's in a bad mood about us trackin' in the mud on her clean floor."

"I don't think she'll make Susie pay for our transgressions."

"Our what?"

"Transgressions. It means doing wrong things."

Melinda hung her head. "I always seem to be doing wrong things around here. I must be very bad."

Faith knelt on the ground and pulled her daughter into her arms. "You're not bad. You just don't understand all the rules yet."

"Will I ever understand them, Mama?"

Faith gently stroked the child's cheek. "Of course you will. It's just going to take a little more time."

"But I want to wear blue jeans and watch TV, and I can't do either of those things here."

Guilt found its way into Faith's heart and put down roots so deep she thought she might choke. Had she done the right thing in taking Melinda out of the modern world she was used to and expecting her to adjust to the Amish way of doing things? Faith had never accepted all the rules when she was growing up. She had experimented with modern things whenever she'd had the chance. Had it really been all those rules that had driven her away, or was it the simple fact that she'd never felt truly loved and acknowledged by her family?

Noah whistled in response to the call of a finch as he knelt in front of a newly planted pine tree. It was still scrawny compared to those around it, and the seedling appeared to be struggling to survive.

"A little more time and attention are what you're needing," he whispered, resolving to save the fledgling. He wanted to see it thrive and someday find its way to one of the local Christmas tree lots or be purchased by some Englishers who would come to the farm to choose their own holiday tree.

The sound of country-western music blared in Noah's ear, and he figured his boss, Hank Osborn, must be nearby. Hank enjoyed listening to the radio while he worked, and Noah had discovered that he rather liked it, too. Of course, he wouldn't let his folks or anyone from their community know that, and he sure wouldn't buy a radio or listen to music on his own at home. But here at work, it was kind of nice. Besides, this was his boss's radio, and Noah had no control over whether it was played.

The man singing on the radio at the

moment also did a bit of yodeling. It made Noah think of Faith and how she had given up her entertaining career and moved back home. He wondered if she had enjoyed the cake he'd given her and what she thought about the verse of scripture he'd attached to it. Had it spoken to her heart, the way God's Word was supposed to? He hoped so, for Faith seemed to be in need of something, and Noah couldn't think of anything more nourishing to the soul than the words found within the Bible.

"Did you bring any of your baked goods in your lunch today?"

Noah turned his head at the sound of his boss's voice. He hadn't realized Hank had moved over to his row of trees. "I made some oatmeal bread last night," Noah said. "Brought you and your wife a loaf of it."

Hank lowered the volume, set his portable radio on the ground, and hunkered down beside Noah. "You're the best! Sure hope your mama knows how lucky she is to have you still living at home."

Noah snickered. "I think she appreciates my help in the kitchen, but I'm not sure how lucky she is."

"A fellow like you ought to be married and raising babies, like those nine brothers of yours have done. Between your cooking and baking skills and the concern you show over a weak little tree, I'd say you would make one fine husband and daddy." Hank nodded toward the struggling pine Noah had been studying before he let his thoughts carry him away.

Noah felt a flush of heat climb up the back of his neck and spread to his cheeks. He hated how easily he blushed.

"Didn't mean to embarrass you. I'm glad to have someone as caring as you working here at Osborns' Christmas Tree Farm." Hank clasped Noah's shoulder. "Besides that, you're easy to talk to."

"Sure hope so." It was then that Noah noticed his boss's wrinkled forehead. "Is there something wrong, Hank? You look so thoughtful."

Hank ran his fingers through his thick, auburn-colored hair. "To tell you the truth, something's bothering me."

Noah got to his feet, and Hank did the same. "Is there a problem with your business? Are you concerned that you won't sell as many trees this year as you have before?"

"It's got nothing to do with business. It's about me and Sandy."

"What's the problem?" Noah kicked a clump of grass with the toe of his boot. "Or would you rather not talk about it?"

Hank shook his head. "I don't mind telling you. In fact, it might do me some good to get this off my chest."

Concern for his boss welled in Noah's soul,

and he clasped Hank's shoulder. "Whatever you say will remain between the two of us; you can be sure of that."

"Thanks. I appreciate it." Hank drew in a breath and let it out with a huff. "The thing is. . .Sandy and I have been trying to have a baby for the last couple of years, and yesterday afternoon we went to see a specialist in Springfield and found out that Sandy's unable to conceive."

"I'm sorry to hear that. I'm sure you would both make good parents."

"We've wanted children ever since we got married ten years ago, but we were waiting to start our family until I got my business going good." Hank sighed. "Now that we can finally afford to have a baby, we get hit with the news that Sandy is barren."

Noah wasn't sure how to respond. Among his people, folks didn't wait until they were financially ready to have a baby. Children came in God's time, whether a couple felt ready or not.

"After we left the doctor's office, Sandy acted real depressed and would barely speak to me. I have to admit, I was pretty upset when I heard the news, too." Hank grunted. "Then last night when we were getting ready for bed, she said, 'I think you don't love me anymore because I can't give you children.'"

"What'd you say to that?"

"I tried to convince her that I do love her, but she wouldn't listen to me."

Noah rubbed his chin thoughtfully as he contemplated his reply. "She probably needs time to adjust to things, and if you let her know through your kind words and actions, she'll soon realize that your love isn't conditional."

"You're right. It's not. I would love Sandy no matter what. Even though it would be nice to have a baby of our own, it's not nearly as important to me as having Sandy as my wife."

"Maybe if you keep telling her that, she'll begin to realize it's true."

"Yeah, I hope so."

Noah didn't know why he was telling Hank all this; he was sure no expert on the subject of marriage. Even so, he felt he had to say something that might help his boss feel better about things.

"Have you thought about taking in a foster child or adopting a baby?" Noah asked.

Hank shook his head. "Oh, I don't know. . . . I don't think Sandy would go for that idea."

"Why not?"

"Because she wants her own child. She said so many times during the two years we tried to have a baby."

"She might change her mind now that she knows she's unable to have children of her own."

"I—I suppose she could, but she's so upset right now. I don't think it's a good time to talk about adoption." Hank stared at the ground.

"Maybe not, but it's something to consider." Noah paused and reflected on his next words, knowing that Hank wasn't a particularly religious man. "I want you to know that I'll be praying for you."

"Thanks." Hank looked up and clasped Noah's shoulder. "You're a good man, and I count it a privilege to have you as my employee and my friend."

"Same goes for me." Noah smiled. "And I really enjoy working with all these," he added, motioning to the trees surrounding them.

"You might not say that come fall when things get really busy."

"I made it through last year and lived to tell about it," Noah said with a laugh. The month or so before Christmas was always hectic at the tree farm. In early November, trees were cut, netted, and bundled for pickup by various lots. Many people in the area came to the Osborns' to choose and cut their own trees, as well. Some folks dropped by as early as the first of October to reserve their pine.

Hank's wife ran the gift shop, located in one section of the barn. She took in a lot of items on consignment from the local people, including several who were Amish. Everything from homemade peanut brittle to pinecone-decorated wreaths was sold at the gift store, and Sandy always served her customers a treat before they left the rustic-looking building Hank had built for her a few years ago. Last year Noah had contributed some baked goods, and his desserts had been well received. He hoped things would work out for Sandy and Hank, because they were both nice people.

"I appreciate you listening to my tale of woe, but now I guess I'd better move on to the next row and see how Fred and Bob are doing," Hank said, breaking into Noah's thoughts. "Want me to leave the radio with you?"

Noah shook his head. "No, thanks. The melody the birds are making is all the music I need."

Hank thumped Noah lightly on the back. "All right, then. See you up at the barn at lunchtime."

"Sure thing." Noah moved on down the row of pines to check several more seedlings. As a father would tend his child, he took special care with each struggling tree. He figured that like everything else the good Lord created, these future Christmas trees needed tender, loving care.

As Noah thought about Hank's comment concerning him making a good husband and father, an uninvited image of Faith Andrews popped into his mind. He could see her look of confusion when he'd given her the cake.

"Now why am I thinking about her again?" he muttered. No question about it—Faith was a fine-looking woman. From what he remembered of the way Faith used to be, she could be a lot of fun. But Noah was sure there was no hope of her ever being interested in someone like him.

I'm shy; she's outgoing. I'm plain; she's beautiful. I'm twenty-four; she's twenty-eight. I'm firmly committed to the Amish faith, and she's— what exactly is Faith committed to? Noah determined to find that out as soon as he got to know her better.

Chapter 8

Noah stood on the front porch of his folks' rambling, two-story farmhouse, leaning against the railing and gazing into the yard. Pop had built this place shortly after he and Mom moved to Missouri from the state of Indiana. Twenty-three other families had joined them in establishing the first Amish community on the outskirts of the small town of Seymour. Now, nearly two hundred Plain families lived in the area. Some had moved here from other parts of the country, while others came about from marriages and children being born to those who had chosen to stay and make their home in the area.

Noah and his brothers were some of those born and raised in Webster County, and Noah had never traveled any farther than the town of Springfield. He had no desire to see the world like some folks did. He loved it here and was content to stay near those he cared about so deeply.

His brothers Chester, Jonas, and Harvey had moved to northern Missouri with their wives and children. Lloyd, Lyle, Rube, and Henry now lived in Illinois. Only William, Peter, and Noah had chosen to stay in the area. Each had his own farm, although some had opened businesses to supplement their income.

Noah's thoughts darted ahead to his plans for the next day. Church was held every other Sunday, and since tomorrow was a preaching Sunday, Noah planned to speak with Faith. He wanted to find out if she had enjoyed his lemon sponge cake and see what she thought of the verse he'd attached. He contemplated the idea of taking her another one of his baked goods but decided she might think he was being pushy. From the few minutes they'd spent together, Noah guessed Faith felt uncomfortable and probably needed a friend. Maybe he could be her friend, if she would let him.

He gulped in a deep breath of the evening air and flopped into Pop's wooden rocking chair. It smelled as if rain was coming, and with the oppressing heat they'd been having lately, the land could surely use a good dousing.

A short time later, a streak of lightning shot

across the sky, followed by a thunderous roar that shook the whole house.

"Jah, a summer storm's definitely coming," he murmured. "Guess I'd best be getting to bed, or I'll be tempted to sit out here and watch it all night." Noah had enjoyed watching thunderstorms ever since he was a boy. Something fascinated him about the way lightning zigzagged across the sky as the rain pelted the earth. It made Noah realize the awesomeness of God's power. Everything on earth was under the Master's hand, and Noah never ceased to marvel at the majesty of it all.

He rose from his chair just as the rain started to fall. It fell lightly at first but soon began to pummel the ground. He gazed up at the dismal, gray sky. "Keep us all safe this night, Lord."

❧❦❧

Faith shuddered and pulled the sides of her pillow around her ears as she tried to drown out the sound of the storm brewing outside her bedroom window. She'd been afraid of storms since she was a child and had often been teased by her older brothers about being a scaredy-cat. But she couldn't help it. Everyone had something they were afraid of, didn't they?

"Mama, I heard an awful boom," Melinda said as she crept into Faith's room, wearing one of Susie's long white nightgowns and holding the vinyl doll her father had given her on the Christmas before he'd been killed.

Faith motioned Melinda over to the bed. "It's just some thunder rumbling," she said, hoping she sounded braver than she felt.

"I don't like the thunder, and I've got a tummy ache. Can I sleep with you?"

"Is Susie awake, too?"

"Nope. She's sound asleep. Didn't even budge when I got out of bed."

"Okay, come on in." Faith pulled the covers aside and scooted over.

Another clap of thunder sounded, and Melinda hopped into bed with a yelp. Faith figured her own fear of storms must be hereditary. No wonder Melinda had a stomachache. Seeing the way the windows rattled and hearing the terrible boom of the thunder was enough to make anyone feel sick.

"I hope Susie won't be too disappointed when she wakes up in the morning and discovers you're not in her room," Faith said as Melinda snuggled against her arm.

"Why would she be disappointed?"

Faith swallowed a couple of times as she thought of the best way to say what was on her mind. She wanted Melinda to bond with Susie and the rest of the family so that, when Faith headed back on the road, Melinda would feel like she belonged here. "I've. . .uh. . .seen how well you and Susie have been getting along since we came here, and I'm hoping the two of you can always be friends."

"You're my friend, too, Mama," Melinda said as her voice took on a sleepy tone. "Always and forever." The child's eyes drifted shut, and her breathing became heavy as she drifted off to sleep.

Another rumble of thunder sounded, and Faith turned her head toward the window. "Dear God, give me the strength to leave when it's time to go," she murmured. It was her first prayer in a long time. "Now where did that come from?" For many years, Faith had done everything in her own strength, and she'd come to believe that she didn't need anyone's help, not even God's. So why had she prayed out loud like that? And why, as she snuggled against her daughter, did she find herself wishing she didn't have to leave Webster County? If she stayed, she would have to give up yodeling and telling jokes, and she didn't think she could endure the somber life her folks would expect her to live. No, she had to go.

***

Noah sat up with a start. He'd been having a strange dream about Pop's squealing pigs when something awakened him. *Strange,* he thought as he slipped out of bed. *I don't even like my daed's smelly critters, so it makes no sense that I'd be dreaming about them.*

It was still raining. Noah could hear the heavy drops falling on their metal roof and the wind whipping against his upstairs bedroom window, rattling the glass until he feared it might break.

Noah padded across the wooden floor in his bare feet and lifted the dark shade from the windowpane. He gasped at the sight before him.

Flames of red and orange shot out of the barn in all directions, as billows of smoke drifted toward the sky.

Noah threw on his clothes and dashed down the stairs. He pounded on his parents' bedroom door, shouting, "Pop, get up! *Schnell!* The barn's on fire! Hurry!"

The next couple of hours went by in a blur as Noah, his father, and several neighbors, including Noah's brothers William and Peter, tried unsuccessfully to save the Hertzlers' barn. Only by a miracle were the animals rescued, although they lost one aged sow, and several other pigs seemed to be affected by the smoke.

One of their English neighbors had phoned the Seymour Fire Department, but they hadn't arrived in time to save the barn. Noah felt sick at heart as he and his folks stood in the yard, surveying the damage. From the slump of his father's shoulders and his downcast eyes, Noah knew Pop felt even worse than he did.

"I'm sorry about your barn," Noah said with a catch in his voice. "If I'd only been awake when it was struck by lightning, maybe we could've caught it in time to keep the whole place from burning."

"It's not your fault," his father said hoarsely, reaching up to wipe away the soot on his cheeks. "Trouble comes to all, and at least no human lives were taken."

Mom slipped an arm around Pop's waist. "We can have a new barn raised as soon as this mess is cleaned up."

Noah nodded. "And I'm sure we'll have plenty of help." Folks in their community always rallied whenever anyone lost a barn or needed major work done on a house.

"There's nothing more we can do here," Mom said. "I say we go on back to bed and try to get a few more hours' sleep before we have to get up for preaching."

Pop nodded and took hold of her hand; then the two of them shuffled off toward the house.

"You coming, son?" Mom called over her shoulder.

"I'll be in after a bit."

Noah heard the back door click shut behind his folks, but he just stood on the grass. The huge white barn he had played in as a child was gone. Its remains were nothing more than a pile of charred lumber and a heap of grimy ashes.

Soon there would be a new barn in its place. At least that was something to be thankful for.

⁂

Faith awoke on Sunday morning feeling groggy and disoriented. She'd spent most of the night caring for Melinda, who had come down with the flu. The child was running a temperature and had vomited several times. It was no wonder she'd complained of a stomachache.

Faith glanced over at her daughter, now sleeping peacefully on the other side of the bed. She would let the child sleep while she went downstairs for a bite of breakfast, then she'd come straight back to her room.

Faith slipped out from under the covers and plucked her lightweight robe off the wall peg. A short time later, she found her mother and three sisters in the kitchen, scurrying about to get the table set and breakfast on. The tantalizing aroma of eggs cooking on the stove made her stomach rumble. Until this moment she hadn't realized she was hungry.

"You're not dressed," Mama said, scowling at Faith and pointing to her nightgown. "And where's Melinda? The two of you are going to make us late for preaching if you don't get a move on."

"Melinda came down with the flu during the night." Faith reached for the teakettle near the back of the stove. "We'll be staying home from church today."

"I'm sorry to hear that," Mama said.

"Sorry to hear Melinda's sick or that we won't be going to church?" Faith knew her voice sounded harsh, but she didn't like the feeling that her mother disapproved of her staying home from church in order to care for Melinda.

"I don't appreciate the tone you're using," Mama said, pushing her glasses to the bridge of her nose. "I'm sorry to hear Melinda is sick, and I understand why you won't be going to preaching today."

A sense of guilt stabbed Faith's conscience. In times past, Mama had seemed so judgmental, and Faith had assumed nothing had changed. Apparently she'd been wrong. Maybe Mama did care about Melinda being sick.

"Sorry for snapping," Faith mumbled. "Guess I'm a mite edgy this morning. Between that awful storm and Melinda getting sick, neither of us got much sleep last night."

"I'm sorry if I sounded irritable, too," her mother said.

"Am I gonna get sick, too, Mama?" Susie spoke up. She'd been setting the table but had stopped what she was doing when Faith mentioned that Melinda had come down with the flu.

"I hope not," Faith said. "That's why I kept Melinda in my room all night."

"If the child stays in your room while she's got the bug, maybe none of us will get it," Mama added.

"What about Faith?" Esther's pale blue eyes narrowed with obvious concern. She handed her mother two more eggs. "If Melinda's been sleeping with Faith, hasn't she already been exposed? Won't she likely get the flu?"

"Guess that all depends on how strong her immune system is," Mama replied. She broke one egg into the pan and reached for another.

"That's right," Grace Ann put in as she retrieved a jug of milk from the refrigerator and set it on the table. "Some people can be exposed to all kinds of things and never get sick. Maybe our big sister's one of those healthy people."

Faith could hardly believe the way her sisters and mother were discussing her as though she weren't even in the room. Irritated with their lack of manners and feeling the need to say something on her own behalf, she said, "I hardly ever become ill, but have no fear. If I do come down with the bug, I'll be sure to stay put in my room." Faith grabbed a stash of napkins and added them to the silverware Susie had set next to each plate.

"If anyone else should get sick, we'll deal with it as it comes," Mama said with a nod. "Your daed and the brothers will be in soon, so right now the only thing we should concern ourselves with is getting breakfast on the table."

Grace Ann and Faith exchanged glances, but neither said a word, and Faith was glad the discussion was over. All she wanted to do was eat a little breakfast, fix a cup of mint tea for Melinda, and head back upstairs to her room.

⟨⟨⟨❀⟩⟩⟩

Once breakfast was over and Faith had gone upstairs to check on Melinda, Wilma began washing the dishes while Susie dried them. Grace Ann swept the floor, and Esther wiped off the stove and countertops.

"I don't understand why Faith gets upset so easily," Esther said as she handed her mother the wet rag she'd been using.

"She did seem a mite testy," Wilma agreed.

"It didn't sound like she got much sleep last night," Grace Ann put. "I can understand that, because I'm always cranky whenever I don't get enough sleep."

"Ha!" Esther grunted. "You're cranky every morning, no matter how much sleep you've had the night before."

"I am not."

"Are so."

"Am not."

"Girls," Wilma said with a frown, "you're acting like a couple of ornery old hens, not two young women who should know better than to carry on in such a way."

"Bawk! Bawk!" Susie flapped her arms and

waved the dish towel. "My sisters are a couple of fat red hens."

"I didn't say your sisters were fat," Wilma corrected. "And I'll thank you to tend to your own business or you might end up making a visit to the woodshed this morning."

Susie dropped her gaze to the floor and turned toward the plates waiting to be dried on the plastic dish drainer. Wilma went back to washing the rest of the dishes. It was good to have Faith home again, but her presence had created a few problems. Her three younger sisters had become a bit disagreeable since Faith's appearance, and young Susie was much more vocal than she used to be.

"I wonder what it must have been like for Faith living in the English world and entertaining folks on a stage somewhere," Esther said as she leaned against the counter near the sink with a dreamy look on her face.

"That's not for us to know, so don't go asking Faith about it," Wilma said with a shake of her head.

"I'd like to see one of those shows sometime," Esther went on to say. "Just so I'd know what it must have been like for Faith."

Wilma dropped her rag into the dishwater with a splash, sending several bubbles floating to the ceiling. "There'll be no more talk like that in this house. It was hard enough to lose one daughter to the world, and I'll not lose another." She paused and shook her finger. "So you'd better think twice about such foolish notions."

Esther nodded solemnly and moved away from the sink, just as John entered the house and announced that the horses and buggies were ready to go. "Papa said for me to tell you womenfolk that it's time to leave for church," he added.

"We're coming," Wilma said as she dried her hands on the clean towel she'd pulled from a cupboard drawer.

John looked around the room. "Where are Faith and Melinda? Aren't they going to church today?"

Wilma lifted her gaze toward the ceiling. "Where were you during breakfast this morning?"

"At the table, same as you."

"Then you must have heard Faith tell us that Melinda took sick during the night, and that she'd be staying home in order to care for the child."

John shrugged and gave a noncommittal grunt. "Jah, okay. See you outside in the buggy."

As Wilma followed her daughters out the door, she offered a silent prayer for all her brood.

❦

Late that afternoon, Faith stepped outside to the front porch. She'd spent the early part of the day resting and caring for Melinda and was glad the child was feeling somewhat better and had eaten a bowl of chicken broth around noon. Melinda was napping now, so Faith decided to spend a few minutes on the porch swing where she could enjoy the fresh, rain-washed scent still permeating the air after last night's storm. It had been a nasty one, and even if Melinda hadn't kept Faith up all night, the wind and rain surely would have. A bolt of lightning could do a lot of damage, and so could the howling winds. Buildings might catch on fire, roofs could be blown off, and flash floods often occurred. Any of those tragedies meant lots of hard work.

When a ball of white fur jumped up beside Faith, she shifted on the swing and stroked the top of the cat's fluffy white head. "You needed to get away from your hungry babies for a while, didn't you, Snowball?"

The cat meowed in response, curled into a tight ball, and began to purr.

Faith smiled. Oh, to live the life of a cat, whose only concern was licking its paws, batting at bugs, and chasing down some defenseless bird or mouse once in a while. Cats didn't have to answer to anyone. They could pretty much do as they pleased.

She leaned her head against the back of the swing and closed her eyes. It was so peaceful here, where the birds chirped happily and no one competed with anyone else to get ahead. Nothing like Faith's life on the road had been. There were so many demands and pressures that went along with being an entertainer. Days and nights spent in travel, hours of practicing for shows, and the burden of trying to please an audience had taken their toll on Faith. Still, she would gladly put up with the discomforts in order to do what she liked best. *If only my folks would have accepted my humor when I was a girl. Was it really so wrong to tell jokes and yodel whenever I felt like it?*

Had her family's disapproval been the reason for Faith's lack of faith? Or had it come about when she'd married Greg and been mistreated by him? Faith believed in God— had since she was a girl. But God had never seemed real to her in a personal way.

Faith's eyes snapped open, and she bolted upright when she heard the thudding of horses' hooves and the rumble of buggy wheels pulling into the yard. Her family was home from church. As John led the horses to the barn, everyone else came streaming up the path toward the house, talking a mile a minute.

"You were missed at preaching today," Mama said as she stepped onto the porch. "Noah Hertzler asked about you."

Faith nodded.

"The Hertzlers' barn burned to the ground last night," her brother Brian said, his dark eyes looking ever so serious. "There's gonna be a barn raising later this week."

"Sorry to hear about their misfortune. Was the barn hit by lightning?"

"It would seem so," Papa said as he came up behind Mama. "Sure hope everybody in this house is well by Friday, because all hands will be needed at the Hertzlers' that day."

All hands? Did that mean Faith and Melinda would be expected to go and help out?

"The little ones will remain at home," Mama said before Faith could voice the question. "Esther can stay with them, so Grace Ann, Faith, and I will be able to help with the meals for the men."

Faith clenched her teeth. She wanted to stand up to Mama and say that she was treating her like a child, and that she could decide for herself if she was going to help at the barn raising. She remained silent, however. No point in getting Mama all riled. Faith needed to keep the peace as long as she chose to stay here; it would help ensure her daughter's future. Besides, she did feel bad for the Hertzlers. Nobody should have to lose their barn.

Chapter 9

By eight o'clock on Friday morning, the air was already hot, sticky, and devoid of any breeze. It would be a long, grueling day as the men worked on the Hertzlers' new barn. Faith didn't envy them having to labor under the sweltering sun. At least she and the other women who had come to help serve the men could escape the blistering heat now and then. Their work wouldn't be nearly as difficult, either.

When Faith entered the Hertzlers' kitchen along with her mother and Grace Ann, she saw several other Amish women scurrying around, getting coffee and lemonade ready to serve the men when they became thirsty or needed a break.

Already the kitchen was warm and stuffy,

making Faith long to be anywhere else but there. A dip in a swimming pool would surely be nice.

Faith leaned against the wall and thought about the last time she'd gone swimming with Melinda and Greg. It had been at a hotel pool in Memphis, Tennessee. Greg was in good spirits that Sunday afternoon, probably because he'd won big at a poker table the night before.

When Faith closed her eyes, she saw an image of Greg carrying Melinda on his shoulders. Tall and slender, his jet-black hair and aqua-colored eyes made Faith think he was the most handsome man she'd ever met. The three of them had stayed in the water for over an hour that day, laughing, splashing around the pool like a model, loving family.

Only we weren't model, and Greg may have been handsome and charming, but his love was conditional. Faith blinked away the stinging tears threatening to escape her lashes. *Why didn't Greg love me the way a man should love his wife? Why couldn't we be a happy family?*

"It's good to see you," Barbara said, jolting Faith away from her memories. "I was hoping you'd be here today. It'll give us a chance to get reacquainted and catch up on one another's lives."

Faith nodded. Truth was she couldn't allow herself to reestablish what she and Barbara once had, because she knew she wouldn't be staying

around long enough to develop any close ties—
not even with family members. It would make
it easier to say good-bye when it was time for
Faith to leave.

"Are you okay?" Barbara asked with a note
of concern. "You look kind of sad today."

"I'm fine." Faith nibbled on her lower lip.
"Just standing here waiting to be told what I
should do."

Barbara looked a little uncertain, but she
handed Faith a pitcher of lemonade and grabbed
one for herself. "Let's take these outside to the
menfolk. Then we can sit a spell and visit before
it's time to start the noon meal."

Faith followed Barbara out the door. They
placed their pitchers on a wooden table beside
a huge pot of coffee. As warm as it was today,
Faith didn't see how anyone could drink the hot
beverage, but then she remembered something
her father used to say: *"If I'm warm on the inside
when it's hot outside, then my body believes it's
cold."*

That made no sense to Faith, and she was
pretty sure it was just Dad's excuse to drink
more than his share of the muddy-looking
brew. She had never acquired a taste for coffee
and planned to keep it that way.

"Let's sit over there," Barbara said, motioning to a couple of wicker chairs under a shady
maple tree.

Faith flopped into one of the seats and

fanned her face with her hands. "Sure is warm out already. I can only imagine how hot and muggy it'll be by the end of the day."

Barbara nodded. "Pity the poor men working on that barn."

Faith's gaze drifted across the yard to where the Hertzlers' barn was already taking shape. Rising higher than the family's two-story house, the framing of the new structure looked enormous. Men and older boys armed with saws, hammers, and planes were positioned in various sections of the barn. It would be a lot of work, but they would probably have most of it done by the end of the day.

"An English barn is built using all modern equipment, but it doesn't come together in twice the time it takes for an Amish barn raising," Faith noted.

"That's because we all pull together when there's a need. I wouldn't be happy living anywhere but here among my people."

If Barbara's comment was meant to be a jab at Faith and her wayward ways, she chose to ignore it. "No, I don't suppose you would be."

"Tell me what it's like out there in the world of entertaining," Barbara said, redirecting their conversation. "Is it all you had hoped it would be?"

"It's different—and exciting. At least it was for me."

"Do you miss it?"

Faith swallowed hard. How could she tell Barbara how much she missed entertaining without letting on that she didn't plan to stay in Webster County indefinitely? She moistened her lips with the tip of her tongue as she searched for the right words. "I miss certain things about it."

"Such as?"

"The response of an appreciative audience to one of my jokes or the joy of yodeling and not having anyone looking down their nose because I'm doing something different that they think is wrong." Faith hadn't planned to say so much, but the words slipped off her tongue before she could stop them.

"You think that's how your family acted?"

Faith nodded.

"Do you believe they saw your joke telling and yodeling as wrong?"

Faith could hardly believe her friend had forgotten all the times she'd told her about her folks' disapproval. Maybe Barbara had become so caught up in her adult life that she didn't remember much about their younger days when they had confided in one another and been almost as close as sisters. The truth was, Barbara had gotten after Faith a few times. Not for her joke telling and sense of humor, but for her discontent and her tendency to fool around.

"Papa used to holler at me for wasting time

when I should've been working. He thought my yodeling sounded like a croaking frog, and many times he said I was too silly for my own good." Faith's voice was edged with bitterness, but she didn't care. It was the truth, plain and simple.

"There are a few others in the area who like to yodel," Barbara reminded. "As you know, yodeling is part of the Swiss-German heritage of some who live here, and it's been passed from one generation to the next."

"That may be true, but Papa has never liked me doing it, and it took English audiences to appreciate my talent."

Barbara's raised eyebrows revealed her apparent surprise. "Did you enjoy being English?"

Faith wasn't sure how to respond, so she merely nodded in reply.

"Then why'd you come back?"

"I—I thought it was best for Melinda."

"Your mamm tells me you've been widowed for several months."

"That's right. My husband stepped out into traffic and was hit by a car."

Barbara slowly shook her head. "Such a shame it is. I'm real sorry for you, Faith. I can't imagine life without my David. We work so well together in the harness shop, and he's such a good father to our boys, Aaron and Joseph. I don't think I could stand it if something happened to David. It's hard enough to lose a parent or grandparent, but losing a husband? That would be unbearable pain." She glanced over at Faith and offered a half smile. "Might be a good thing for you and your daughter if you found another husband. Don't you think?"

Faith felt her fingers go numb from clutching the folds in her dress so tightly. She had no intention of finding another husband. Not now. Not ever.

"How old are your sons?" Faith asked, hoping to steer their conversation in another direction. She didn't want to talk about her dysfunctional marriage to Greg, his untimely death, or the idea of marrying again. Remembering was easy; forgetting was the hard part. Thinking about a relationship with another man was impossible.

"Aaron's four, and Joseph just turned two." Barbara patted her belly and grinned. "We're hoping to have another *boppli* soon. Maybe a girl this time around."

"You're pregnant?" Faith couldn't imagine having two little ones to care for, plus a baby on the way.

"Not yet, but soon, I hope. I love being a mamm."

Faith enjoyed motherhood, too, and she had hoped to have more children someday. But with the way things were between her and Greg, she was glad it hadn't happened. His unreliability and quick temper were reason enough not to want to bring any more children into their unhappy marriage, not to mention his drinking and gambling habits. Now that Faith was widowed and had no plans of remarrying, she was certain Melinda would be her only child.

Faith shifted in her chair. *At least Melinda will have her aunt Susie to grow up with. That's almost like having a sister.*

"You'll have to excuse me a minute," Barbara said as she stood. "David's waving at me. He must want something to drink."

Faith stood, too. "Guess I'll go on back to the house and see what needs to be done for the noon meal."

Just before Faith and Barbara parted ways, Barbara touched Faith's arm and said, "I always enjoyed your joke telling."

"Thanks." Faith headed around the back side of the Hertzlers' place, not feeling a whole lot better about things. Barbara's compliment was appreciated, but it didn't replace the approval of Faith's parents. That's what she longed for but was sure she would never have.

She was almost to the porch when she spotted Noah coming out the door. He carried a jug of water and lifted the container when he saw her. "It's getting mighty hot out there. Thought some of the men would rather have cold water to quench their thirst."

Faith's cheeks warmed. "Sorry," she mumbled. "I should have realized not everyone would want coffee or lemonade."

Noah tromped down the stairs, his black work boots thumping against each wooden step. He stopped when he reached Faith. "I haven't had a chance to talk to you since I gave you that lemon sponge cake after church a few weeks ago. I was wondering how you liked it."

"It was very good."

"Glad you liked it," he said with a friendly grin. "What'd you think about the verse of scripture?"

Faith sucked in her breath, searching for words that wouldn't be an outright lie. "Well, I. . .uh. . .I think it may have gotten thrown out before I had a chance to read it."

Noah's forehead wrinkled. "I'm sorry to hear that. It was a good verse. One about faith, in fact."

"There's a verse in the Bible about *me*?" Faith giggled and winked at him, hoping he wasn't one who had a dislike for the funny side of life.

A slow smile spread across Noah's face, and he chuckled. "You do still have a sense of humor. You seemed so solemn when we last talked, and I couldn't help but wonder if you'd left your joke telling back in the English world."

She shrugged. "What can I say? Once a comedian, always a comedian." So much for being careful to watch her tongue and keep her silliness locked away.

"Do you miss it?" This was the second time today that Faith had been asked the question, and she wondered what Noah's reaction to her response would be.

"Sometimes," Faith admitted. "But I'm afraid there's no place for my joke telling here in Webster County."

"You don't have to set your humor aside just because you're not getting paid or standing in front of a huge audience anymore."

She pulled in her lower lip as she inhaled deeply and then released her breath with a groan. "It's kind of hard to be funny when everyone around you is so serious."

Noah took a seat on the porch step and motioned for Faith to do the same. "We're not all a bunch of sourpusses sucking on tart grapes, you know. In case you haven't noticed, many among us like to have fun." He nodded toward two young men who stood across the yard. They'd been drinking lemonade a few minutes ago but were now sprinting across the grass, grabbing for one another's straw hats.

Faith smiled, realizing Noah had made his point.

"Now back to that verse of scripture."

Oh no. Here it comes. I think I'm about to receive a sermon from this man.

"It was from Hebrews, chapter eleven, verse six."

"And it's about faith, right?"

He nodded. " 'But without faith it is impossible to please him: for he that cometh to God must believe that he is, and that he is a rewarder of them that diligently seek him.' "

She contemplated his words. "If it's impossible to please God without having faith, then I must be a terrible disappointment to Him."

Noah tilted his head to one side. "Now why would you say something like that?"

"Because my faith is weak. It's almost nonexistent."

"Faith isn't faith until it's all you're holding on to. Some folks get the idea that faith is making God do what we want Him to do." He shook his head. "Not so. Faith is the substance of things not seen."

"Hmm."

"Abraham was the father of faith. When he heard God's voice telling him to leave and go to a new land, he went—not even knowing where he was going."

Faith could relate to that part a little. When she'd first left home to strike out on her own, she hadn't had a clue where she was going. She had ended up waiting tables at a restaurant in Springfield for a time.

"Faith's like a muscle you've got to develop. It takes time and patience." Noah grinned at her. "Guess that's a little more than you were hoping to hear, jah?"

She shrugged, then nodded. "Just a bit."

"Oh, and one more thing."

"What's that?"

"Your name is Faith, so I think that means you've got to have faith."

"No, it doesn't." She jumped up and dashed for the house before he had a chance to say anything more.

Chapter 10

One Saturday morning a few weeks after the Hertzlers' barn raising, Faith decided to take Melinda into Seymour to check out the farmers' market. It would give the two of them some quality time together, which they hadn't had much of since they'd arrived in Webster County. Faith knew she'd be leaving soon. She'd driven one of her father's buggies into town last week and phoned the talent agency in Memphis again. This time she was told that one of their agents, Brad Olsen, was interested in representing her as soon as she was ready to go back on the road. He asked that she contact him at her earliest convenience, and Faith planned to do so as soon as she could leave.

Faith felt a need to speak to Melinda in

private today, encouraging her in the ways of her Amish family and helping her adjust to their new lifestyle. Besides, getting away from the farm for the day would allow Faith to do something fun—something she was sure she would be criticized for if she did it at home. It would give Faith a chance to make another phone call, too. She needed to check in with the agency and make sure they knew she was still interested in being represented by Mr. Olsen.

After they finished browsing the market, Faith had every intention of taking Melinda to one of the local restaurants where they could listen to some country-western music. Baldy's Café had been one of her favorite places to go when she was a teenager, so she thought about taking Melinda there. Not only did they serve succulent country fried steak, tasty pork chops, and smothered chicken, but lively country music was played on the radio.

Gathering the reins in her hands and waving good-bye to her mother, who stood watching them from the front porch, Faith guided the horse down the gravel driveway and onto the paved road in front of their farm. It was another hot, sticky day, and the breeze blowing against her face was a welcome relief. There was something to be said for riding in an open buggy on a sultry summer day.

"Too bad it's such a pain in the wintertime," she muttered.

"What's a pain, Mama?" Melinda questioned.

Faith sucked in her breath. She hadn't realized she'd spoken her thoughts out loud. The last thing she needed was for Melinda to hear negative comments about living as the Amish.

"It's nothing to worry about." Faith reached across the seat and patted her daughter's knee. "Mama was just thinking out loud."

"What were you thinking about?"

"It's not important." Faith smiled at Melinda. "Are you excited about our day together?"

Melinda nodded. "Sure wish Susie could have come, too."

"Maybe some other time. Today I want to spend time alone with you."

"Will we buy something good to eat at the market?"

"We should find plenty of tasty things there, but I think we'll have lunch at one of the local restaurants."

"Can I have a hot dog with lots of ketchup and relish?"

"Sure," Faith said with a nod. "You can have anything you want."

Melinda's lower lip protruded. "Grandma Stutzman makes me eat things I don't like. She says I have to eat green beans and icky beets whenever they're on the table. How come she's so mean?"

Faith's heart clenched. How could she leave Melinda with her parents if the child felt she was being mistreated? "Vegetables are good for you," she replied.

"I still don't like 'em."

"Maybe someday you will."

Melinda shrugged.

"Are you still missing TV and other modern things?"

"Not so much. I'd rather be out in the barn helping Grandpa with the animals than watching TV."

"I'm glad to hear it."

"Mama, are you ever gonna get married again?"

Melinda's unexpected question took Faith by surprise, and she answered it without even thinking. "No!"

"How come?"

Faith thought before replying this time. She couldn't tell Melinda she was against marriage because she was bitter and angry over the way Greg had treated her. The child loved her father and had no idea what had gone on behind closed doors when she'd been sound asleep. Faith had managed to keep Greg's abusiveness hidden from their precious child, and she wouldn't take away the pleasant memories Melinda had of her father.

"Mama, how come you don't want to get married again?" Melinda persisted.

Faith reached for her daughter's hand and gave it a gentle squeeze. "Because you're all I need."

Melinda seemed satisfied with that answer, for she smiled, leaned her head against the seat, and closed her eyes. "Wake me when we get there, okay?"

Faith smiled and clucked to the horse to get him moving a bit faster. "I will, sweet girl."

***

"That Melinda sure has a way with animals," Menno said as he joined his wife at the table for a cup of coffee. "You should have seen how easily she picked up on milking the cows." He took a drink from his cup and set it down on the table. "I think she's going to be a real big help to me when it comes to any of the farm chores that involve working with animals."

Wilma grunted. "Jah, well. . .don't get too attached to that idea. Melinda might not be around much longer."

"Why's that?"

"Faith might leave again—you said so yourself, remember?"

"True, but Melinda is settling in pretty well, and I really enjoy being around her." He smiled. "So I'm hoping they'll stay."

"I hope so, too, but the way Faith has been acting makes me think she might not be happy living here, and if she leaves, who knows if we'll ever see her or Melinda again?"

"You really think she's going to leave us again?"

"Can't say for sure, but she's as restless as a cat walking on a hot metal roof, and I have a hunch it's because she's not happy here."

He groaned. *"Mir lewe uff hoffning."*

"I know we live on hope, but we also need to face facts. And the fact is our daughter left home once because she wasn't happy being Amish, so what's to say she won't do it again?"

He shrugged. Wilma was right; Faith had always had a mind of her own, and the truth was, he'd never quite gotten over her leaving home when she was eighteen, nor had he completely forgiven her. He'd not said the words out loud, but he'd missed her something awful when she was away, and if she left home again, he would not only miss Faith, but her daughter, as well. "What can we do to keep them here?" he asked, reaching over to touch Wilma's arm.

"Don't guess there's a whole lot we can do other than pray that she won't leave."

"Maybe she would stay if she knew how much her daughter liked it here." His head bobbed up and down. "Jah, that could be all it would take. I'll keep letting Melinda help me in the barn with the animals, and she'll like it so much she'll convince her mamm that living here is the best place for them to be."

"Or maybe," Wilma said as a slow smile spread across her face, "Faith needs to find a good Amish man and settle down to marriage like she should have done in the first place."

"What are you saying?"

"I'm saying that if our daughter married an Amish man, she'd have to join the church and would have no reason to leave the faith."

He picked up his cup again and took a long, slow drink. "And I suppose you have an idea as to who that prospective husband might be?"

Wilma toyed with the ribbons on her head covering. "I might."

"Mind if I ask who?"

"Well. . .I was thinking Noah might be a good catch."

Menno lifted one eyebrow. "Noah Hertzler?"

"Jah. He's single, not too bad-looking, seems to be kind and helpful to his folks, and he's a real good cook."

Menno coughed and nearly choked on the coffee he'd put in his mouth, spitting some onto his shirt. "You're going to try and get Faith and Noah together?"

"Maybe just give them a bit of a nudge."

He reached for a napkin and swiped at the coffee that had dribbled onto his chin and shirt. "My advice is for you to mind your own business and let Faith do her own husband picking."

Faith couldn't believe how many Amish folks were at the farmers' market. When she was a teenager, only a few from her community had attended. Now several Amish families had booths and were selling fresh produce, quilts, and homemade craft items. Others, Faith noticed, were there merely to look, the same as she and Melinda.

Melinda pointed to a booth where an English woman was selling peanut brittle. "That looks yummy. Can we buy some, Mama?"

"I might get a box, but it will be for later—after we've had our lunch."

"You like peanut brittle?" asked a deep voice from behind.

Faith whirled around. Noah Hertzler stood directly behind her, holding his straw hat in his hands and smiling in that easygoing way of his.

"Noah. I'm surprised to see you. Are you selling some of your baked goods here today?" Faith asked.

Noah twisted the brim of his hat and shuffled his feet a couple of times. "Naw, I just came to look around."

"We're looking around, too," Melinda piped up. "And Mama's gonna take me to lunch soon."

Noah grinned at the child. "I was fixin' to do that, as well." He glanced over at Faith. "Would you two care to join me?"

The rhythm of Faith's heartbeat picked up, and she drew in a deep breath, hoping to still the racing. She wasn't sure whether it was Noah's crooked grin or his penetrating dark eyes that made her feel so strange. No Amish man had ever affected her this way, and she found it a bit disconcerting.

Melinda tugged her hand. "Can we, Mama? Can we eat lunch with Mr. Noah?"

"Noah's his first name, Melinda. Hertzler's his last name."

The child looked up at Faith with an expectant expression. "Can we have lunch with Noah?"

Faith was surprised to see her daughter's enthusiasm over the possibility of sharing a meal with Noah. Was it because she missed her father so much, or had she taken a liking to Noah?

If Noah had been this friendly when I was a teenager, I might have taken a liking to him myself. She popped a knuckle on her right hand. *Now where did that thought come from? Noah's four years younger than me, so even if he had been friendly and kind to me back then, I wouldn't have given him a second glance. Besides, his kindness could just be an act. Greg had acted kind and caring for a while, too, and look how that turned out.*

"I had planned to take Melinda to Baldy's Café," Faith said, pushing her troubling thoughts aside and turning to face Noah. "It was one of my favorite places to eat when I was a teenager."

Noah waggled his dark eyebrows. "That's one of my favorite places, too. They have some finger-lickin' good chicken there, not to mention those yummy corn dogs."

Melinda jumped up and down. "Yippee! We're going to Baldy's Café!"

※

Sitting across the table from Faith and her daughter, Noah felt strangely uncomfortable. Faith had seemed friendly enough at the farmers' market, but she'd become quiet all of a sudden and would barely make eye contact with him. Melinda, on the other hand, had been talking nonstop ever since they'd entered the restaurant.

He smiled at the child, who had a splotch of ketchup smeared on her chin from the hot dog she'd eaten. "Did you get enough to eat, Melinda?" he asked.

She bobbed her head up and down. "But I left room in my tummy for some ice cream."

Noah chuckled and was surprised when Faith laughed, too. "I think I'll have my ice cream on top of a huge piece of blackberry cobbler," he announced. "How about you, Faith? Do you like cobbler?"

She smiled at Noah, and he felt a strange stirring in his heart. "Sure. Most anybody raised in these parts has a taste for that delicious dessert." Faith swiped a napkin across her daughter's face. "You look a mess, you know that?"

Melinda scrunched up her nose. "I don't care. It ain't no fun eatin' a hot dog unless you make a mess."

"*Isn't* any fun," Faith corrected.

"Isn't," the child repeated. "Anyway, can I have some ice cream now?"

"Sure, why not?" Noah blurted out before Faith had a chance to respond. "That is, if it's okay with your mamm," he quickly amended.

Faith nodded. "I guess it would be all right."

When the waitress returned to their table, they placed an order for one bowl of strawberry ice cream for Melinda and two blackberry cobblers topped with vanilla ice cream for Faith and Noah.

While they waited for their desserts, Noah listened to the blaring country music and watched with interest as Faith tapped her fingers along the edge of the checkered tablecloth, keeping perfect time to the beat.

The woman who was singing on the radio also yodeled, and Noah marveled at her ability to make her voice warble in such a pleasant way. "Oh–le–ee—Oh–le–dee–ee—Oh–de–lay–dee—" Faster and faster the song went, until Noah could no longer keep up with the intriguing sounds.

He glanced over at Faith and noticed her staring out the window. She appeared to be a million miles away. Maybe in her mind she was back onstage, telling jokes or yodeling like the woman on the radio.

"You really do miss it, jah?"

"What?"

"Entertaining."

Melinda, who had been twisting her straw into funny shapes, spoke up. "Mama don't tell jokes no more. She gave that up when we came here to become Amish."

"Is that so?"

Melinda nodded, but Faith shrugged her shoulders.

The waitress showed up with their desserts just then, and the conversation was put on hold.

When Noah finished his cobbler several minutes later, he leaned his elbows on the table and studied Faith. She seemed so somber. It was hard to believe she had ever been a comedian. Didn't the woman realize she could still tell jokes and have fun, even though she was no longer an entertainer?

She looked at him and frowned. "You're staring at me, and it makes me nervous."

His face grew warm. "Sorry. Didn't mean to stare."

"I'll bet you were lookin' at her 'cause she's so pretty."

Melinda's candid statement must have taken

Faith by surprise, for her mouth fell open and her blue eyes widened. "Really, Melinda—you shouldn't try to put words in Noah's mouth."

"She doesn't have to," he said. "Your daughter's right. You're a fine-looking woman."

Faith stared at the table. After a few seconds, she looked over at Melinda and said, "Did you hear about the restaurant that just opened on the moon?"

Melinda's eyebrows lifted. "Really, Mama?"

Faith nodded as she looked over at Noah and winked.

"Tell us about it," he said, deciding to play along.

"Well, they have lots of good food there, but there's absolutely no atmosphere."

Noah chuckled.

"See, I do still have some humor left in me," Faith said with a lift of her chin.

He nodded. "I'm glad."

"Tell us another joke, Mama."

"Not now." Faith looked back at Noah. "Why don't you share something about yourself?"

He plunked his elbows on the table and rested his hands under his chin. "What would you like to know?"

"Do you farm with your dad, or have you found some other kind of work to keep you busy?"

"Actually Pop doesn't farm much anymore.

He's been raising hogs for the last nine years." Noah rubbed his hands briskly together. "I work at a nearby Christmas tree farm, and I truly like it."

Melinda's eyes seemed to light right up. "A Christmas tree farm? Does Santa Claus live there?"

He snickered as he shook his head. "No, but it's sure a great place to visit. In fact, I think you would enjoy seeing all the pine trees that are grown especially for English people at Christmastime."

Melinda licked the last bit of strawberry ice cream off her spoon and turned to face her mother. "Could we go to Noah's work and see the Christmas trees?"

"Well, I—"

"That's a great idea," Noah cut in. "I'll talk to my boss next week and see what we can arrange." He glanced over at Faith. "That is, if you're in agreement."

She deliberated a few seconds and finally nodded. "Sure, that sounds like fun."

"I'll let you know as soon as I get it set up."

❦

As they traveled home that afternoon, Faith thought about Noah and how at ease he had seemed with her and Melinda during their meal at Baldy's. He wasn't the same shy boy she'd known when they were growing up. Faith had enjoyed Noah's company today and had actually felt relaxed. Noah's gentle way had settled over her like a soft, warm quilt.

She shook the reins, and the horse began to trot. *Makes me wonder why the man's never married. It seems like he would make a good father.* In the years Faith and Greg had been married, he'd never looked at her, or even Melinda, with the tenderness she'd seen on Noah's face today. Was it merely an act, or did Noah have the heart of a kind, considerate man? Should she have agreed to his invitation to take them to the tree farm?

She glanced over at her daughter, whose head lolled against the seat as her eyes closed. Melinda seemed excited about the idea, and it would certainly be a nice change from all the work Faith had been expected to do since she'd come home. A visit to the tree farm would be fun for Melinda and maybe for Faith, too. It might be the only fun thing she would get to do while she was here in Webster County.

Faith grimaced as her thoughts moved in a different direction. *Oh no. I got so caught up in the enjoyment of the day that I forgot to call the talent agency in Memphis again.*

Chapter 11

It's nice we could have this time to visit," Wilma said to Noah's mother, Ida, as the two of them sat at Ida's kitchen table. "We've both been so busy lately, and it's been awhile since we've had a chance to get caught up on each other's lives." She lifted her glass. "This iced tea sure hits the spot on such a warm day."

Ida nodded and handed Wilma a plate of ginger cookies. "Please, help yourself. Noah made these last night, and they're sugar free."

"Danki," she said as she plucked a cookie off the plate then took a bite.

"How are things at your house?" Ida asked, as she also reached for a cookie. "Are your *dochder* and *grossdochder* adjusting fairly well?"

"My granddaughter's doing well, but with

Faith, I'm not so sure."

Ida's eyebrows lifted slightly. "How's that?"

"Faith has seemed so despondent since she's returned home—hardly cracks a smile and doesn't say much unless she's spoken to."

"That's too bad. You think she'll stick around this time?"

"I don't know, but if it's within my power to keep her, I surely will."

"How are you going to do that? It's not like Faith is a little girl and you can order her to do as you say."

Wilma sighed. "How well I know that. If I'd been able to make her listen to me when she was a teenager, she wouldn't have left home in the first place."

Ida reached for another cookie. "I'm glad none of my kinner ever got the notion of leaving the Amish faith. Don't think I could stand it if they did."

Wilma stared at the table. "I'll never forget the shock of awakening one morning and discovering a note from Faith saying she was running off to find a new life—one where she could yodel and tell jokes."

"She could have done that here, couldn't she?" Ida asked. "I mean, there are some in our community who like to yodel."

"That's true, but Faith had it in her mind that her yodeling wasn't appreciated. Of course, that's partly her daed's fault; he never did like to hear her yodel. Said it sounded like a bunch of croaking frogs or like she had something caught in her throat." Wilma grimaced. "I'm sure I didn't help things any when I got after her for acting so silly all the time. Seemed like she never had a serious word and was always playing some kind of prank on her brothers and sisters. Now Faith barely cracks a smile, much less tells any jokes."

"If she's unhappy, then she might leave. Isn't that what you're thinking?"

"Exactly."

"What if Faith married someone from our community? Then you'd be assured of her sticking around."

Wilma nodded. "That thought did cross my mind."

Ida snapped her fingers. "I think I've got the perfect solution."

"What might that be?"

Ida leaned closer to Wilma, and her voice lowered to a whisper, which Wilma thought was kind of silly, since they were the only ones in Ida's kitchen. "Levi and I have been hoping Noah will find a good woman and settle down to marriage, and I'm thinking if we got our two together, it could be an answer to prayer for both our families."

Wilma's lips curved into a smile. "You know, that's exactly what I've been thinking."

When Noah stepped into the kitchen and found Faith's mother sitting at the table, visiting with his mom, he halted. He'd just arrived home from work and hadn't expected any guests.

Wilma looked up at Noah and smiled.

"It's good to see you, Wilma. What brings you out our way on this hot afternoon?" he asked.

"Just came by for a little chitchat with your mamm."

Noah took down a glass from the cupboard and got himself a drink of water at the sink. "Want me to make myself scarce so you two can talk?"

"That's okay; I think we're pretty much talked out," Wilma responded.

Noah shrugged and gulped down the glass of water.

"So, Noah, how are you doing these days?" Wilma asked.

He wiped his mouth with the back of his hand. "Pretty good. And you?"

"Oh, fair to middlin'."

"Glad to hear it. How's the rest of the family?"

"Most are doing okay. Grace Ann is still working at Graber's General Store, and Esther's helping out at the Lapps' place now. Sally Lapp had triplets awhile back, you know."

Noah nodded and went to the refrigerator. "What did you have planned for supper, Mom?"

"That can wait awhile. It's too hot to do any cooking, so I might fix cold sandwiches."

"Okay. Maybe I'll go out for a walk then." He gave his mother's shoulder a gentle squeeze. "You look tired. Are you feeling all right?"

"I'm fine." Mom fanned her face with the corner of her apron. "Just feeling the heat is all."

"Is there anything I can do for you before I take my walk?"

She shook her head. "But I appreciate the offer."

Noah headed back to the sink to get another drink of water.

"That's a good boy you've got there, Ida," Wilma said.

"I think so, too."

"It's good that you know how to cook," Wilma said to Noah. "Most women would appreciate a man who can cook."

Noah grunted. He wasn't used to getting such praise.

"Faith has never liked to cook that much," Wilma went on to say. "But when I told her I was running a few errands and would probably be stopping here to see your mamm, she said she'd have supper waiting when I got home."

Noah's ears perked up at the mention of Faith's name, but he tried not to appear too interested. No point in giving Wilma or

Mom the wrong idea.

"Even if Faith's not the best of cooks, she does seem to be a good *mudder*." Ida nodded at Wilma. "After all, she gave up her worldly ways and brought her daughter home."

"That's true," Noah said as he made his way over to the table to get a cookie.

"I just hope Faith isn't planning to leave again." Wilma's tone sounded resentful, and when Noah took a sideways glance, he saw her mouth quiver.

"What makes you think she's aiming to leave? Have you come right out and asked if that's what she's planning to do?" Noah asked before he even had time to think.

Both women turned to look at him, and Noah's face heated up. He scrubbed his hand across his chin, realizing he'd forgotten to shave that morning. "Sorry for butting into a conversation that was none of my business."

"It makes no never mind," Wilma said. "To answer one of your questions—I haven't asked her outright because I'm afraid of what the answer will be."

"But what makes you think she has leaving on her mind?" Noah persisted.

"I've caught her yodeling a few times when she didn't think anyone was around."

"But as we said earlier, others in our community yodel," Noah's mother said.

"True, but Faith knows her daed doesn't like

it, and besides, she's been acting real strange since she and Melinda came to our place."

"Strange? In what way?" Noah asked.

"She won't make a decision to be baptized and join the church. Not even after talking with the bishop. And she doesn't seem the least bit interested in reading her Bible." Wilma drew in a deep breath and released it with a groan. "A smart mamm knows when her daughter's trying to pull the wool over her eyes."

Noah felt as if his heart had sunk clear to his toes. He was just beginning to get acquainted with Faith and had hoped she'd be sticking around.

"I think what Faith needs is a little encouragement—a reason to want to stay in Webster County. Don't you think so, Noah?" Mom asked as she reached for her iced tea.

Noah nodded, then glanced over at Faith's mother. "Would it help if I had a talk with Faith—maybe tried to become her friend?"

Wilma smiled, and so did Mom. "That'd be real good," they said at the same time.

In that moment, Noah made a decision. If Faith had any thoughts of leaving and had no plans to join the church, then he would do all he could to help her see the need for God as well as her family. He was glad he'd spoken to Hank this morning about taking Faith and Melinda to see the tree farm on Saturday.

"Guess I'll go out for that walk now," he

said, turning to face his mother. "So I might be late getting home for supper."

"No problem," she replied. "Take all the time you need, and if you're not back in time for supper, your daed and I will just have a sandwich."

⁂

As Faith stood in front of the stove, stirring a pot of chicken broth, she thought about her lack of cooking skills and hoped the meal she was making would turn out all right. She'd been left in charge of fixing supper while Mama ran some errands. Grace Ann and Esther were in the garden picking peas, which would be added to the steaming broth. The dumpling dough had already been mixed, and Melinda and Susie were busy setting the table.

A knock at the door startled Faith, and she nearly dropped the wooden spoon into the broth.

"I'll get it," Melinda offered.

A few seconds later, Faith heard the back door creak open. When she turned from the stove, she was surprised to see Noah holding his straw hat in one hand.

"Look who came to visit, Mama." Melinda motioned to Noah.

"If you came to see Papa or one of the brothers, they're out in the barn." Susie placed a glass on the table and moved over to where

Noah and Melinda stood near the kitchen door.

"Actually it's you I'm here to see," Noah said, patting Melinda on top of her head. "You and your mamm." His gaze shifted to Faith.

"What do you need to see me and my daughter about?"

Noah took a few steps toward her. "I—uh—wanted to tell you that I arranged with my boss to give you and Melinda a tour of the Christmas tree farm this Saturday. Would you be able to go then?"

Melinda bounced up and down. "Yes! Yes! The Christmas tree farm! Can we go, Mama? Can we, please?"

"Well, I—"

"Me, too?" Susie begged. "I've never been to the tree farm before."

Noah looked down at Susie and smiled. "You, too, if it's okay with your mamm."

"Oh, I'm sure it will be. I'll go outside and see if she's home yet." Susie raced out the back door.

"How about it, Faith?" Noah asked. "Can I come by on Saturday morning around ten o'clock?"

Faith pursed her lips, uncertain how to reply. She didn't want to disappoint Melinda or Susie. But did she really want to spend several hours in the company of a man who confused her thinking and made her hands feel clammy every time he came near? She'd been through all those giddy feelings with Greg and wasn't about to set herself up for that again. She didn't need a man. She'd had one before, and look how that had turned out. Sure, Greg had gotten her plenty of shows, but it had been for his own selfish gain, not because he loved Faith and wanted her to succeed.

"We could take along a picnic lunch and have a meal at one of the tables under the maple tree in front of Sandy's Gift Shop," Noah suggested.

"Who's Sandy?" Faith questioned, as she brought her thoughts back to the present.

"Hank's wife. She runs a little store in one half of their barn, and she sells everything from peanut brittle to pot holders."

"Sounds like an interesting place. If it had been there when I was a girl, I'm sure I would have wanted to visit."

He grinned. "Popping into the gift store from time to time is an added bonus to working at the tree farm. I've even donated some of my baked goods for Sandy to share with her customers." Noah grabbed a handful of napkins from the wicker basket in the center of the table and folded each one, then placed them beside the plates.

Is this man for real? Greg was never so helpful. Faith shook her head and mentally scolded herself for comparing Noah to her deceased husband. It was pointless to do so. She would be leaving soon, and besides, she didn't know if Noah was merely putting on an act.

The back door collided with the wall as Susie raced into the room, her forehead glistening with sweat and her cheeks flushed like ripe cherries. "Mama just got home, and she says I can go with you to the tree farm on Saturday."

"Yippee!" Melinda grabbed her aunt's hands, and the girls jumped up and down like a couple of hopping toads.

"Now hold on a minute," Noah said, shaking his head. "Faith hasn't agreed to go yet."

The children stopped their exuberant jumping and stared up at Faith with expectant expressions. She lifted one hand in defeat. "Okay. We'll go to the Christmas tree farm."

"Yeah!" Melinda grabbed Susie and gave her a hug.

"You'd better get busy and fill those water glasses." Faith pointed to the table.

Noah turned toward the door. "Guess I'd best be getting on home."

"Why don't you stay for supper?" Faith asked, without thinking. She wasn't sure she wanted Noah, the good cook, to sample anything she had made. But she had extended the invitation, so she couldn't take it back now.

Noah pivoted around to face her, a smile as wide as the Missouri River spreading across his face. "It's nice of you to offer, and since my mamm's only planning to make sandwiches for supper, I'm sure she won't miss me." With that, Noah plunked his hat on a wall peg, rolled up his shirtsleeves, and sauntered back across the room. "What can I do to help?"

Faith pointed to the salad fixings on the counter. "Guess you can whip up a green salad if you've a mind to."

"It would be my pleasure," he said with a nod.

Faith turned back to the stove. She had a feeling tonight's meal would be better than most.

⁂

As Noah sat at the Stutzmans' table a short time later, he was glad he'd decided to stop by their place. He was being treated to some fine chicken and dumplings, not to mention such good company. Eating with Mom and Pop every night was all right, but Noah really enjoyed the fellowship of the Stutzmans—from Menno right down to Melinda, the youngest child present. It made him wonder what it might be like if he had a wife and children of his own. Of course, that was nothing but a foolish dream. He didn't think any woman would want a shy man with a big nose who liked to cook. At least, that's what Noah's brother Rube had told him many times. Mom said Rube was only kidding, but truth be told, Noah figured his older brother was probably right.

"Noah, would you like to join me out in the living room for a game of checkers?"

Menno's question pulled Noah from his musings, and he pushed away from the table. "I might take you up on that after I help with the dishes."

Menno's forehead creased as he shook his head. "Are you daft? Nobody volunteers to do dishes."

Noah glanced at Faith, who sat to his left, and said, "I just ate a tasty supper, so it's only right that I show my appreciation by helping out."

"You already helped by fixing the salad and setting the table," Faith reminded him.

He shrugged. "I help my mamm do the dishes most every night."

Faith slid her chair back and stood. "Okay. I'll wash, and you dry."

❦

"It's good Noah was able to join us for dinner, jah?" Menno said to Wilma, as he set up the checkerboard in the living room and she lit a few of their kerosene lamps.

She nodded and smiled. "Couldn't have planned it better myself."

"Want me to plant a few ideas in Noah's head while we're playing checkers?"

"What kind of ideas?"

He lifted a folding chair from behind the

sofa and snapped it open. "You know—about him getting together with Faith."

Wilma shook her head. "I don't think you want to be that obvious, husband."

"Why not? I don't see any point in beating around the shrubbery, do you?"

She lifted her gaze toward the ceiling. "Maybe you could just mention how nice it is to have Faith home and how we're hoping she'll get baptized and join the church real soon."

His eyebrows scrunched together. "How's that gonna get 'em together?"

"It probably won't, but it's a start." Wilma lit the lamp closest to the table where he'd set out the checkerboard. "Would you like me to stay in the room and direct your conversation?"

Menno grunted. "No way! I'll be better off on my own with this. Besides, if you're in the room talking to Noah and asking a bunch of questions, it'll throw my concentration off, and he might win the game."

Wilma pinched his arm and turned toward the door leading to their bedroom. "I'll be in our room reading a book in case you need me." She hurried from the room before he could respond.

A few minutes later, Noah showed up with his shirtsleeves rolled up to his elbows.

"How'd everything go in the kitchen?" Menno asked, motioning for Noah to take a seat in the folding chair opposite him.

"It went fine. Got the dishes washed, dried, and put away."

"I still don't see why you'd want to get your hands all wrinkled in soapy dishwater."

Noah seated himself. "I've been helping my mamm in the kitchen since I was a kinner, and I'm used to having dishpan hands."

"Whatever you say." Menno nodded toward the checkerboard. "You go first."

"I don't mind if you'd like to start the game."

Menno shook his head. "That's okay. I'm the champion of checkers, so I'd better give you the edge by letting you begin."

"Okay," Noah said with a shrug.

They played in silence for a time as each of them racked up a few kings. About halfway through the game, Menno leaned back in his chair with his hands clasped behind his head and said, "Say, I've been wondering something."

"What's that?" Noah asked, as he studied the board.

"How come a nice fellow like you, who likes to cook and do other things in the kitchen, isn't married and raising a passel of kinner by now?"

Noah's eyebrows shot up. "Well, I. . ." He jumped one of Menno's checkers and then another. "To tell you the truth, I've never found a woman who showed much interest in me."

"Is that so?"

Noah nodded. "It's your turn, Menno."

Menno contemplated his next move as he

thought about what he should say. This conversation wasn't going nearly as well as he had hoped. "I should think with your kitchen skills that all the single women in our community would be chasing after you like hound dogs in pursuit of a rabbit," he said as he moved his checker piece.

Noah took his turn again, this time jumping three of Menno's checkers. "That's it! That's the end of this game!"

Menno stared dumbfounded at the checkerboard. He didn't know how Noah had done it, but he'd managed to skunk him real good. "I. . .uh. . .guess I didn't have my mind on the game," he mumbled. "That's what I get for trying to. . ." His voice trailed off. He'd almost blurted out that he was trying to help Wilma get Noah and Faith together.

"Trying to what?" Noah asked with a puzzled expression.

"Nothing. Nope, it was nothing at all." Menno pushed a stack of checkers in Noah's direction. "You take the red ones this time." He gritted his teeth. *And from now on, Wilma can do her own matchmaking.*

Chapter 12

Faith didn't know why she felt so nervous, but the idea that Noah was coming by soon to take them to the Christmas tree farm had her feeling as jittery as a cat with a bad case of fleas. She'd been pacing the kitchen floor for the last ten minutes, periodically going to the window to see if he had arrived.

"It was nice of Noah to invite you out for the day. It'll be good for you and the kinner to have some fun."

Faith whirled around at the sound of her mother's voice. She hadn't realized anyone had come into the kitchen. "I—I'm sure the girls will enjoy themselves."

Mama's eyebrows furrowed. "And what about you, daughter? Won't you have a good time, as well?"

"I suppose I will."

"Noah's a nice man, don't you think?"

Faith shrugged. "It will be interesting to see how Christmas trees are grown," she said. No use giving Mama any ideas about her and Noah becoming an item.

Her mother grunted and helped herself to a cup of the herbal tea she'd brewed a few minutes earlier. "It wonders me the way our English neighbors put so much emphasis on bringing a tree into the house at Christmas, then throwing all sorts of fancy decorations and bright lights onto the branches. Why not just enjoy the trees outdoors, the way God intended us to?"

Faith didn't bother to answer. Mama had never approved of Faith showing an interest in modern things, and if she gave her opinion now, it might be misconstrued as Faith wanting to have a tree in the house. She helped herself to a glass of water at the sink and headed for the back door. "Think I'll wait outside with the girls," she said over her shoulder. "See you when we get home."

Out on the porch, Faith took a seat in one of the wicker chairs and watched Melinda and Susie as they took turns pushing each other on the old wooden swing hanging from one of their maple trees.

"I remember the days when I was that carefree," she murmured, closing her eyes and imagining herself as a child again. Faith and her sisters used to play on the swing whenever they had a free moment. Sometimes when Barbara came to visit, she and Faith would take turns, just as Melinda and Susie were doing now. Those were untroubled days, when Faith was more content with her life—always joking and playing tricks on her siblings. She'd actually enjoyed much of her early childhood. It wasn't until Faith became a teenager that she had decided she wasn't happy being Amish. Mama and Papa had seemed more critical, saying things like, "Why don't you grow up and start acting your age?" and "Quit playing around and get to work."

Faith remembered the time she and Dan Miller had hitchhiked into Springfield and gone to the movies. When she returned home in the evening, she'd gotten into trouble for that little stunt. Papa had shouted at her something awful, saying if she were a few years younger she'd have been hauled to the woodshed for a sound *bletsching*. He said she was rebellious and irresponsible for taking off without telling them where she was going. When it came out that they'd hitchhiked and gone to see a show, Papa blew up and gave Faith double chores for a whole month. He said what she and Dan had done was not only worldly but dangerous. What if some maniac had been the one to give them a ride? They could have been beaten, robbed, or worse. Faith couldn't believe Dan had spilled the beans. It was a good thing he and his family had moved to Illinois, or she might tell him what she thought about all that even now.

Mama, who had also been quite upset, had made Faith learn a whole list of scripture verses over the next several weeks. Faith had used that as an excuse for not reading her Bible after that.

The *clip-clop* of a horse's hooves drew Faith's musings to a halt, and she opened her eyes. Noah had arrived. She drew in a deep breath, smoothed the wrinkles in her dark blue cotton dress, and stood. "Come on, girls," she called to Melinda and Susie. "Noah's here, and it's time to go."

❦

Noah was glad to see Faith waiting on the front porch, and he chuckled as the girls surrounded him, both begging, "Hurry up and let's go."

Soon he had the children loaded into the back of his open buggy and Faith settled on the front seat beside him.

"Sure is a nice day," Noah said, glancing over at Faith with a grin.

She nodded.

"I hope the girls like the tree farm."

"I'm sure they will."

"Hank's wife has been looking forward to your coming. She really likes kinner."

"That's nice."

"Hank has a couple of beagle hounds,

Amos and Griggs. I'm guessing the girls will enjoy playing with them."

"Could be."

Noah grimaced. Couldn't Faith respond to anything he said with more than a few words? Didn't she want to go to the tree farm, or was she just being quiet because the girls were chattering so loudly in the seat behind them that it was hard to make conversation over their voices?

Deciding it might be best to keep quiet for the rest of the trip, Noah concentrated on guiding the horse down the highway. A short time later, he pulled into the driveway of Osborns' Christmas Tree Farm. He stopped in front of the hitching post Hank had built for Noah, got out, and headed around back to help the girls out. When they were safely on the ground, he turned to Faith, but she'd already climbed down.

He led the way, taking them into the area where the rows of Scotch and white pines had recently been sheared and shaped.

"Look at all the trees!" Melinda shouted as she ran down the lane. "I wish we could see them decorated for Christmas."

"You can," Noah called. "My boss's wife, Sandy, has some artificial trees in her gift shop. We'll stop in there after we've seen the real trees, and you can take a look."

For the next hour, Noah showed Faith

and the girls around the farm, explaining the procedure that began in the late winter months and continued up to harvest, shortly before Christmas the following year. From late December until early June, dead trees were cut down, and new ones were planted in their place. From the first of April all the way through summer, the grass around the seedlings had to be kept mowed. The larger trees were sheared and shaped during the summer months, and by fall, certain trees were selected to be sold to local lots and shipped to other markets farther away.

"By the first of November, we start cutting the trees; then they're netted, packed, and ready for pickup on Thanksgiving weekend. The Christmas tree lots are usually open for business on the Friday after Thanksgiving," Noah explained.

"Do all Englishers buy their trees from the lots?" Susie questioned.

Noah shook his head. "Some come out here and reserve their trees as soon as October, rather than going to a lot to pick out a tree." He motioned to a group of nearby pines. "This place is really busy during the month of December, and many folks come back year after year to get a tree. Hank keeps his business operating on weekends until Thanksgiving; then it's open daily for folks to come and get their trees and browse through the gift shop."

"We put up a small tree in our hotel room last Christmas. Ain't that right, Mama?" Melinda asked, giving the edge of her mother's apron a tug.

"Yes, that's right. We did have a tree." Faith tweaked her daughter's nose. "And it's *isn't*, not *ain't*."

"Mama told me yesterday there won't be a tree in Grandma and Grandpa Stutzman's house," Melinda continued, making no mention of her mother's grammatical correction.

"That's right, Melinda. The Amish don't celebrate Christmas by bringing a decorated tree into the house." Noah motioned to the rustic barn nearby. "Now that we've seen the trees, we can go into the gift shop and take a look at all the things Sandy has for sale. After that, we'll eat our picnic lunch."

"Yippee!" the girls chorused.

Faith looked over at Noah. "I think you've made their day."

"I hope you're enjoying yourself, as well."

She nodded. "It's been quite interesting."

When they entered the gift shop a few minutes later, they were greeted by both Hank and his wife, Sandy, a petite red-haired woman with brown eyes.

"Would you all like something to drink?" Sandy asked, once the introductions had been made.

"Maybe in a bit," Noah replied. He turned

to Faith. "How about you?"

"I'm fine for now, too."

The girls, who seemed mesmerized by the artificial trees decorated with white twinkling lights, red balls, and brightly colored ornaments, darted around the room, checking each one out, while the adults found seats near the unlit, wood-burning stove.

"Did Noah explain how I run things here, while he showed you around the tree farm?" Hank asked, looking at Faith.

Faith nodded and bent to pet the Osborns' two beagle hounds, Amos and Griggs. Griggs licked her hand, while Amos nudged her foot with a rubber ball he'd taken from a wicker basket near the front door. "It's all quite impressive," she said, tossing the ball for Amos while she continued to pet Griggs.

"I'm sure glad Noah came to work for me," Hank continued. "He's one of the best workers I've ever had."

Noah's face heated with embarrassment. "I enjoy working with the trees almost as much as I like baking," he mumbled.

"And you're as good a baker as you are a tree farmer." Sandy smiled at Faith. "Noah often bakes some of his goodies for the customers who come into my shop. One of the things folks like best is his lemon sponge cake."

Faith nodded but made no comment. It was obvious that her focus was on the dogs.

Hank stood and placed his hand on Noah's shoulder. "If you'd like to come out to my workshop with me, I'll show you my latest woodworking project."

Noah nodded. "That'd be fine." He glanced over at Faith to get her reaction, but she shrugged and threw the ball for Amos again.

"We'll probably be ready for some apple cider and a few cookies when we get back," Hank said, nodding at his wife.

"They'll be ready whenever you are," she replied.

As Noah followed Hank outside, he smiled at Melinda and Susie, who played under the trees with the other hound dog.

❧

"Are you sure you wouldn't like something to eat or drink?" Sandy asked Faith.

"No, thanks, I'm fine." Faith glanced around the shop, noticing all the gift items as well as the artificial trees. "This place must keep you plenty busy."

"It does fill the lonely hours." There was a tone of sadness in Sandy's voice, and her downcast eyes revealed sorrow.

"Isn't your husband around quite a bit? I would think with his business being near where you live, you would see him a lot."

"Not really. Whenever Hank's not working with his trees, he's in his woodworking shop, making all sorts of things."

"Things like the items you sell here?" Faith asked, gesturing with her hand to one of the birdhouses on a nearby shelf.

Sandy nodded. "He does make quite a few of the things, and I make peanut brittle, but others from the community keep me supplied with their homemade items, as well."

"Do you get a lot of customers?"

"At certain times I do. Mostly around holidays like Mother's Day and Valentine's Day. Of course, Christmastime is especially busy, too."

"I imagine it would be."

"Do you make anything you might consider selling here in the store? I'm always looking for new items," Sandy said.

"The only thing I'm good at is telling jokes and yodeling. Mama's the expert baker and quilter in our house."

"Yes, I knew you yodeled, because Hank and I were at one of your shows in Branson. The day Noah asked Hank if he could bring you and your daughter by our place, he mentioned that you'd given up your career and moved back home." Sandy's forehead wrinkled. "I was really surprised to hear that."

Faith's mouth went dry. She felt guilty every time someone mentioned her quitting her life as an entertainer and returning home. She didn't feel at liberty to tell anyone that she was planning to leave again.

"When I was an entertainer, I dressed in a hillbilly costume," she said, hoping to avoid the subject of why she'd returned home.

"That's right, you were wearing a hillbilly costume the night we saw you."

A vision of her performances flashed onto the screen of Faith's mind. She saw herself onstage, dressed in a tattered blue skirt and a white peasant blouse. A straw hat, bent out of shape, was perched on top of her head, and she'd worn a pair of black tennis shoes with holes in the toes. The audience seemed to like her corny routine, for they'd laughed, cheered, and hollered for more.

"Yodeling sounds like fun. Is it hard to learn?" Sandy asked.

Faith shrugged. "Not for me it wasn't. Ever since I was a little girl, I could whistle like a bird and trill my voice. When I went to town one day, I heard a woman yodeling on the radio at Baldy's Café. After I got home, I headed straight for my secret place in the barn, where I knew I wasn't likely to be disturbed."

"Did you actually try to yodel right then, with no teacher?"

"I did, and much to my amazement, I didn't sound half bad. After that, I practiced on my own every chance I got, but hearing the yodeler on the radio wasn't my only contact with yodeling."

"Oh?"

"A few others in our Swiss-Amish community like to yodel, but not to the extent that I do." Faith bit down on her lower lip. "And no one but me has ever gone off and become an entertainer."

"I'm surprised your family had no objections to your leaving home like that."

"They objected all right. Even before I'd made my decision to leave home, they were always after me for acting silly and sneaking off to listen to country-western music." Faith shook her head. "Papa called my yodeling 'downright stupid' and said it sounded like I was gargling or that I had something caught in my throat."

Sandy reached over and patted Faith's arm in a motherly fashion. "I guess it's safe to say that with most parents, something about their children gets their dander up." She glanced over her shoulder, and Faith did the same. Melinda and Susie were lying on the floor, with both dogs lying on their backs and getting their bellies rubbed. "I used to think that if I ever became a mother, I'd try to accept my kids just as they are." She stared down at her hands. "Hank and I have been married almost ten years, and we recently found out that we can't have any children. So I'll never have the opportunity to try out my mothering skills."

"I'm sorry to hear that. Have you thought of adopting?"

Sandy shook her head. "Hank was pretty upset when he learned that I couldn't give him any babies, and I doubt he would want to adopt."

Faith was trying to think of what she could say to offer comfort, when the men returned to the gift shop.

"We're ready for some refreshments now," Hank said, smiling at Sandy.

She pushed her chair aside and stood. "I'll have something served up in a jiffy."

"I'll help you." Faith started to get up, but Sandy waved her aside. "I can manage. Why don't you stay put and relax?"

Faith didn't know whether to argue or take Sandy up on her suggestion, but when the hound dog Amos trotted over to her with the ball in his mouth, she decided to stay put.

Chapter 13

She likes pets, and so does her daughter, Noah thought, as he watched Faith chuck the ball across the room for Amos, while Melinda stroked Griggs behind his ear.

Sandy returned to the room a few minutes later with a tray of cookies, some of her peanut brittle, and a pitcher of cold apple cider. When she placed the tray down on a small table, the girls scampered over with expectant expressions.

"Are you two hungry?" Hank asked with a chuckle.

"Jah," they said at the same time.

"Just don't eat too much." Faith shook her head. "Or you'll spoil your appetites for the meal Noah's made us."

Susie grinned. "I'm always hungry, so it

won't matter how many cookies I eat."

"Just the same, I don't want you filling up on cookies when there's a meal to be eaten."

The girls each took two cookies and a glass of cider and then settled themselves on the floor again.

After visiting with Hank and his wife awhile and sampling some of Sandy's delicious peanut brittle, Noah finally ushered his guests outside to one of the picnic tables. He opened the small cooler he'd packed that morning and spread the contents on the table. He had invited Hank and Sandy to join them, but they'd declined because of work they had to do.

"How do you expect us to eat all this food?" Faith asked when he placed a plate of golden fried chicken in front of her.

"Just eat what you can." He added a jar of pickles, a plastic container full of coleslaw, a loaf of brown bread, and some baked beans.

They paused for silent prayer and then dug right in. Melinda and Susie ate two drumsticks apiece, and Faith devoured a thigh plus a large hunk of white meat. Noah was glad to see her eating so well. She was far too skinny to his way of thinking. He was also pleased to see how much Faith had relaxed. Either she was feeling more comfortable in his presence or her playtime with Hank's hounds had done the trick. Noah figured he'd made some headway in befriending Faith. Now if he could only think of something to say that might give him an indication of whether she was planning to go back on the road again. He debated about asking her outright but decided that might put a sour note on the day. Besides, what if it wasn't true? Maybe Faith's mother had been wrong.

When the meal was over, Susie looked for wildflowers, while Melinda played with Amos and Griggs. Noah suggested that he and Faith sit on a quilt under a cluster of shady maples, as the afternoon had become hot and humid.

Faith leaned back on her elbows and stared up at the sky. "Sure is peaceful, isn't it? I can see why you enjoy coming to work here every day."

Noah nodded. "Working with the pine trees gives me much satisfaction."

"How come you're not married and raising a family by now?" she asked suddenly.

Noah's ears burned, and the heat quickly spread to his face. "I. . .uh. . .don't think I'm much of a catch."

"I wasn't much of a catch, either, but Greg married me." Faith grimaced. "Of course, he never really loved me."

"What makes you think that?"

"Greg only wanted me because he thought I could make him rich."

"And did you?"

"Not even close. I was doing pretty well for a while, but Greg spent most of our money on alcohol, and he gambled some." Faith's eyebrows furrowed, and she looked away. "I don't know why I blurted all that out. I sure didn't plan on it."

"It's not good to keep things bottled up." He reached out to touch her arm, but she flinched and pulled away.

"Sorry. I didn't mean to startle you."

"I—I get a little jumpy whenever someone touches me unexpectedly." As Faith looked at Noah, he noticed tears in her eyes. "Greg had a mean streak and often took out his frustrations on me, but I've never admitted it to anyone until now."

Noah's eyebrows lifted in surprise. "You mean he was abusive?"

She nodded. "A few times he hit me but usually in places where it didn't show."

"I'm sorry to hear that. No man should ever strike a woman; it's just not right." Noah's heart went out to Faith. He'd had no idea what life had been like for her in the English world.

"Greg did get me some good shows, and I felt that I needed him as my agent." She squinted. "It's not easy to find a good agent, you know."

"Why would you want to go back to that way of living if it was so hard?"

"Who says I want to go back?"

Noah felt like slapping himself. He hadn't meant to say that, and he surely couldn't tell Faith what her mother had told his mother.

"I. . .uh. . .kind of got that impression by some of the things you've said about life as an entertainer. You mentioned that you missed it and all."

Faith shrugged.

Noah decided to change the subject. "Remember that scripture verse I attached to the lemon sponge cake I gave you awhile back?"

She nodded slowly. "It had something to do with faith, right?"

"That's correct."

"Faith might give some people high expectations when things are messed up in their lives, but to me, it's nothing more than false hope."

Noah couldn't believe his ears. His own faith had grown so much over the last couple of years. He couldn't imagine that anyone who had been taught to believe in God would think faith wasn't real. "As I told you the other day at Baldy's, faith is like a muscle, and it needs to be exercised in order to become strong."

Faith looked uncomfortable as she shifted on the quilt, so Noah suggested they talk about something else.

"Okay." She moistened her lips with the tip of her tongue. "Say, did you hear about the elderly man who moved to a retirement home and hoped to make lots of new friends there?"

He shook his head. "Can't say that I have."

"The man met a lady, and they spent a lot of

time together. Soon he realized he was in love with her, so he proposed marriage. But the day after the man proposed, he woke up and couldn't remember what the woman's answer was."

"So what'd he do?"

"He went to her and said, 'I'm so embarrassed. I proposed to you last night, but I can't remember if you said yes or no.'" Faith tapped her fingers against her chin and rolled her eyes from side to side. "'Oh, now I remember,' the old woman quipped. 'I said yes, but I couldn't remember who asked me.'"

Noah chuckled. Faith was beginning to use her sense of humor again, which was a good thing. "That was a great story. Have you got another?" he asked.

She jiggled her eyebrows up and down. "Do bats fly at night?"

He grinned.

"Okay, here goes." Faith drew in a deep breath. "You know, I never got used to driving a car when I lived among the English those ten years I was gone. Especially after I discovered what a motorist really is."

"And what would that be?"

"A person who, after seeing a wreck, drives carefully for the next several blocks."

Noah grinned. Faith could be a lot of fun when she had a mind to. He hoped they would have more opportunities to spend days like this.

"Tell me how you learned to bake such

delicious goodies," Faith said, changing the subject again. "I sure ate my share today."

"It's no big secret. I just started baking when I was a young fellow, found that I enjoyed it, and I've been doing it ever since."

"I see."

"Even though I did plenty of outside chores when I was a kinner, Pop and my nine brothers thought I was a bit strange because I didn't mind helping in the kitchen."

Faith grimaced as she shook her head. "My family thinks I'm odd because I can't cook so well."

"The chicken and dumplings you made the other night were good."

"Maybe so, but that dish is one of the few things I can fix well. I can't bake like you do, that's for sure." Faith took a bite from one of the brownies he'd brought along. "Mmm. . . now this is really good."

"Practice makes perfect," he said with a grin. "I didn't always bake well, but I had fun learning."

"I think I need a lot more than practice." Faith held up the brownie. "I doubt I could ever make anything as good as this."

"Sure you could. Where's your faith?"

"I don't have much faith in anything these days." She looked away. "I told you before—my faith has diminished over the years."

"Have you read your Bible regularly?"

She shook her head.

"That's the only way you can strengthen your faith—that and spending time with the Lord in prayer."

Impulsively, Noah touched her hand and noticed how soft it felt. He was glad she hadn't flinched when he'd touched her this time. "I've been praying for you, Faith," he whispered.

"You—you have?"

"Jah, and I'll keep on praying that your faith will grow so strong that you'll feel God walking right beside you every day."

She stared down at her hands, clasped tightly in her lap.

"I suppose we should gather up the girls and start for home," she murmured a few seconds later.

Noah nodded. "Jah, I guess we should."

During the first half of the ride home, the girls chattered again, but suddenly, their voices died out. When Noah glanced over his shoulder, he saw the two of them leaning their heads together, eyes shut and cheeks flushed.

Faith was quiet, too, as she stared at the passing scenery and spoke only whenever Noah posed a question. Was she thinking about the things they had discussed after their picnic lunch? Could she be mulling over the idea of exercising her faith? He hoped so, for it was obvious that the woman sitting beside him needed a renewed faith in God. He thought she needed the kind of peace that would fill her life with so much happiness she would have no desire for the things the world had to offer. She'd proven by her joke telling today that she could be joyful and funny, even when not on some stage entertaining.

Thinking about Faith and the girls in the backseat, suddenly Noah was overcome with the need for a wife and children. He'd never missed it much until lately, and he wondered if it had anything to do with Faith's return. Noah was sure from some of Faith's comments that she didn't believe in or accept the same kinds of spiritual things he did. He knew he could never take a wife who didn't share his love for and belief in Jesus.

Even though I can't allow myself to become romantically involved with Faith, I'll still try to be her friend, Noah decided.

He glanced over at Faith. "I enjoyed the day. Thanks for agreeing to come."

"I had fun, too. I'm glad you invited us to see where you work."

"Maybe we can get together some other time this summer. I'd like to hire a driver and go to Springfield to see that big sportsmen's store."

"You mean the Bass Pro Shops?"

"Jah, I've never been there, but I hear it's really something to see."

"It's billed as the world's greatest sporting

goods store, and there's even a wildlife museum."

"You've been there then?"

She nodded. "A few times."

"Sounds like the place to be," Noah said, feeling his enthusiasm rise. "I'd also like to visit Fantastic Caverns, just outside of Springfield."

Her pale eyebrows wiggled slightly. "Noah Hertzler, you're a man full of surprises."

"I'm not sure I get your meaning."

"You used to be so shy when we were children, and now you seem to have such a zest for life. I feel as if I'm getting to know a whole different side of you."

He reached under his straw hat and scratched the side of his head. "I guess maybe I have changed some." *Especially since you came back to Webster County. You bring out the best in me, Faith. You just don't know it.*

Chapter 14

As Faith took a seat in a booth at Baldy's Café, her heart started to hammer. When she'd phoned the talent agency in Memphis the last time, they had informed her that Brad Olsen, the agent who'd chosen to represent her, would be in Springfield over the weekend and would like to meet with her. Faith knew she wouldn't be able to get away for that long or come up with a good excuse as to why she wanted to go to Springfield, so she asked if the agent could meet her at Baldy's Café on Monday morning. The meeting had been agreed upon, so here she sat, picking at the salad she'd ordered and waiting for Mr. Olsen to arrive. She hoped he would be here soon, because she'd told her mother she was going shopping in Seymour and that she would be back by late afternoon.

"Are you Faith Andrews?" a deep male voice asked, halting Faith's thoughts.

She looked up and saw a tall, thin man with ebony-colored hair.

"Yes, I'm Faith Andrews."

He extended his hand. "I'm Brad Olsen from the agency in Memphis."

When she reached over and shook his hand, his eyebrows lifted slightly. "I recognized your face from the pictures I've seen of you, but those clothes you've got on really threw me. When did you decide to start wearing an Amish costume?"

"Oh, this isn't a costume." Faith gestured to the bench on the other side of her table. "If you'd like to have a seat, I'll explain my situation."

"Sure thing."

During the next half hour, Faith gave Brad Olsen the details as to why she had temporarily given up her profession and come to Webster County, and she ended by saying, "So as soon as my daughter has adjusted well enough, I'll be ready to return to the stage."

"I see," he said, as he scribbled some notes on the tablet he'd pulled from his briefcase. "Do you have any idea how much longer that will be?"

Faith shrugged. "Hopefully, not long. Melinda's doing fairly well, but I can't leave until I know for sure that she's accepted the Amish way of life."

Brad's eyebrows drew together as he motioned to her plain cotton dress. "Looks to me like you've accepted it pretty well yourself."

Faith's cheeks heated up as she shook her head. "I'm only going through the motions of being Amish so none of my family will question things. It wouldn't be right for me to take off without seeing that my little girl is completely settled in."

"You need to get back in circulation as soon as possible. The longer you're away from performing, the further your name will be from people's minds." He tapped the end of his pen along the edge of the table. "Not to mention that in order for you to keep on top of your skills as an entertainer, you'll need to practice."

"I practice my yodeling whenever I get the chance to be alone, and I tell jokes to whoever's willing to listen." Faith thought about the meal she and Melinda had shared with Noah not long ago and how she'd been able to make Noah laugh.

"Well, I think that about does it for now," Brad said as he slipped his notebook into his briefcase and stood. He handed her a business card. "I'd like you to call me once a week and let me know how things are going so I'll know when to schedule you for a show."

"I'll do that," Faith promised as she followed

him to the checkout counter.

They were about to head for the door when Faith caught sight of Noah sitting in a booth near the back of the restaurant. She hadn't noticed him earlier and didn't know if he'd come in during her visit with Brad Olsen or if he'd been there the whole time. She squinted and stared when she realized someone was in the booth with him—a young Amish woman with medium brown hair. Faith didn't recognize her as anyone from their community, and she wondered if the woman could be from a neighboring community and had come to Seymour to meet Noah. Was she Noah's girlfriend? They were sitting side by side, with their heads close together as though in deep concentration.

Faith considered going over to say hello but thought better of it. It might raise questions as to why she was at Baldy's, and if Noah saw her with the talent agent, he would have questions she didn't want to answer. With a quick glance over her shoulder, Faith slipped out the door.

Noah craned his neck as he watched Faith leave the café with a tall English man. He'd seen the couple walk over to the checkout counter together a few minutes ago and had wondered who the man was. Did Faith have a boyfriend—maybe a fellow entertainer? That's sure what it looked like when they'd been standing near the counter with their heads together.

"Noah, did you hear what I said?"

The soft-spoken voice pulled his attention back to his cousin Mary, who sat on the bench beside him and had been pouring out her heart about the way she'd been jilted by her boyfriend, Mark. Mary and her folks lived near Jamesport, and Mark lived in Webster County with his family. They'd been courting for several months, but two weeks ago, Mary had received a letter from Mark saying he wanted to break up with her and that he would be moving to Illinois to work with his brother who owned a dairy farm there. Mary had caught a bus to Seymour, hoping to talk Mark into changing his mind, but by the time she'd arrived, Mark had already left for Illinois. Heartbroken, Mary had asked Noah to give her a ride back to Seymour so she could catch the bus home.

Noah gave Mary's arm a gentle squeeze. "What was that you said?"

"I was telling you that I'm going to try real hard to forget about Mark and move on with my life. No point in crying over spilled honey, as my mamm likes to say."

"That's good. Glad to hear it."

"Noah, are you okay? You look like you're a thousand miles away."

"It's nothing. I saw someone I know, and I was wondering what she was doing here."

Mary's eyebrows lifted high on her forehead. "You've found yourself an *aldi*?"

"No, no," he sputtered. "It's nothing like that. The woman I saw is just a friend."

"Is she someone I know?"

"I don't think so. She's been gone from home for ten years, and you and your folks have been living in Jamesport longer than that, so— "

"Oh my. . .look at the time!" Mary pointed to the clock hanging on the wall above the checkout counter. "If we don't get a move on, I'm going to miss my bus."

Noah nodded. "You're right. We'd better get over to Lazy Lee's Gas Station right away."

As they left their booth, Noah wondered if he should ask Faith about the English fellow he'd seen her with. *Probably not,* he decided. *Whatever Faith does is her business, not mine.*

As Faith stood at the kitchen sink that afternoon, getting a drink of water, she thought about the young woman she'd seen Noah with. Should she say something to him about it? Probably not. It was none of her business who Noah saw in private. Besides, if she brought it up to Noah, she might have to tell him why she'd been at Baldy's. If Noah knew she had hired an agent, he would realize she planned to leave, and then her folks would find out.

Faith hated to admit it, but she was attracted to Noah, and that scared her a lot. Spending time with him had made her feel different than she'd ever felt in the company of a man. Maybe it was because Noah seemed nothing like other men she'd met during her years of living among the English. He was soft-spoken, seemed to be kind, and had taken an interest in her and Melinda. Could it be an act? Was Noah too good to be true?

Faith had been looking forward to making a trip to Springfield with Noah to see the Bass Pro Shops and Fantastic Caverns, but now that she'd seen him with that woman in town, she was sure those plans had changed. It was probably for the best. She couldn't afford to begin a relationship with a man who was wholly committed to being Amish, even if he did seem to be one of the nicest fellows she'd ever met.

Faith heard shrill laughter coming from outside, and she glanced out the window. Melinda and Susie ran back and forth through a puddle of water in their bare feet, giggling and waving their hands.

"Maybe after supper I should tell Mama and Papa that I'll be leaving soon. There's no point in prolonging it," Faith murmured. "But first, I should tell Melinda."

Faith went out the back door and made her way across the lawn toward the frolicking children. She would take her daughter aside, explain everything to her, and then tell the folks. She hoped Melinda would understand that she was doing this for her own good. Faith would promise to visit as often as she could—whenever she was in the area doing a show or she had time off. Melinda might not care for the arrangement, but someday she would realize her mother had her best interests at heart.

Faith had just approached the girls when she heard a shrill scream near the house. She whirled around but saw nothing out of the ordinary.

"Help! Somebody, help me!"

That sounds like Mama. Faith rushed to the cellar steps and peered down. Her mother lay at the bottom, moaning and holding her leg.

Faith ran down the steps. "Mama, what happened?"

"I—I was going down here to get a jar of green beans, and I must have tripped." Mama winced when Faith touched her leg. "I think it's broken."

"I'd better call Papa and tell him we're going to have to get one of our neighbors to drive you to the hospital." Faith hated to leave her mother lying on the cold, hard concrete, but she had no other choice. "Hang on, Mama. I'll be right back."

She rushed out to the fields, where her father and brothers had been working on broken fences. When she caught sight of them, she began frantically waving her hands.

"What's wrong, daughter?" Papa called with a worried frown. "Has that cantankerous bull been chasing you?"

"It's not the bull. Mama's fallen down the cellar steps, and I think her leg is broken. We need to get one of our neighbors to drive her to the hospital right away."

Papa dropped his wire cutters, and the brothers let go of the shovels they'd been using. "Son," Papa said, motioning to Brian, "you run over to the Jenkinses' place and see if they can give us a ride." He turned to John. "Come with me to see about your mamm."

Brian scampered off toward the neighbors', and Faith followed Papa and John across the field, through the pasture, and into the backyard. Papa dashed down the basement stairs and gathered Mama into his arms. "What happened, Wilma? How did this happen?"

"Clumsy me. I wasn't watching where I was going, and I must have slipped on a step." Mama's lips quivered, and Faith could see the anguish on her mother's face. "Sorry to be such a bother."

"You're no bother," Papa said as he and John made a chair with their interlinked arms and carried Mama up the steps and into the house. Faith followed, and so did Susie and Melinda. After the men placed Mama on the sofa in the living room, Faith put two pillows under her mother's head.

"Is Mama gonna be okay?" Susie's eyes were as huge as saucers.

"I'll be fine, daughter," Mama said, although she was gritting her teeth.

"I wonder what's taking so long for our ride to get here," Papa said as he peered out the window. "I thought Brian would have been back by now."

Faith shook her head. "Papa, it's only been ten minutes or so since you sent Brian. I'm sure Mama's ride to the hospital will be here soon, so in the meantime, you need to relax."

He whirled around and leveled her with a look of irritation. "Don't you be tellin' me what to do."

She flinched and drew back as if she'd been stung by a bee. This was exactly the way her father had treated her when she was a girl. "I wasn't trying to tell you what to do. I just thought if you relaxed, the time would pass quicker."

"Our daughter's right, Menno," Mama put in. "Pacing and fretting won't bring us help any quicker."

He grunted and stood in front of her. "You need anything, Wilma? Maybe some ice for the swelling?"

She looked down at her swollen leg. "Jah, that might be a good idea."

"I'll get it." Faith scooted for the kitchen and returned a few minutes later with an ice bag, which she carefully placed on her mother's leg.

"Danki. You're a good daughter."

Tears stung the backs of Faith's eyes. She couldn't remember the last time her mother had said anything that nice to her.

A horn honked, and John, who had been watching out the window, rushed to the door. "Lester Jenkins and his wife are here!"

The rest of the day went by in a blur. Papa, Brian, and Faith rode with Mama to the hospital, while Elaine Jenkins, Lester's wife, stayed at the Stutzmans' house with Melinda and Susie. After X-rays were taken of Mama's leg, the doctor explained that the swelling needed to go down some before the cast was put on, so Mama was kept overnight. Papa decided to stay with her, but Faith and her brothers returned home to do their chores and wait for their sisters to get home.

As Faith prepared for bed that night, she thought about the events of the day. No way could she leave Webster County now. Esther and Grace Ann had jobs outside the home, so they couldn't be counted on to take care of Mama or run the house while her leg was healing. Faith would have to stick around until her mother's cast came off and she could resume her regular chores. It was a good thing

Faith hadn't said anything about leaving yet.

⁂

The following afternoon, Mama came home from the hospital, and Papa and John helped her into her bedroom. Faith thought it was a good thing her folks' room was downstairs, because with Mama having to rely on crutches for weeks, it would have been difficult for her to navigate the stairs safely.

Once Mama was situated, Faith herded Melinda and Susie into the kitchen and instructed them to set the table while she made supper. She'd no more than taken a package of meat from the refrigerator when a knock sounded at the back door.

"I'll get it!" Melinda hollered. She scurried across the room and flung open the door.

A few seconds later, Noah entered the kitchen, holding a loaf of gingerbread in one hand and his straw hat in the other.

"I heard about your mamm's broken leg, and I thought she might like this." He handed the bread to Faith.

"That was nice of you. Would you care to join us for supper?" she asked.

"I appreciate the offer, but I can't stay that long. Mom isn't feeling well today, so I promised I'd get right home to make supper." Noah smiled. "Guess I could stay long enough to have a glass of iced tea, though."

Noah took a seat at the table, and Faith handed him some iced tea. "This sure hits the spot," he said after taking a drink.

"Can Susie and I go out back and play now?" Melinda asked her mother.

Faith nodded her consent, and the girls raced for the back door, giggling all the way.

"Must be nice to be young and full of energy, don't you think?" Noah asked when Faith took the seat across from him.

"I'd give up dessert for a whole week to be able to carry on the way those two do. Even with chores to do, they still find time for fun and games."

"That's the way it should be. We adults need pleasure and laughter in our lives, too." Noah pulled a slip of paper from the pocket of his trousers and held it up.

Faith seemed interested as she leaned across the table. "What have you got there?"

"A scripture verse. I read it this morning before I left for work, and I copied it down."

Faith sat back in her chair with a look of indifference. "Oh, I see."

Noah couldn't understand why she acted so remote whenever he brought up the Bible. It worried him. Her disinterest could mean she would never get baptized and join the church, which pointed to the fact that she wasn't happy here and wanted to return to the English way of life. And if that English fellow Noah had seen Faith with at Baldy's was her boyfriend, then she might be planning to leave home.

"Don't you want to know what the verse says?" he prompted.

She shrugged.

"It's Philippians 4:4: 'Rejoice in the Lord always: and again I say, Rejoice.'"

When she made no comment, Noah added, "The Bible also says in the book of Proverbs, 'A merry heart doeth good like a medicine.' I think everyone needs a bit of God's merry medicine, don't you?"

"I'm a comedian, so it's my job to try to make everyone laugh when I'm onstage."

He shook his head. "I'm not talking about entertaining, Faith. I'm referring to good, old-fashioned, God-given humor."

"I used to get into trouble with my folks for acting silly and playing tricks on my siblings."

Noah lifted his eyebrows. "Acting silly isn't so bad, but playing tricks is another matter."

"You're too good for your own good, do you know that, Noah Hertzler?"

"I don't think my daed would agree. He took me to the woodshed for my fair share of bletchings when I was a boy."

Faith shook her head. "You're such a nice man; I find that hard to believe."

"It's true."

"Well, be that as it may, I think you're a do-gooder."

"Is that a bad thing?"

"No, of course not."

Noah fought the temptation to tell Faith that he'd seen her at Baldy's Café, but he decided it was best not to mention it. Faith had enough on her mind right now, and being put on the spot about the Englisher he'd seen her with might only upset her.

Swallowing the last of his iced tea, Noah pushed his chair back and stood. "Guess I'd better head for home."

Faith scooted her chair away from the table. "Thanks for stopping by with the gingerbread. I'm sure Mama will appreciate it."

She followed him to the door, and just before he exited, Noah handed her the scrap of paper with the Bible verse. "I'd like to leave this with you as a reminder that it's okay to have fun and tell jokes."

Faith took the paper and placed it on the counter but made no comment.

"Let me know if there's anything I can do to help out while your mamm's recuperating."

"Thanks, I will."

Noah bounded down the porch steps, waved to the girls, and climbed into his buggy.

Faith watched until Noah drove out of sight. He really did seem like a nice man. Just not the right man for her. Besides, she was fairly sure

Noah already had a girlfriend.

She turned to the stove, where she added the potatoes she'd peeled to the pot of stew, and when she turned back to the counter to cut up some carrots, she spotted the verse Noah had given her. Did God really find pleasure in hearing people laugh and rejoice? Was Noah all he seemed to be? Faith's head swam with so many unanswered questions. "I have to leave Webster County before I go crazy with a desire for something I can't have. I'll go as soon as Mama's back on her feet."

"Go where?"

Faith whirled around. "Nowhere! I—I didn't know you were here, Grace Ann."

"Jah. Got home from work a few minutes ago." Grace Ann headed over to the kitchen sink. "When I was putting my horse away, I saw Papa out in the barn, and he said Mama came home from the hospital."

Faith nodded. "She's in her bedroom resting."

"Is she in much pain?"

"Probably would be, but the doctor gave her some medication, so I think she's fairly comfortable."

"That's good to hear." Grace Ann looked around the room. "Where's the rest of the family?"

"The boys are doing their chores, and the girls are outside playing."

"Esther's not home yet?"

"Nope."

"Would you mind if I slip into Mama's room and say hello before I help you with supper?"

Faith shrugged. "Go ahead. The stew won't be done for another half hour or so anyway."

When Grace Ann left the room, Faith turned back to the stove. Her thoughts, however, returned to Noah.

Chapter 15

The next several weeks were difficult, with Faith working from sunup to sunset. Everything in the garden seemed to come ripe at the same time, and much of it had to be canned. Mama did all she could from a sitting position, the girls helped with the simpler tasks, and a few Amish women from their community dropped by to offer assistance. Faith gladly accepted everyone's help—even Noah's. He'd come over a few times on his way home from work and had helped Faith fix supper and do some outside chores. Last Saturday Noah had worked in the garden, helped with the canning, and done some baking, as well. It was hard to believe, but he was as much help in the kitchen as he was outdoors.

Faith hated to admit it, but she liked having Noah around. His cheerful disposition as he helped with the chores made her workload seem a bit lighter. Even so, she felt trapped like a mouse caught between a cat's paws. Would she ever be able to go back on the road? It was beginning to seem as if the time would never come.

On this Saturday, Noah had come over to help. He was out in the garden picking tomatoes. Faith had helped him earlier, but she'd gone into the house to get them some water.

When Faith stepped inside the kitchen, Melinda and Susie, who were making a batch of lemonade, greeted her. She chuckled at the sight. Two little girls squeezed lemons into a glass pitcher, but more juice was running down their arms than was making it into the container.

"Need any help?" she asked as she stepped up to the table.

"We can do this," Susie said, a look of determination on her youthful face. "Mama told us how."

"That's right, and we wanted to surprise you and Noah with a glass of lemonade," Melinda added.

"Then surprise us you shall." Faith gave her daughter a smile, then turned on her heel. "You can bring the lemonade outside when you're finished."

Faith was still smiling when she stepped

outside. Melinda was adjusting so well. School would be starting in a few weeks, and as soon as Melinda was settled into that routine and Mama was back on her feet, Faith planned to leave.

❧

"That Noah's sure a nice man," Melinda said to Susie, as they scurried over to the refrigerator to get out some more lemons.

"Jah, he sure is," Wilma answered before Susie could respond. She'd been sitting at the table, reading the latest issue of *The Budget* and couldn't help hearing Melinda's comment.

"Noah's a lot of fun, and he's real smart, too." Melinda fairly beamed as she carried a handful of lemons back to the counter across the room.

"That's right," Susie agreed. "With all the help he's given you, you'll be the smartest scholar in the first grade."

Melinda's cheeks turned pink. "I might not be the smartest, but I'm doing a lot better now that Noah's been working with me."

Wilma tipped her head and studied Melinda. Oh, how she hoped Faith would never leave and take the child away. She'd grown attached to the girl, and from the looks of Melinda's exuberant smile, she had a hunch the child was happy to be living here, too.

"Say, Melinda," Wilma asked, "do you think your mamm's happy living here?"

"Sometimes, when she's laughing and playing silly games with me, she seems happy, but other times, she acts kind of sad." Melinda squinted as she turned to face Wilma. "I think she misses my daddy, and it makes me wish Mama would get married again."

Susie plunked a sack of sugar on the counter next to the lemons. "Maybe she'll marry Noah. He seems to like her, and truth be told, I think she likes him, too."

Wilma smiled. If that were true, then she and Noah's mother wouldn't have to work so hard at getting Noah and Faith together. Maybe the young couple would begin courting on their own.

Just then, Grace Ann stepped into the kitchen. "Whew, it sure is hot out there," she said, wiping the perspiration from her forehead. "I don't know how Faith and Noah can keep working in the heat of the sun like that."

Wilma motioned to the girls. "If you'd like something to drink, some lemonade is in the making."

"Sounds good. Need any help?" Grace Ann asked, stepping up to the counter.

Susie shook her head. "We can do this by ourselves, can't we, Melinda?"

Melinda nodded. " 'Course we can."

Grace Ann chuckled and took a seat at the table beside her mother. "How's that leg feeling, Mama?"

"It's getting better every day," Wilma replied.

"Glad to hear it. I'm sure you'll be relieved when the cast comes off and you can get back to walking without your crutches."

"That's for sure."

Wilma and Grace Ann chatted about everyday things, while Melinda and Susie finished making the lemonade. When the girls took the pitcher of lemonade outside, Grace Ann leaned closer to Wilma and whispered, "I've been wanting to tell you something, but there never seemed to be a good time."

"What's that?"

"The day you came back from the hospital, I overheard Faith mumbling something to herself about leaving."

Wilma's eyebrows drew together. "Leave here?"

"I think so," Grace Ann said with a nod. "She was fixing stew for supper, and I heard her say, 'I'll go as soon as Mama's back on her feet.'"

Wilma's heart clenched. It was as she'd suspected. Faith wasn't happy here, and she had no intention of staying. That meant she probably wasn't as interested in Noah as Susie thought, either. "Danki for sharing that with me," she said. "You haven't told anyone else, have you?"

Grace Ann shook her head.

"Good. I think it'd be best if you didn't."

"How come?"

"Because if Faith thinks we're talking about her, it might make her want to leave all the more." Wilma patted her daughter's arm. "The best thing we can do for Faith is think of some way to make her like it here well enough to stay."

"How are we going to do that?"

"I'm working on that," Wilma said with a nod.

When Barbara pulled her rig into the Stutzmans' yard, she spotted Faith sitting on the porch with her daughter and Susie. Noah was also there, which gave Barbara a little hope that things might be getting serious between Noah and Faith.

Susie waved to Barbara and called, "Come join us for some lemonade."

Barbara tied her horse to the hitching rail and hurried toward the house. "It's plenty hot today, so something cold to drink will surely hit the spot," she said as she stepped onto the porch.

"This is real tasty, too." Noah lifted his glass in the air. "Susie and Melinda made it."

"Did they now?" Barbara patted both girls' shoulders and took a seat in the empty chair beside Faith.

Faith poured some lemonade into one of

the empty glasses sitting on the small table nearby. "See for yourself how good it tastes," she said, handing the glass to Barbara.

Barbara lifted it to her lips and took a sip. "Umm. . .you're right, this is *gut* lemonade."

Both girls beamed, and then Susie said, "Maybe we should go inside and see if there's any cookies we can have."

"Good idea." Melinda jumped up, and the two girls disappeared into the house.

"Where are your boys today?" Faith asked, turning to face Barbara.

"They're home with my mamm. David thought I needed some time to myself, so he said I should leave the shop for a while and go somewhere on my own."

"Sounds like a good man to me," Noah said.

"Jah, he's the best." Barbara smiled at Noah. "What brings you over here today?"

"Came to help Faith work in the garden."

"How thoughtful of you." Barbara had to bite her tongue to keep from saying what she was thinking. Noah would make the perfect husband for Faith, and if Faith was courted by someone as nice as Noah, it might help her smile more, the way she used to do when they were children.

Noah lifted himself from the chair. "This has been a nice break, but I think I'll get back to work and let you two women visit."

"Is there anything going on between you

and Noah?" Barbara asked once Noah was out of earshot.

Faith's mouth dropped open. "Why would you ask such a question?"

"I couldn't help but notice the way he looked at you—like he thinks you're something special."

"No way! Noah and I are just friends; nothing more."

"But I heard he's been coming around here a lot lately, and—"

Faith held up her hand. "Noah's been coming over to help out since Mama broke her leg, but there's nothing special between us. Fact is, Noah already has a girlfriend."

"He does?"

Faith nodded.

"Who is she?"

"I don't know her name, but I saw Noah sitting with her at Baldy's Café sometime back. I didn't recognize her as anyone from our community."

"Hmm. . ."

"Has Noah ever said anything to you about having a girlfriend?"

Barbara shook her head. "But then, most courting couples don't broadcast their intentions until they're ready to get married."

"You think he's planning to marry this woman?"

"I have no idea. Want me to ask him?"

"No!" Faith's face heated up. "He might not like it if you started prying into his business." She shrugged. "Besides, what Noah does is his business. I sure don't care."

Barbara was tempted to say more on the subject but decided to keep quiet.

"So, how are things going in the harness shop?" Faith asked.

"Real well. David and I enjoy working together."

Faith grunted. "I still can't believe you're helping him make and repair harnesses and other leather items. That seems like hard work for a delicate woman."

Barbara patted her stomach. "After having two kinner, I'm afraid I'm not so delicate anymore."

Faith stared out at the garden, where Noah worked.

"I guess I should get going and let you get back to work," Barbara said as she rose from her seat.

Faith stood, too. "Yes, I should probably help Noah."

Impulsively, Barbara gave Faith a hug. "It's sure good to have you back in Webster County. I missed you."

"Thanks."

Barbara stepped off the porch and headed across the yard. She stopped at the garden to say good-bye to Noah, then climbed into her buggy, whispering a prayer for her childhood friend.

✧❀✧

Noah looked up as Faith joined him at the row of beans he'd been weeding. "Did you and Barbara have a nice visit?"

"It was okay."

"Just okay? I thought the two of you used to be good friends."

"*Used to be* is the correct term. I was away from home a long time, and we barely know each other anymore."

Using the back of his hand, Noah wiped the sweat rolling down his forehead. "She cared enough to come over and see how you're doing. To me that says she wants to be your friend."

Faith shrugged. "Maybe so."

"I'd like to be your friend, too."

To his surprise, she smiled. "I'd say you've already proven that by the acts of kindness you've shown me and my family."

Noah wanted to tell Faith that he was interested in her as a woman, not just as a friend who needed his help, but he held himself in check. If there was any hope of them having a relationship, he needed to take it slow and easy with Faith. He also needed to accept the fact that she might never be romantically interested in him—especially if she was involved with an English man.

Should I come right out and ask her? Noah thumped the side of his head. *I need to quit thinking such thoughts and just be her friend.*

Chapter 16

Faith didn't know where the summer had gone. But here it was nearing the end of August, and today was the first day of school for Melinda and Susie. They'd been so busy they still hadn't made it to Springfield with Noah to see Fantastic Caverns or the Bass Pro Shops. The only trips Faith had made were into Seymour for groceries and to phone her agent.

"Maybe next spring," Noah had said a few days ago, but Faith knew otherwise. By spring she would be gone.

It's just as well, Faith decided as she hung a freshly washed towel on the clothesline. *Thanks to Mama's accident and Noah coming over to help so often, I've already seen him more than I should have. Each time we're together it makes me long for. . .*

She grabbed another towel from the wicker basket and gave it a good shake. *I long to be back onstage entertaining—that's what I long for. I won't let anything stand in my way once Mama's up and around and able to resume her chores. I plan to be on a bus heading for my next performance by the end of September.*

A short time later, Faith hitched her favorite horse to one of Papa's buggies and drove Melinda and Susie to school. The one-room schoolhouse was only a half mile down the road, but this was Melinda's first time in school, and Faith figured her little girl might need some moral support. At least it made Faith feel better to see that her daughter was dropped safely off at school on her first day.

"Do I have to go to school today, Mama?" Melinda asked from her seat behind Faith. "Can't I stay home and let you be my teacher?"

Faith glanced over her shoulder and grimaced when she saw the look of despair on her daughter's face.

"She'll be okay once we get there," Susie said before Faith could respond. "I was *naerfich* last year when it was my first day, too."

Melinda's lower lip quivered. "Were you really nervous?"

"Jah." Susie tapped Faith on the shoulder. "See how well Melinda's learning Pennsylvania Dutch? She knows what *naerfich* means."

"Good job, Melinda." Faith smiled. "Susie,

why don't you tell Melinda what school is like? Maybe give her an idea of what to expect."

"Well," Susie began, "the first thing we do when we get to school, after we've taken a seat behind one of the desks, is to listen to our teacher, Sarah Wagler, read some verses from the Bible. Then we all say the Lord's Prayer, and after that we sing a few songs."

"That seems easy enough," Melinda said, her voice sounding much brighter. "What happens after the songs?"

"Then it's time for lessons to begin." Susie paused, and Faith wondered if her little sister was finished sharing the details of school or trying to think of what to say next. "Sarah usually gives the older ones their arithmetic lesson, and then she or her helper, Nona Shemly, works with the younger ones who need to learn English," Susie continued.

"But I already know how to speak English."

"Then you'll be given some other assignment."

Melinda released a little grunt, and Faith figured the child was probably mulling things over. Hopefully, she would come to grips with the idea of school and get along fine.

When Faith pulled the buggy into the school's graveled parking lot a short time later, she handed the girls their lunch pails, waved a cheery good-bye, and drove away with a lump lodged in her throat. *My baby is growing up, and soon I'll be saying good-bye for much longer than just the few hours she'll be in school every day.*

The thought of leaving Melinda behind was always painful, but nothing good could come from Faith staying in Webster County. Nor could any good come from hauling her child all over the countryside while they lived out of a suitcase in some stuffy hotel room. Melinda would be better off with her Amish grandparents.

But she won't have her mother, Faith's conscience reminded her. She pushed the thought aside and concentrated on the pleasant weather. Breathing deeply, she filled her lungs with the fresh, crisp air. Soon the leaves on the maple trees would transform into beautiful autumn colors. As colder weather and winds crept in, the leaves would drop from the trees, making a vibrant carpet of color.

She had never had much time to enjoy the beauty of nature when she was entertaining. Sometimes she did two or three shows a day, and when she wasn't performing, she was practicing or sleeping. The only quality time she'd had with Melinda was on her days off. Greg had been responsible for their daughter the rest of the time, and he sometimes hired a babysitter so he could be free to do his own thing.

There was no doubt in Faith's mind—it was better for Melinda to stay in Webster County.

For as long as Faith was here, she planned to enjoy every minute spent with her daughter. And she needed to make another trip to town to call her agent and let him know how things were going. While she was there, she'd pick up a few groceries, too

❀

Noah wasn't glad Wilma Stutzman had broken her leg, but he was grateful for the extra time it had given him to be with Faith. Not only was he doing something he enjoyed, but the hours they'd spent together seemed to be strengthening their friendship. At least he thought so. Faith always acted friendly whenever he came by to help out, and Noah took that as a good sign. She hadn't told him to stop quoting scripture or talking about God, either. *Maybe it's just wishful thinking,* he told himself as he headed down the road after leaving work for the day. *Might could be that the strong feelings I'm having for Faith have clouded my thinking. It's not good for me to be so attracted to her when I'm not sure if her relationship with God has grown. Besides, I still don't know if that man I saw her with at Baldy's plays a part in her life. I need to ask, but I'm afraid of her answer.*

Noah's thoughts came to a halt as he approached the Amish schoolhouse and noticed Faith's horse and buggy pulling into the lot. On impulse, he did the same. It would be nice to say hello and see how Melinda had fared on her first day of school.

Faith apparently hadn't seen him, and she hopped out of the buggy and sprinted toward the school without a glance in his direction. The children were filing out the front door, and Noah sat in his buggy, watching. He would wait and speak to Faith as soon as she had Melinda and Susie in tow.

A few seconds later, Susie came out and climbed into the buggy, but there was no sign of Faith or her daughter. He figured she was probably talking to the teacher—maybe checking to see if Melinda had any homework to do.

Susie turned in her seat and waved at Noah. He lifted his hand in response. Then, deciding that Faith's little sister might like some company, he hopped down from his buggy, secured the horse to the hitching rail, and ambled over to Faith's carriage.

"Hi, Noah," Susie said. "You're not married and you've got no kinner, so how come you're here at school?"

Noah leaned against the side of the buggy and grinned at the little girl. She was cute and spunky like her big sister. "I saw your rig and thought I'd drop by and say hello to Faith," he said.

The skin around the corners of Susie's coffee-colored eyes crinkled, and she leveled him with a knowing look. "You're sweet on my sister, aren't ya?"

The child's pointed question took Noah by surprise. When it came to owning up to his feelings for Faith, he couldn't deny them to himself, but he surely wasn't going to admit such a thing to young Susie. She would most likely blab. If word got out that he was interested in Faith, Noah would not only be the target of teasing by friends such as Isaac Troyer, but he was sure Faith would find out, as well. If that happened and she didn't return his feelings, Noah wouldn't be able to stand the humiliation.

"Do you care for Faith or not?" Susie pried.

"Of course I care for her," Noah said, carefully choosing his words. "She's a friend, and I care about all my friends."

Susie snickered. "That's not what I meant."

Noah was busy thinking up some kind of a sensible comeback when he caught sight of Faith and Melinda leaving the schoolhouse. As they drew closer, he noticed Faith's furrowed brows and puckered lips. She looked downright flustered. He was tempted to rush over and see what was wrong but waited at the buggy until they arrived.

"It's good to see you, Faith," he said.

She nodded, and her frown deepened.

"What's the trouble? You look upset."

"Sarah Wagler. She's the trouble."

"What's the problem between you and the schoolteacher?"

Faith helped Melinda into the buggy and then turned to face Noah. "That woman had the nerve to say that my daughter seems spoiled and didn't show any interest in learning how to read." Her blue eyes narrowed, and she clamped both hands against her hips. "Can you believe that?"

Noah opened his mouth to respond, but Faith cut him off.

"Sarah insisted that Melinda is behind for her age, and she even said I was being defensive when I assured her that my little girl is as smart as any child in her class." Faith pulled her hands away from her hips and popped the knuckles on her left hand.

Noah took a step toward Faith. "I've been around Melinda a fair amount, and I can tell how smart she is. I think she'll catch on quickly to book learning if she's encouraged to keep trying. I know you've got your hands full caring for your mamm, so I'd be happy to drop by on my way home from work a few nights a week or on Saturdays to help Melinda learn to read."

"It's kind of you to offer, but—"

"I really would like to do this."

"You've already done so much, and I don't feel right about asking you to do more."

"Please, Mama? I want Noah to help me." Melinda's tone was pleading.

"Oh, all right," Faith finally conceded. "Noah can help you study."

"Great," Noah said, clapping his hands together. "We can get started Saturday afternoon."

Chapter 17

When Noah showed up on Saturday afternoon, he held a small box in his hand. "I made some chocolate chip cookies this morning," he said, leaning his head over and sniffing the box.

Melinda, who had been sitting at the table with her reading book, jumped up and dashed across the room. "Yippee! I love chocolate chip!"

"Not until your homework is finished," Faith said with a shake of her head.

"Your mamm's right." Noah placed the box of cookies on the counter. "You can have some when your lessons are done."

Faith watched Noah take a seat at the table next to Melinda, with Melinda's early reader placed between them, and as Faith finished washing their lunch dishes, Noah read from the book, pointing to each word and asking Melinda to repeat what he'd read.

"I'll be in the next room helping my mother with some mending," Faith said when the dishes were done. "Give a holler if you need me for anything."

Noah nodded and smiled. "Jah, okay. When we're finished, I'll let you know. Maybe you'd like to have a few cookies with us."

"Sounds good. Susie's outside helping Esther and Grace Ann dig potatoes. They'd probably like to have some cookies, as well."

"I brought three dozen. Should be plenty for everyone."

"Okay."

Faith headed for the living room and found her mother sitting in the rocker. Her leg, which was still encased in a heavy cast, was propped on a wooden footstool.

"Was that Noah I heard come in?" Mama asked, looking up from her needlework.

Faith nodded. "He's here to help Melinda with her reading, and he brought along some freshly baked cookies. When they're done, we'll have some. Would you care to join us?"

Mama patted her stomach. "I'd better not. Since I broke my leg and have had to sit around so much, I think I've put on a few extra pounds."

Faith took a seat on the sofa across from

her mother and gathered up the sewing basket sitting on the end table. "I hardly think one or two cookies will make you fat, Mama."

"Maybe not, but with me not getting much exercise these days, everything I eat goes right here." She thumped her midsection again.

Faith shrugged. "Whatever you think best."

For the next hour, Faith and her mother darned socks, patched holes in the men's trousers, and hemmed school dresses for the younger girls. Faith had just finished hemming a dress for Melinda when Noah emerged from the kitchen. "We're done with our studies. Anyone ready for some cookies?"

"I am. I need a break from all this sewing," Faith was quick to say.

"None for me, danki," Mama said with a smile.

Faith rose from her chair. "Is it all right if we help ourselves to some goat's milk to go along with the cookies?"

Mama's glasses had slipped to the middle of her nose, and she pushed them back in place. "It's fine by me. The goats are producing heavily right now, so we've got plenty of milk to go around." She nodded at Noah. "Would you like to stay for supper?"

"That offer's tempting, but I really should get home soon. Preaching is at our place tomorrow, and even though my two sisters-in-law have been helping my mamm get the house ready, I think she'll have a few things she wants me to do yet today."

Mama looked disappointed. She'd obviously been hoping Noah would stay for supper. "I hope Ida knows how fortunate she is to have a son like you," she said. "My boys are all hard workers when it comes to outside things, but I can't get them to do much inside the house."

"My daed's the same way." Noah smiled. "I like doing many outside chores, but kitchen duty doesn't make me the least bit nervous."

Faith followed Noah through the kitchen doorway just as Melinda darted for the back door. "Where are you going?" she called after her daughter. "Don't you want some cookies and milk?"

"I'll have some later. Right now, I'm going out to the barn to see the baby goat that was born this morning. Grandpa told us about it during lunch, remember?"

Faith nodded. "And I said you'd have to wait to see it until your studies were done."

"They're done now; just ask Noah." Melinda bounded out the door before Faith could respond.

"That girl," she muttered. "Anything that pertains to an animal captures her attention. I hope she becomes that conscientious where her schoolwork is concerned."

Noah grinned as he scooped Melinda's book off the table. "If she had stayed living in the English world, she might have grown up to be a veterinarian."

Faith shrugged. Had she done the right thing bringing Melinda here to be raised? Would the child have been better off in the English world, where she could further her education and become a vet or whatever else she wanted to be? She shook her head, as though it might get her thinking straight again. If she had kept Melinda in the English world while she entertained, the child might have ended up becoming an entertainer and would never have had the opportunity to be with so many farm animals. Melinda seemed happy here, and Faith was sure she had been right to have her daughter be raised by her Amish family. She glanced over at Noah and was surprised to see him wiping a spot on the cupboard where some sticky syrup must have dripped from that morning's breakfast. She still couldn't get over how helpful the man was. For one moment, she let the silliest notion take root in her mind. *What would it be like to be married to someone as kind and ready to lend a hand as Noah?*

❦

"I'll get the milk while you set out the cookies," Faith said.

Noah grunted as he bit back a chuckle. "You like bossin' me around?"

She halted her steps and turned to face him.

"Is that how I come across—like I'm bossy?"

He shook his head. "Not really, but just now you sounded a lot like my mamm."

Faith grimaced. "I didn't mean for it to seem as if I was trying to tell you what to do."

Noah shrugged. "It's not a big thing. I'm more than willing to set out the cookies."

"Okay." Faith got out a bottle of goat's milk, and Noah piled a stack of chocolate chip cookies on a plate, then placed it on the table.

"We could take a few of these to your mamm if you think she might change her mind and have some," he said.

Faith shook her head. "When Mom says no to something, she means it."

Noah noticed the bitter tone in Faith's voice. Obviously, Faith and her mother still had problems. Should he say something about it. . .maybe offer a listening ear if Faith wanted to talk? "I. . .uh. . .sense some bitterness in the way you spoke of your mamm," he said hesitantly. "Would you like to talk about it?"

"No!" She set the bottle of milk down on the table with such force Noah feared it might break.

"Sorry. I didn't mean to upset you," he apologized.

Faith's hands shook as she took two glasses from the cupboard. "The problem between me and my folks goes back to when I was a kinner, and I don't think talking about it will change a thing."

Noah was tempted to argue the point but thought better of it. No point in upsetting her further. "If you ever change your mind and need a listening ear," he said, moving to stand beside her, "I'd be more than willing."

She gave a brief nod, then hurried across the room with the glasses.

A short time later after Noah had gone home, Faith decided to take a walk out to the barn to see what Melinda was up to, as she still hadn't come back to the house. She found her daughter hanging over one of the stall doors, staring at a baby goat while talking to Faith's father, who stood beside her.

"Look at Tiny, Mama," Melinda said when Faith stepped up to them. "Isn't he cute?"

Faith nodded. "So you've named him already, huh?"

"Sure did. Grandpa said I could pick the name, and I chose Tiny because the goat's so small."

Papa chuckled. "He won't be so tiny once he's grown."

"Did you forget about coming to the house for cookies and milk?" Faith asked, tapping Melinda on the shoulder.

The child looked up at her and grinned. "Guess I got so busy watching the baby goat and talking with Grandpa that my stomach forgot it wanted cookies."

Faith smiled. It was good to see her daughter so happy and satisfied. It made her wish she could have been that content when she was a child. If only she'd been more accepted. If only. . .

"How's your mamm doing?" Papa asked, breaking into Faith's thoughts. "Has she been resting that leg like she's supposed to?"

"As far as I know, she's still in the living room doing some mending," Faith replied.

Papa lifted one eyebrow. "I wouldn't call that resting."

"She had her foot propped on a footstool and was sitting comfortably in the rocker with the mending in her lap, so I'm sure it didn't cause any discomfort to her leg."

"Are you trying to be *gchpassich*?" her father asked in a clipped tone.

Faith gritted her teeth as she struggled with the desire to defend herself. *Here we go again. . . being accused of trying to be funny when I was merely trying to explain something. Why is it that everything I say to him seems to be taken wrong?*

"Are you going to answer my question or not?" her father persisted. "Were you trying to be gchpassich?"

"Mama's good at being funny," Melinda interjected before Faith could respond. "Telling funny stories used to be her job before we moved here, you know." When she looked up at Faith, a look of pride shone in her eyes.

Faith figured if her father saw that look, he would accuse Melinda of being filled with *hochmut*, and then she would be in for a lecture the way Faith used to be whenever she'd said or done anything that could have been considered proud.

Much to Faith's surprise, however, Papa made no comment about what Melinda had said. Instead, he took hold of the child's hand and steered her toward the barn door. "How's about you and me going up to the house for some of those cookies you missed out on?"

Melinda nodded eagerly. "Are you coming, Mama?" she called over her shoulder.

"In a minute."

When the barn door clicked shut, Faith dropped to a bale of straw near the goat's stall. She sat there a few minutes, staring at the mother goat and her baby. Then she let her head fall forward in her hands, and she wept. She needed to get away from this place as soon as possible.

Chapter 18

The day finally came when Mama's cast was removed. Faith wasn't sure who was more relieved—she or Mama. The cumbersome cast must have been heavy, not to mention hot and sweaty during the warm days in late summer. The only trouble was, Mama's leg, though healed, was now stiff and shriveled from being stuck inside the cast and not used for six weeks. The doctor had told Mama that she would need physical therapy to regain strength in her leg. That meant more expense for Faith's folks, and it also doomed Faith to stick around a few more weeks. It wouldn't be right to leave when Mama wasn't able to function at 100 percent.

Faith had agreed to go to Springfield with her mother once a week for her therapy treatments, as her father and brothers were busy with the beginning of harvest, and Grace Ann and Esther were working at their jobs all day. Faith hired one of their English neighbors to drive them.

On the day of the first appointment, Faith hurried to make the girls their lunches, sent them off to school with a reminder not to dawdle, and rushed around to clean up the kitchen. She'd begun to wipe off the table when she noticed one of Melinda's reading books. She hurried outside, calling, "Melinda, come back! You forgot something!"

The children were already halfway down the driveway, but Melinda must have heard, for she spun around and cupped her hands around her mouth. "What'd I forget?"

Faith held up the book. "Come back and get it!"

Seconds later, Melinda had the book and was running down the driveway to catch up to Susie. Faith clicked her tongue against the roof of her mouth as she headed back to the house. At least one good thing had happened over the last few weeks. Noah had been able to teach Melinda enough to make Sarah Wagler happy. The teacher said she was pleased with Melinda's progress and that the child seemed a bit more sure of herself.

Faith knew her daughter liked Noah a lot. She often talked about him, saying she wished he could be her new daddy. Faith tried to dissuade Melinda, reminding her that Noah had his parents to care for, and she and Melinda had Grandpa and Grandma Stutzman to help out. No point getting her daughter's hopes up over something that was never going to happen.

When Faith entered the kitchen a few minutes later, she found her mother limping around the room, putting clean dishes in the cupboard.

"Why don't you take a seat at the table and have a cup of tea?" Faith suggested. "I'll finish up here, and we'll be ready and waiting when Doris Moore comes to pick us up."

Mama's eyebrows were pinched as she sat down. "I'm beginning to wonder if I'll ever get the strength back in my leg."

"I'm sure with some therapy you'll be good as new."

"I hope so, because I'm getting awful tired of sitting around trying to do things with one leg propped up." Mama heaved a sigh and took a sip of tea. "Will Noah be coming over this afternoon when he gets off work?" she asked with a hopeful expression.

Faith shook her head as she slipped a stack of clean plates into one of the cupboards. "When I saw Noah at church yesterday, I told him we were going to Springfield this morning for your therapy. Since I didn't know what time we might get home, I suggested he wait until

Tuesday to work with Melinda."

"I guess that makes sense." Mama smiled. "That man sure does have the patience of Job, don't you think? I can't get over what a good cook he is, either."

"You're right—Noah is a good cook, and he does seem to have more patience than most men." Faith's thoughts went immediately to Greg. He'd been so short-tempered. Especially when it came to Faith. He'd expected more than she could possibly give. He'd always pushed her to do multiple shows and reprimanded her whenever she wanted to take time off. And he'd let his temper loose on Faith more times than she cared to think about.

She rubbed her hand along the side of her face, thinking about how hard he had hit her one night shortly before his death. It had left a black-and-blue mark, but she'd hid it under a layer of heavy makeup.

"Susie thinks Noah might be sweet on you," Mama said, pulling Faith out of her disconcerting thoughts. "I'm wondering if the feelings might be mutual."

Faith clenched her teeth. *Not this again.* "Susie should mind her own business." She slammed the cupboard door with more force than she meant to, and it rattled the dishes. She jerked it open again and checked to be sure nothing had broken. To her relief, all the dishes were intact.

"Faith, did you hear what I asked?"

Faith whirled around. "I heard you, Mama. I just don't have anything to say."

"Oh, I see."

Maybe now was the time to tell Mama her plans. Faith opened her mouth, but the words stuck in her throat like a glob of gooey peanut butter. Maybe this wasn't the right time. Not with Mama's leg still trying to heal.

She popped two knuckles and frowned. *Shouldn't be doing that either, I guess.*

"Faith, what's wrong? You seem kind of agitated," Mama said softly. "Why don't you come over here and have a cup of tea with me while we wait for Doris?"

Faith moved back to the counter, where a stack of clean plates waited on the sideboard to be put away. "I–I'm fine, Mama, and I really do need to get the rest of these dishes put away." *Chicken. You're afraid to tell her what's troubling you.*

"All right, then. Guess we can visit while you work and I sip my tea."

For the next several minutes, they talked about the weather, who in their community was expecting a baby, how the girls were doing in school—anything but the one thing that weighed heavily on Faith's mind. If only she felt free to tell Mama the truth: that she'd come home only so Melinda would have a place to stay while Faith was on the road entertaining, and that she felt ready to leave now, knowing Melinda had adjusted to being Amish, but she didn't want to leave Mama in the lurch.

"Your teacup is empty," Faith said after turning from the sink and glancing at her mother's cup. "Would you like me to pour you some more?"

"Jah, sure, that'd be nice."

Faith dried her hands and got the simmering teakettle. She had just finished pouring hot water into her mother's cup when someone tapped on the back door.

"I wonder if that could be Doris," Mama said. "I didn't hear a car pull into the yard, did you?"

"No, I didn't." When Faith opened the door, she was surprised to see Barbara standing on the porch.

"*Wie geht's?*" Barbara asked.

"I'm all right. How about you?"

"Fine and dandy."

"Would you like to come in and have a cup of tea? Mama's having some while we wait for Doris to give us a ride to Springfield for Mama's first therapy session, and I'm finishing up the dishes." Faith held the door open.

With an eager expression, Barbara nodded. "I always enjoy a good cup of tea."

Faith led the way to the kitchen and pulled out a chair for Barbara. "Have a seat, and I'll get another cup."

"Wie geht's, Wilma?" Barbara asked, smiling at Faith's mother.

"I'm doing all right," Mama replied. "The bone in my leg's healed, although I do need some therapy." She smiled at Barbara. "My oldest daughter's been taking real good care of me."

"Glad to hear it." Barbara sat down, and Faith scurried to get tea and cups for both herself and her friend. Then she joined the women at the table.

"What brings you over our way, and where's your horse and buggy? We never heard you pull in," Mama said, looking at Barbara.

"I walked over today. Thought I could use the exercise." Barbara patted her thick hips. "The reason for my visit, Wilma, is to invite you and your daughters to an all-day quilting bee at my house next Thursday."

"That sounds like fun," Mama said. "I'd like to come, but Esther and Grace Ann will both be working, so they won't be able to make it." She glanced over at Faith. "How about you? Would you like to go to the quilting bee?"

"How can you host a quilting bee when you work at the harness shop with your husband?" Faith asked Barbara.

"We're fairly well caught up on things right now." Barbara took a sip of tea. "So David suggested that I take a few days off and do something fun with my friends. He said I'm in the shop too much and need to fellowship more." She rested her hand on Faith's arm. "Please say you'll come."

Faith felt like a helpless fly trapped in a spider's web. The last thing she wanted to do was spend the day with a bunch of somber women who could sew better than she could and whose idea of fun was to talk about the weather, who'd been sick in their family, or who'd recently had a birthday. But she hated to say no, since Mama wanted to go and would need someone to drive her there. "Jah, okay," she finally said. "Mama and I will be at your quilting bee."

❧

"I was wondering something, Mama," Faith said after Barbara left for home.

"What's that?"

"How did you and Papa meet, and how'd you know he was the one you should marry?"

Wilma smiled as she stared across the room, allowing herself to remember the past. "Well, as you know, your daed's two years older than me."

Faith nodded.

"All through our school days, I had an interest in him, but he never gave me more than a second glance." She took a sip of tea. "Anyway, when I went to my first young people's singing, I made up my mind I was going to get your daed to notice me one way or another."

"What happened?"

"Menno—your daed—had taken off his straw hat and laid it on a bale of straw in the Millers' barn. When he wasn't looking, I snatched the thing up and hid it behind some old milk cans."

Faith leaned her elbows on the table and cupped her chin in the palms of her hands. "Then what?"

"Well, your daed spent the next half hour searching for his hat, and in the meantime, my two brothers, Henry and Levi, decided to head for home. Only thing is, they left without me." She snickered. "I think they did it on purpose because they knew how much I cared for your daed."

Faith added more water to her teacup. "I can't believe you would do such a thing, Mama. It doesn't sound like you at all."

Wilma slowly shook her head. "I'm not perfect, Faith. Never claimed to be, neither. Besides, I had to do something to get that man to look my way."

"I assume he did, since you're married to him now."

"After I discovered my brothers had run off without me, I conveniently found your daed's hat. When I gave it to him, I just happened to mention that Henry and Levi had gone home and I had no ride."

"Of course, Papa volunteered to give you a

lift in his buggy."

"He sure did." Wilma grinned. "Not only did he drive me home, but when he dropped me off, he let it be known that he thought I was pretty cute. Even said he might like to give me a ride in his buggy after the next singing."

Faith opened her mouth as if to comment, but the tooting of a car horn closed the subject. "Guess that must be Doris."

"We'd better not keep her waiting," Wilma said. "Wouldn't be good for me to be late to my first appointment."

Noah whistled as he flagged a group of six-foot pine trees with white plastic ribbon. The ones that were six and a half feet would get green and white ribbons. The trees he selected would be sold to wholesale Christmas tree lots. Amos and Griggs were at his side, vying for attention.

"Go play somewhere else, fellows," Noah scolded. "Can't you see that I'm a busy man?"

The hound dogs responded with a noisy bark and a couple of tail wags; then they bounded away.

A short time later, Hank showed up, offering Noah a bottle of cold water. Noah took it gratefully, as it had turned out to be a rather warm day.

"Thanks. With the weather being so hot,

one would never guess it's fall. Sure hope it cools off some before folks start coming to choose their trees."

"That won't be long," Hank said as he flopped onto the grass between the rows of trees where Noah had been working. Noah followed suit, and the two of them took long drinks from their bottles, then leaned back on their elbows.

"I brought you and Sandy one of my lemon sponge cakes," Noah said. "Dropped it off at the house before I started work."

Hank licked his lips. "Umm. . .sounds good. Maybe we can have a piece after we eat the noon meal."

Whenever Noah made lemon sponge cake, he thought about Faith and the cake he'd given her that first Sunday after she'd returned. He'd gotten to know her better since then, and the more time he spent with her, the more he cared about her. He hadn't heard any more from either his mother or Wilma about Faith leaving Webster County, so he hoped she might have given up on the idea. Either that or she'd never planned to go in the first place. Could be that Wilma Stutzman had misread her daughter's intentions. Maybe Noah had, as well, for Faith certainly seemed to have settled into the Amish way of life again, except for not being baptized and joining the church. Noah saw Faith's staying as an answer to prayer and figured in time she would make things permanent by joining the church—if she wasn't involved with that English fellow he'd seen her with, that is. Oh, how he wished he could get up his nerve to ask about that, but he'd let it go so long now that it might seem odd to Faith if he questioned her about it.

"So what's new in your life?" Hank asked, pulling Noah's thoughts aside.

"Not so much."

"Are you still helping that little Amish girl with her reading?"

Noah nodded. "Melinda's doing better in school, but I've had such a good time helping her that I think I'll keep going over awhile longer."

Hank shot him a knowing look. "You sure it's not the child's mother you're going to see?"

"As I've said before, Faith and I are just friends." Noah's face heated up. Hank was right. Even though Noah enjoyed helping Melinda with her studies, the real reason he wanted to keep going over to the Stutzmans' place was to see Faith. He took another swig of water and clambered to his feet. "Guess I'd best get back to work. These trees won't flag themselves."

Hank stood, as well. "If you don't want to talk about your love life, it's fine by me." He winked at Noah. "Just be sure I get an invitation to the wedding."

Noah nearly choked on the last bit of water

he'd put in his mouth. Was the idea of marriage to Faith a possibility? He doubted it, but it sure was a nice thought. "Changing the subject," he said, "I was wondering how things are going with you and Sandy these days."

Hank shrugged and reached up to rub the back of his neck. "About the same, I guess. She keeps busy with her things, and I keep busy with mine. We don't talk much unless there's something that needs to be said."

"Have you thought any more about adopting a baby?"

"Nope. I've been afraid to bring it up for fear she'll say no."

"I'll continue to pray for you," Noah said. "But if you want my opinion, I think you should come right out and tell Sandy you'd like to adopt."

"I'll give it some thought." Hank gave Noah's shoulder a squeeze. "Thanks for being such a good friend." He started to walk away but turned back. "Oh, and if you ever decide to start courting that woman you're *not* interested in, you can count on me for some good advice."

Chapter 19

As Faith and her mother headed down the road in their buggy toward the Zooks' house the following week, Faith found herself dreading the day ahead. Spending time with Barbara made her think about the past, something she would rather forget. But Mama had been insistent about them going to the quilting bee, and since they'd been getting along pretty well of late, Faith didn't want to do anything to upset the applecart. Soon enough, she would tell her folks about her plans to leave Webster County, and she wanted the time they had together to be free of disagreements.

"I've sure been looking forward to the quilting bee," Mama said, glancing over at Faith and smiling. "I've been cooped up so much since I broke my leg that I like any reason to get out."

"Does that include going to physical therapy?" Faith asked.

"Jah. Even that."

"Did the last session hurt much?"

"Some, but the therapist said it'll get better as time goes on."

"Then I'm sure it will."

They rode in silence for a while. Mama pointed to the schoolhouse as they drove by and said, "It's good that Melinda's doing better in school."

Faith nodded. "That's mostly because of the help Noah has given her."

"Noah's a good man," Mama said, reaching over to touch Faith's arm. "He's kind, trustworthy, and can cook better than most women I know. I think he'll make a fine husband and father some day."

"I'm sure he will." Faith thought about the young woman she'd seen Noah with some time ago and wondered if she might be his future wife.

"I was wondering. . ."

"What were you wondering, Mama?"

"I was wondering if you're feeling ready to take classes to prepare for church membership and baptism yet."

Here it goes again. Faith's teeth snapped together with an audible *click*. Maybe if she didn't respond, Mama would drop the subject.

"Faith, did you hear what I said?"

"Yes, I heard; and no, Mama, I'm not ready."

"Oh."

They rode along in silence awhile longer; then Mama spoke again. "Melinda seems to like Noah a lot."

"Uh-huh."

"And I believe the feeling's mutual."

"You're probably right."

"How do you feel about Noah?"

Faith shook the reins to get the horse moving faster but gave no reply.

"Faith, are you listening to me?"

"I heard you, Mama. Just didn't know how to respond, so figured it was best not to say anything."

"You don't know how you feel about Noah?"

Faith released a sigh and squinted as she looked over at her mother. "Noah seems like a nice enough man, but I don't feel any particular way about him."

Mama grunted. "Have you tried?"

"What's that supposed to mean?"

"It means, have you allowed yourself to get to know Noah well enough so you can tell whether you might have a future with him?"

Faith's hands shook as she pulled back on the reins and guided the horse and buggy to the side of the road.

"Why are we stopping?"

"So I can concentrate on what I'm saying to you without worrying about driving off the road because I'm feeling so upset."

Mama's eyebrows furrowed. "Now why would you be upset?"

Faith curled her fingers into the palms of her hands as she resisted the temptation to pop her knuckles. "I'm upset because you keep bringing up Noah and listing his many virtues."

Mama opened her mouth as if to comment, but Faith rushed on. "I'm not interested in a relationship with Noah or any other man, so please stop trying to match me up with him."

Mama blinked a couple of times. "I—I just thought—"

"I know what you thought." Faith drew in a deep breath to steady her nerves. "My husband abused me, Mama," she blurted out. "And I—I don't think I could ever get married again."

Mama's mouth dropped open, and her eyes widened. "He—he abused you?"

Faith nodded. "Greg had a terrible temper, and whenever he drank, he became mean and physically abusive."

"Did he hurt Melinda?"

"No, just me. But I was worried that if she ever said or did the wrong thing, he might take his anger out on her, too." Faith swallowed hard. "Our marriage was not a happy one, but Greg was a good agent, and he got me lots of shows."

Mama touched Faith's hand. "I'm real sorry. I had no idea you had been through so much."

Faith took up the reins again. "I'd rather not talk about this anymore. It's too painful, and the past is in the past."

"Oh. Okay."

In silence, Faith guided the horse onto the road again.

A short time later, she found herself sitting in the Zooks' living room, surrounded by eight other women. Besides her and Mama; Barbara, and her mother, Alice; Noah's mom, Ida; and four other women from the community attended.

The women enjoyed lots of friendly banter as they worked with needle and thread, bent over a quilting frame, making hundreds of tiny stitches that would hold the top of the Double Wedding Ring quilt together. Barbara's mother, who was a left-handed quilter, sat at the corner of the frame. "I imagine it's been awhile since you did any kind of quilting," she said, looking over at Faith.

Faith nodded. "That's true, but even when I helped my mother work on quilts during my younger days, I never did so well."

"Quilting's like anything else one wants to do well—it takes practice and patience," Ida put in. "I've always enjoyed the challenge of working on a circular design such as this, but I didn't learn to quilt overnight, that's for sure."

"One thing I like about this pattern is that the pieces are small so we can use a lot of scraps," Barbara said.

"So true," Faith's mother agreed. She released a dreamy-sounding sigh. "I can still remember the five quilts I received for my wedding. Three were from my mamm, and the other two came from Menno's family. Those quilts have been used on my family's beds for a good many years now, even though some are getting pretty worn."

Faith began to relax, and before she knew it, she was drawn into the conversation by telling a few jokes.

"Has anyone heard about the English man who met his wife at a travel agency?" she asked.

"Can't say as I have," Barbara said. "Tell us about it."

"Well, he was looking for a vacation, and she was the last resort."

To Faith's surprise, most everyone laughed—except for her mother. She gave Mama a sidelong glance. *Just accept my silliness. Can't you understand who I really am?*

"Tell us another joke," said Ellen Troyer.

"Let's see. . . . An English man approached the gate of an Amish farmhouse one day and was about to enter when he noticed a large dog lying under a bush. The dog seemed to be eyeing him in an unfriendly way, so the man called out to see if anyone was at home." Faith leaned slightly forward, making sure she had the women's full attention. "Now, both the Amish man and his wife came to the front door. 'Come in,' said the woman. 'But what about the dog?' asked the Englisher. 'Will he be apt to bite me?' 'Don't rightly know,' said the Amish man. 'We just got him yesterday, and we're eager to find out.' "

Barbara howled at this joke, and Faith quickly launched into another tale.

"The same English man visited another Amish farm, and he was shocked to see yellow bundles of feathers zooming all around the yard. They were going so fast he couldn't see them clearly. 'What are those things?' the man asked the Amish farmer who lived there. 'Oh, those are my four-legged chickens. They're pretty quick, don't ya think?' The man replied, 'I'd say so, but why do you want four-legged chickens?' The Amish man pointed to his wife, who stood on the front porch. 'Me, Nancy, and our two kinner all cotton to the drumstick. Now whenever we have fried chicken, there'll be a leg for each of us.' The Englisher pondered the Amish man's words a few minutes; then with a nod, he said, 'So does it taste like normal fried chicken?' 'Don't know yet,' the Amish man answered. 'We haven't been able to catch any.' "

Barbara's mother almost doubled over with laughter at the end of that joke, and Faith smiled triumphantly. This was the first time she remembered feeling so accepted or appreciated among those in her community.

Barbara nudged Faith's arm with her elbow. "Have you got any more jokes to tell?"

Faith nodded, as her confidence soared. "Does anyone know the sure sign that the honeymoon is over for a new bride and groom?"

"What's the sign?" asked Barbara's sister-in-law, Margaret Hilty, as she leaned closer to Faith.

"When the husband no longer smiles as he scrapes the edges of his burnt toast."

More snickers and chuckles filled the room.

"I know one that's true but not so funny," Barbara piped up. All heads turned toward her, but she kept her focus on Faith. "It's been proven that having a mate is healthy. Single people die sooner than married folks. So if you're looking for a long life, then you'd best get married!"

Faith squinted at her so-called friend. *Not another hint at me finding a mate? Won't Barbara ever let up?*

"Speaking of marriage, it won't be long now until we have a few fall weddings," Noah's mother commented. "I'm thinking maybe my son Noah might be a candidate for marriage."

Faith's ears perked up. Noah was getting married? He hadn't said anything to her. Could he have become betrothed to that woman she'd seen him with at Baldy's Café?

The fun Faith had been having with the women drifted away like a leaf on the wind. She didn't know why, but she felt a sense of loss. Noah had become a good friend, and if he married, everything between them would change.

It shouldn't matter to me. I'll be leaving soon, and what Noah does is his own business. I have no say in it, nor do I wish to have any. Even as the words popped into Faith's head, she knew they weren't true. She did care, and that's what scared her. She cared too much.

As Faith and Wilma traveled home from Barbara's, Wilma determined to keep the conversation light and cheery, the way it had been during the quilting bee. It had been wonderful to see the way Faith had opened up, laughed, joked, and shared stories with the other women. If only Faith could be that joyful at home, instead of acting so serious all the time. Of course, at home, Faith had responsibilities that kept her busy, especially since Wilma had broken her leg, making even more chores for Faith and the others to do.

"I'm curious about some of those jokes you told today," Wilma said, glancing over at Faith.

"What about them?"

"Were those the kind of jokes you told when you entertained onstage?"

"Yes, and I have a bunch more up here," Faith said, tapping the side of her head.

Wilma pushed her weight against the seat. She wished Faith wouldn't look so wistful whenever she talked about her days as an entertainer. If Faith enjoyed being in the limelight too much, she might become dissatisfied with her life and head out on her own again.

Faith lifted one hand from the reins and held up her index finger. "I don't know how many times I pricked my finger today, but I did better at sewing than I figured I would," she said.

Wilma smiled. A change of subject—that was better. "Jah," she said with a nod. "Your stitches were nice and even."

"Not like when I was a girl and all my sewing projects turned out bad."

"Guess you had your mind set on other things besides sewing."

Faith nodded. "I always preferred to be out in the barn talking to the animals and yodeling."

"Melinda likes to hang out there, too. Have you taught her how to yodel?"

"Not really. I figured if she learned how, she might want to. . ." Faith's voice trailed off.

"Want to what?"

"Never mind. It's not important."

"Are you worried that Melinda might want to follow in your footsteps and take to the stage?"

"Maybe so, but that won't happen, because she's here with you now."

Wilma was tempted to mention that Faith had been here once, too, and that hadn't stopped her from running off to chase after her dreams in the English world. She thought better of bringing it up, not wishing to have any unpleasant moments on the trip home.

When Faith guided the horse and buggy up the driveway a short time later, Menno stepped out of the barn. As soon as Faith stopped the buggy, he began to unhitch the horse. "If you don't mind putting old Ben away," he said, nodding at Faith, "I'll help your mamm into the house."

"That's fine with me." Faith grabbed the horse's bridle and led him to the barn.

"She had a good time today," Wilma said as Menno assisted her into the house. "Fact is, our eldest daughter was the life of the party."

He quirked an eyebrow. "Is that so?"

"Jah. Faith was real talkative, and she ended up telling one joke after another. Had everyone in stitches, she did."

Menno frowned. "She didn't try to entertain you with that awful yodeling, I hope."

Wilma shook her head. "No, but she sure told some funny stories. At one point, Alice Raber almost fell off her chair, she was laughing so hard."

"Oh great," Menno said with a groan.

"Faith was showing off her worldly ways then, huh?"

"I don't think so. I believe she just got caught up in having a good time, but I was kind of worried that all that joke telling might make her dissatisfied about not being able to be onstage entertaining English folks."

"Did you discourage her from telling those jokes?"

"Well, no, but I didn't laugh at them, either." Wilma snickered. "Although it was hard not to when she was saying such funny things and had everyone else in stitches."

"Guess no harm was done," Menno said. "As long as she doesn't start with that yodeling stuff when I'm around, I won't complain."

They entered the house, and Wilma took a seat on the sofa in the living room. "Whew! I'm all done in. Didn't realize a whole day like that would wear me out so."

"Why don't you stretch out on the sofa and rest awhile?" Menno suggested.

She shook her head. "I've got to get supper going."

"The girls can do that. Faith's here, Grace Ann and Esther will be home from their jobs soon, and Susie and Melinda will be home from school shortly, I expect. There's no reason they can't get supper on without any help from you."

She smiled up at him. "You're right. We've got four capable daughters and one granddaughter to prepare the meal, so I think I will rest my eyes for a bit."

"And your leg, too," he said, helping her to lie down and placing a pillow under her leg.

"Danki, Menno. You're a good man."

He grunted. "Too bad our oldest daughter doesn't think so."

Wilma took hold of his arm. "Things have been strained between you and Faith since she came home, but after seeing how she was today, I think given some time, she's bound to come around."

Menno shrugged and headed for the door. "We'll have to wait and see how it goes."

Chapter 20

It wasn't until the end of October that Faith's mother finished her physical therapy. Only then was she able to get around well enough on her leg so that Faith felt Mama could handle things on her own.

As Faith got ready for bed one night, she made a decision. In the morning, she would tell Melinda and then her folks that she would be leaving at the end of the week. She had put it off long enough, and there was no good reason to stay now that Mama was better and Melinda had adjusted so well to Amish life. All she needed to do was contact the agent in Memphis and let him know she was available. Until the agent got her a show, she would probably have to launch out on her own, doing one-night stands wherever she could find work. She'd done it before Greg came into her life, and if necessary, she could do it again.

As Faith glanced at the calendar on the wall, her thoughts went to Noah. November was almost here. He would probably be getting married soon. After church last week, she had overheard Noah's mother telling his friend Isaac that Noah was interested in someone— probably the woman he'd had lunch with at Baldy's. Faith had wanted to ask Noah about it, but she'd lost her nerve. Besides, it was none of her business. She had her career to think about, and Noah's life was here in Webster County with his family and friends.

Faith stared out her open bedroom window at the night sky overflowing with thousands of twinkling stars. She drew in a deep breath, filling her lungs with fresh air. It had rained earlier in the day, and everything smelled so clean. She blinked away sudden tears. *If only my soul felt as pure as this air. If I just didn't feel so confused about things.*

❧❦❧

The following morning, Faith busied herself at the stove, helping Mama fix pancakes and sausage for breakfast, while Melinda and Faith's three sisters set the table.

Who should I tell first about my plans to leave? Faith had intended to give her daughter some advance notice, but now she wondered if it might not be best to lay out her plans in front of everyone at once. Or maybe she should tell her mother first and get her reaction. If Mama didn't shy from the idea of caring for Melinda in Faith's absence, then Faith would inform the child.

Faith moved closer to Mama. "There's something I need to tell you," she whispered.

"What's that? I can't hear you, Faith."

"I was wondering if. . ." She gripped the spatula in her hand. Why was it so difficult to say what was on her mind? "I've. . .uh. . .made a decision."

Her mother's eyebrows lifted high on her forehead. "What sort of decision?"

"I think it would be best if I—"

The back door swung open and Papa rushed into the kitchen. His face was flushed, and his eyes looked huge as silver dollars.

Mama left the stove and hurried to his side. "Menno, what's wrong?"

He tried to catch his breath. When Mama handed him a glass of water, he shook his head and pushed it away. "Always trouble somewhere."

"What kind of trouble?" she asked in a tone of concern.

"Old Ben's dead. Found him lying on the floor in his stall this morning."

Mama gasped, and everyone else stood like statues.

"I blame myself for this." Papa clasped his hands together. "I've been using that horse in the fields every day this week, and I think I must have worked the poor creature to death."

Mama touched Papa's arm. "Menno, think about what you're saying. You've had Ben for nigh onto twenty-five years. A year ago, you tried to put him out to pasture, but he wasn't content. He liked to work with the other horses and was bound to die sooner or later." She sighed deeply. "At least the horse perished doing what he liked to do best."

Papa blinked a couple of times, and Faith wondered if he was struggling not to cry. "Mama's right," she agreed. "You shouldn't blame yourself for this."

He stared past her as though he hadn't heard her. "The boys and I are in the middle of harvest, so I need that animal. Jeb and Buck can't do the work of three horses, and I can't afford to buy another one just now."

Mama pushed the skillet of pancakes to the rear of the stove, and she dropped into a seat at the table with a moan. Grace Ann and Esther went immediately to her side, each of them patting her on the back. Melinda and Susie, obviously uncomfortable, scooted quickly out of the room. Faith, unable to think of anything more to say, stood off to the side with her arms folded.

"If you hadn't had to spend most of our

savings on doctor bills and physical therapy because of my leg, we'd have the money we need to buy a new horse," Mama said with a shake of her head.

"It's not your fault, Wilma. Falling down the cellar stairs was an accident, plain and simple." Papa took a seat across from Mama and let his head fall forward into his hands. "Guess I could ask some of our church members to help out, but others have needs, too, and I hate to be asking for more money."

Faith moved to the side of the table and placed her hand on her father's shoulder as she made a painful decision. "I have some money saved up from when I was entertaining. I'll give it to you so you can buy a new horse."

Papa sat up straight and turned in his chair to look at Faith. His beard jiggled as a muscle in his jaw quivered. "You—you'd be willing to do that?"

Faith didn't understand why he was so surprised. Amish family members and friends helped each other all the time. Of course, most offers didn't come from wayward daughters returning home with money they'd made entertaining worldly English folks. Faith had been holding on to this money so she could start over when she left Webster County. If she gave her father the cash, she would be staying here even longer. Even so, this was a chance to prove that she wasn't such a bad daughter, after all—maybe even show Papa she cared about the welfare of her family. "I want you to use the money," she insisted.

He sat silently and then finally nodded. "Jah, okay, but I plan to pay the money back as soon as I'm able."

"Der Herr sie gedankt," Mama said with a catch in her voice.

Faith swallowed hard in an attempt to push down the lump that had formed in her throat as she heard her mother thank God. She was happy to be helping her folks in their moment of need, but at the same time, she felt a sense of sadness. She had no idea how long it would take for Papa to pay her back. Certainly not until the harvest was over and he'd been paid for his crops. At the rate things were going, would she ever see the bright stage lights or hear the roar of the audience's laughter again?

Chapter 21

Noah shifted on the backless wooden bench as he glanced over at the women's side of the room and spotted Faith. Ever since the preaching service had begun this morning, he'd had a hard time concentrating on anything other than her. He hoped he might be able to speak with Faith after the noon meal, and he had brought an apple crumb pie to give her with Romans 5:1–2 attached to it: "Therefore being justified by faith, we have peace with God through our Lord Jesus Christ: by whom also we have access by faith into this grace wherein we stand, and rejoice in hope of the glory of God."

Noah wasn't trying to be pushy, but as Faith's friend, it was his Christian duty to help strengthen her faith. Truth be told, he was beginning to see her as more than a friend, and if there was any chance for them to have a permanent relationship, he had to be sure she had an interest in him and most of all that she was secure in her faith in God. But how would he know if there was another man in her life or if her faith had grown unless he came right out and asked? Did he dare take the chance? What if she got angry and turned away from him? What if because he questioned her, she decided to leave? He didn't want to be responsible for Faith leaving Webster County.

Noah squeezed his eyes shut and offered a silent prayer. *Dear Lord, please help Faith be receptive to the scripture verses I plan to give her today. And I'm hoping she will be receptive to the questions I have for her, as well.*

When Faith finished eating her meal and had taken a seat under the weeping willow tree on the south side of Jacob Raber's house, she spotted Noah heading her way. He held a pie in his hands, and she licked her lips in anticipation. As far as she was concerned, Noah was the best baker in Webster County, and she hoped the pie was for her.

"Would you like to have a seat?" Faith asked as Noah approached the quilt she'd spread on the ground.

"Jah, sure." He sat down beside her and placed the pie pan in her lap. "This is for you. It's an apple crumb pie."

"Thanks. I needed something to cheer me up today."

The wrinkles in Noah's forehead showed his obvious concern. "What's wrong? Is your mamm's leg acting up again?"

Faith shook her head. "It's not Mama this time. One of my dad's workhorses died yesterday, and now he's faced with buying a new one." She chose not to mention that she'd offered to loan him the money. No point making it seem as though she was bragging. Faith was well aware of the stand her people took on hochmut. She also wasn't about to share her disappointment in not being able to return to entertaining.

"That's a shame about the horse. With this being harvesttime and all, everyone needs all the help they can get. That includes the assistance of their horses and mules." He offered her a sympathetic smile. "Once the word gets out, others in the community will help—either with the loan of a horse or some money."

"That won't be necessary. It's been taken care of."

"That's good. Glad to hear it."

Faith popped a couple of knuckles, then clasped her hand tightly to keep from doing the rest. If Papa found her habit annoying, Noah might, too. She was glad he hadn't asked who had provided the money. "My family has sure had their share of problems lately. It doesn't seem fair, and it worries me that something else might happen."

"The rain falls on the just, same as it does the unjust," Noah reminded.

Faith had heard that verse before, but it didn't make it any easier to deal with things when they went wrong. Besides, she wasn't sure she was one of the "just." If Noah or her family had any idea she was planning to return to the English world, they might see her as a sinner.

"All these problems don't do much to strengthen my faith," she muttered.

Noah motioned to the pie. "I attached another verse. Maybe that will help."

She groaned inwardly. *Another reminder of the error of my ways. Just what I don't need this afternoon.* Maybe what she needed was to change the subject.

"I've been wanting to ask you something, Noah, but I wasn't sure if I should."

He tipped his head. "What's that?"

"I overheard your mother talking to my mother awhile back, and then she said something to Isaac Troyer."

"About what?"

Faith moistened her lips with the tip of her tongue. "Well, I got the impression that you might be planning to be married in November."

Noah's face flamed, and he looked away.

Was he too embarrassed to talk about it? "I probably shouldn't have brought it up," she murmured. "It's none of my business anyway."

"I don't know where my mamm got the impression I'm about to be married."

"Then it's not true?"

He shook his head.

"But what about that woman I saw you with at Baldy's Café a few months ago?"

"Huh?"

"I saw you sitting in a booth, having lunch with a young Amish woman, and I assumed it was—"

"Oh, you must mean Mary. She's my cousin, and she had come down from Jamesport to speak with her boyfriend, who'd jilted her. He'd left for Illinois before she got here. Then she asked if I would give her a ride to the gas station so she could catch a bus home, but we had lunch at Baldy's first."

Faith inhaled deeply, feeling as if the breath had been squeezed clean out of her lungs. All this time she'd thought Noah had a girlfriend, when he'd just been having lunch with his cousin. She toyed with the strings on her prayer kapp. "But if you don't have a girlfriend, then why would your mother think you were seeing someone?"

A deep shade of red spread across Noah's cheeks. "Well—uh—she knows I've been seeing you."

"Me?" Faith's heart began to hammer. Surely Noah didn't see her in any light other than friendship.

He nodded. "We went to see Hank's Christmas tree farm, and I've gone over to your place several times to help with Melinda's studies and to give you a hand with some chores." He snatched up a blade of grass and bit off the end. "Guess maybe Mom could have assumed *we* were courting."

If Noah's mother thought that, did others, as well? While Faith felt a sense of unexplained relief to hear Noah wasn't courting anyone, she didn't think it was good if others had linked her and Noah together as a couple. No telling what rumors might be flying around.

"It would probably be good if you made sure your mother knows the truth," Faith said after a long pause. "So she doesn't tell others there's going to be a wedding come November."

Noah chewed on the blade of grass and looked at Faith in such a tender way it made her stomach do little somersaults. "Uh, Faith, there's something more I'd like to say. A question I want to ask you."

"What's that?"

"The day I was with my cousin at Baldy's, I saw you there with a tall English man."

Faith grimaced. *Oh great. How am I going to explain things to Noah without telling him I was talking to my future agent?*

"Was that fellow your boyfriend, Faith?"

"What? Oh no, definitely not," she sputtered. "He was just. . .uh. . .an acquaintance from the entertainment business, nothing more."

A look of relief flooded Noah's face, but Faith barely noticed. All she wanted to do was nip this thing in the bud about her and Noah being an item.

Holding on to the pie, she clambered to her feet. "I—I'd better get going." She wasn't sure what he planned to say, but she knew it was important for her to let folks know they weren't courting. She would start with Barbara, who was sitting on the Rabers' porch, blowing bubbles with her two young sons.

"Thanks for the pie," she called over her shoulder.

Faith made a beeline for the house, where she put the pie in the refrigerator. Then she headed for the front porch.

Barbara turned when Faith stepped outside. "Hey! Want to join us in some fun?" She lifted a bubble wand in the air and waved it about.

"Actually, I'd like to have a little heart-to-heart talk, if you don't mind."

Barbara scooted over, making room for Faith on the step. "Have a seat, and tell me what's on your mind."

Faith sat down and cleared her throat a couple of times. "I'd kind of hoped we could talk in private."

"Oh sure. No problem at all." Barbara leaned over and said to her boys, "Why don't you two go find Susie and Melinda? They'd probably like to blow a few bubbles, too."

Aaron and Joseph nodded, grabbed their bottles of bubbles, and bounded away.

Barbara turned back to Faith. "Now, what did you want to talk to me about?"

"Noah and me."

Barbara smiled. "Ah, so you two *are* an item. I've been hearing some rumors to that effect, and—"

Faith held up one hand, as her forehead wrinkled. "Noah and I are *not* an item."

"But Ida Hertzler told my mamm that—"

"It's not true. None of it."

Barbara tapped the toe of her black leather shoe against the step below her. "I was hoping those stories had some merit."

"What stories have you heard?"

"Just that you two went out to Osborns' Christmas Tree Farm awhile back, and—"

"We took Melinda and Susie along, so it wasn't a date."

"What about all the times Noah's been over to your folks' place? Wasn't he going there to see you?"

"Noah dropped by to help after Mama

broke her leg, and he came over to assist Melinda with her studies. That's all there is to it—nothing more."

Barbara pursed her lips. "I'm sorry to hear that. As I've told you before, I think it would be good for both you and Melinda if you found another husband."

"I've been down that road, and it only brought heartaches."

"You mean because your husband was killed?"

"That and other things."

"Such as?"

"There was no joy in my marriage, Barbara." Faith's jaw snapped shut with an audible *click*. "My husband was an alcoholic who liked to gamble and smack me around whenever he wasn't happy. You get the picture?"

Barbara flinched, feeling as if she'd been slapped. "Ach! I—I didn't know."

"No one did. I never want Melinda to know what her father was really like." Faith blinked, and a few tears trickled onto her cheeks. "There's nothing good in marriage. Not for me, anyway."

Barbara slowly shook her head. "Don't say that, Faith. Never give up on the idea of marriage or God's will for your life. There's certainly a lot of joy in marriage if you have the right man."

Faith grunted. "That's easy for you to say.

I'll bet you've never been slapped around by your husband."

"That's true. David has been nothing but kind since we first got married. I've always felt loved and safe with him."

"With Greg, I felt about as safe as a mouse trapped between a cat's paws." Faith's tone was one of bitterness, and her eyes narrowed into tiny slits.

Barbara touched her friend's arm in what she hoped would be seen as a comforting gesture. "There's joy all around, if you only look for it."

"Maybe for some, but not for me." Faith stood. "Noah and I are only friends, and we won't be finding any joy with one another." She walked away without another word.

Barbara bowed her head. *Heavenly Father, my friend is hurting and is probably confused about some things. Please give her a sense of joy that only You can bring.*

Chapter 22

As Faith stood on the front porch, staring across a yard covered with a blanket of freshly fallen snow, she thought about Noah and how she had tried to avoid him these last couple of weeks. The way he had looked at her that day under Jacob Raber's willow tree had made her suspicious that he might be romantically interested in her. She couldn't let Noah think their relationship could go beyond friendship, even though she was beginning to have strong feelings for him. She would be leaving soon, so any kind of permanent relationship was impossible.

Faith drew in a deep breath. While she wanted to return to her life in the English world, the idea of leaving home didn't hold nearly as much appeal as it had when she'd first returned. She would miss Melinda terribly, even with occasional visits, and now there was another reason to stay. These last few months, she'd found comfort and security being with family. Life as an entertainer could be lonely, and she felt as if a war raged within her. She needed to go yet wanted to stay. Maybe she could postpone leaving until after the holidays. A few more weeks wouldn't matter. It might be better if she waited until after Christmas to head back on the road.

Faith was glad she and Barbara had talked. At least now Barbara wouldn't be expecting a wedding for Faith and Noah. If others saw them together, more rumors would float around the community, and Faith sure didn't need that. But she'd promised Melinda and Susie they could go one more time to the Christmas tree farm. Noah had said he wanted to show them Sandy's Gift Shop when it was decorated for the holidays. Faith figured it would probably be her and Noah's last time together, and since the girls would be there, no one could accuse them of courting.

Her thoughts shifted gears. The harvest was over. Papa said he was pleased that Sam, the horse he'd bought with Faith's money, was a hardworking animal and had done his fair share of the pulling as they cut and baled the hay. She'd felt relief when Papa came to her a few days ago and returned the money he'd borrowed. Now, except for her shifting emotions, nothing stood in the way of her going back to the life she had made for herself in the English world.

⁂

"What are you doing out here in the cold?" Wilma asked as she stepped up to the porch railing where Faith stood staring out at the yard.

Faith smiled. "Watching Melinda and Susie play in the snow while we wait for Noah to pick us up to visit Hank Osborn's tree farm."

Wilma grunted. "I'm glad you're seeing Noah, but I don't see why you want to take the girls back there again."

Faith's smile faded. "Why must you always throw cold water on everything I want to do?"

"I'm not, but those fancy Christmas trees are worldly, and—"

"And you think I'm trying to convince Melinda and Susie that having a Christmas tree in the house is a good thing to do?"

"It's not that. I just don't want Susie exposed to anything that might make her dissatisfied with our way of life."

Faith's eyes blazed with anger. "So she won't turn out like me? Isn't that what you're saying, Mama?"

Wilma could have bitten her tongue. She

shouldn't have mentioned her concerns about the girls visiting the tree farm. After all, she had given her consent, so it was too late to go back on her word. Bringing it up had obviously upset Faith, and the last thing Wilma needed was to put distance between her and Faith.

"I'm sorry. I shouldn't have said anything." Wilma touched Faith's arm. "I hope you'll have a good time today."

Faith's face softened some. "You mean it?"

"Jah." Wilma swallowed around the lump in her throat. She did want them to have a good time, and she didn't want to make an issue of how she really felt, so she would say nothing more on the subject. She would be praying, however, that neither of the girls came home wanting to put up a Christmas tree.

❦

When Noah showed up at the Stutzmans' place, he wasn't the least bit surprised to see Melinda and Susie playing outside in the snow. What he hadn't expected was to see Faith and her mother standing on the front porch, with Wilma wearing no coat. He'd no more than climbed down from the buggy, when the girls dashed over to him, wearing huge smiles on their rosy faces.

"Yippee! We're going to the tree farm!" Melinda shouted as she hopped up and down.

Susie nodded in agreement. "I can't wait to

see them all decorated."

"Only the ones inside Sandy's Gift Shop will be decorated," Noah said as he rapped his knuckles on the tops of the girls' black bonnets.

Melinda giggled and smiled up at him. "Maybe Sandy will serve us some cookies and hot chocolate."

"I wouldn't be a bit surprised." Noah nodded toward the house. "Shall we see if your mamm's ready to go?"

"Oh, she's ready," Susie put in. "She's been standing on the porch for some time."

Noah smiled. The thought that Faith had been waiting gave him a good feeling. Maybe she looked forward to spending the day together as much as he did. He'd been relieved to learn that she didn't have a boyfriend, and as much as he'd fought against it, he found himself wanting to be with her more all the time.

"Looks like the girls are ready to go; how about you?" he asked, stepping onto the porch and smiling at Faith.

She nodded but didn't return his smile.

He looked over at Wilma and noticed that she wasn't smiling, either. "You're welcome to join us if you like."

Wilma shook her head. "I appreciate the offer, but I've got housework and baking to finish." She glanced down at Susie, who stood beside Melinda. "Be good now, daughter, and do whatever Faith says."

"I will, Mama."

Noah clapped his hands together. "All right, then. Let's be off."

The girls bounded down the steps, and as Wilma turned to go inside the house, Noah followed Faith out to his buggy. She seemed so quiet and reserved, and he wondered what could have happened to make her cool off toward him. Until that day he'd given her the apple crumb pie with the scripture verse attached, he had thought they'd been drawing closer. Had he been too pushy in trying to help strengthen her faith? Or had it been their discussion about his mother believing them to be a courting couple? Maybe he could get Faith to open up to him today. Then again, it might be better if he backed off and kept his distance—instead of him trying to meddle and make things happen the way he wanted them to, let the Lord work in Faith's life.

As they headed down the country road in the open buggy, Noah continued to scold himself. Mom had told him time and again that he had a habit of taking things into his own hands. He hoped he hadn't botched it up where Faith was concerned—with their friendship or with her relationship with Christ. He would try to keep their conversation light and casual today and not mention anything spiritual. And he had to be careful not to let Faith know he was romantically interested in her.

"Looks like winter's got a mind to come early this year," Noah said, directing his comment to Faith.

"It would appear so," she answered with a slight nod.

"You warm enough? I could see if there's another quilt underneath the seat."

"I'm fine."

"You girls doing okay back there?" Noah called over his shoulder.

"Jah, sure," Susie shouted into the wind. "This is fun!"

Noah got the horse moving a bit faster, and soon they were pulling into the driveway leading to the tree farm. Amos and Griggs bounded up to the buggy, yapping excitedly and wagging their tails.

"The trees look like they're wearing white gowns," Melinda said, pointing to the stately pines that lined the driveway and were covered with snow.

"You're right about that," Noah agreed.

Hank and his wife stepped outside just as Noah helped Faith and the girls down from the buggy. The hounds ran around in circles, and the children squealed with delight while they romped in the snow.

"Come inside and get warm," Sandy said, motioning toward her rustic-looking store.

Everyone but the dogs followed, and soon

squeals of delight could be heard as the girls ran up and down the aisles, oohing and aahing over the brightly decorated Christmas trees. Sandy took hold of Faith's arm and led her toward the side of the store where the crafts were located. Noah figured they wanted to have a little woman-to-woman talk, so he moved over to the wood-burning stove where Hank stood. Soon they both had a mug of hot coffee in their hands and were warming themselves by the crackling fire.

Noah glanced around the room. "I'm glad we got here before the rush of customers."

"You're right. By noontime, this place will probably be swarming with people," Hank said. "Usually is, right after Thanksgiving."

When Noah looked over at Faith, he wondered if she would miss having a Christmas tree with colored lights and all the trimmings. An Amish Christmas was a simple affair compared to the way most Englishers celebrated the holiday, yet it was just as special—at least he thought so. A Christmas program would be presented at the schoolhouse a few weeks before Christmas, and all the relatives of the scholars would be invited. Then on Christmas Day, families would gather for a big meal, and a few gifts would be exchanged. The emphasis would be on spending time with family and friends and remembering the birth of Jesus, not on acquiring material things or looking at tinsel and fancy colored lights decorating a tree.

"Yep, this is a busy time of the year," Hank said, nudging Noah with his elbow and bringing his mind back to the conversation.

Noah nodded. "I was in Seymour yesterday after work, and the tree lot there was doing a booming business, as well."

"That's usually the case," Hank said. He turned away from the fire and looked at Noah, his hazel-colored eyes ever so serious. "I know this is probably none of my concern, and if you want me to mind my own business, just say so."

Noah waited silently for his boss to continue.

"You seem kind of down in the mouth today, and I'm wondering if there's something wrong at home."

"Except for Mom's bouts with her diabetes, everything's fine."

Hank took a sip of coffee. "Your sullen attitude couldn't have anything to do with one pretty little blond, could it?"

Heat flooded Noah's ears and quickly spread to his cheeks. "I'm afraid I might have ruined my friendship with Faith," he muttered.

"How so?"

Noah lowered his voice. "I've been trying to help strengthen her faith in the Lord, and I've attempted to make her my friend."

"Nothing wrong with that."

"The thing is I'm worried that I might have

pushed too far and scared Faith off, because she seems to be keeping her distance and didn't say much on the way over here." Noah leaned closer to Hank, to be sure what he said wouldn't be overhead. "She might move further from me and the Lord if she thinks I'm trying to force things on her."

"Give her some time and a bit of space," Hank said. "If Faith's anything like Sandy, she doesn't want anyone telling her what to think or do."

Noah snickered. He had heard Hank's wife speak on her own behalf a time or two and knew Hank was telling the truth. "I came to that conclusion, and I've decided to back off and let God do His work in Faith's life instead of me trying to do it for Him."

Hank tapped Noah on the back. "Smart man."

"How are things with you and Sandy these days?"

"About the same. We talk but only when there's something to say." He grunted. "Every time Sandy sees a baby, I notice a look of sadness on her face."

"And you haven't brought up the subject of adoption yet?"

"No, but I'm thinking about it."

"That's good to hear." Noah gave Hank's arm a squeeze. "You're still in my prayers."

"I appreciate that, and even though I don't

talk much about my religious convictions, I do believe in God, and I'll say a prayer for you and Faith, too."

Noah grinned. "Thanks. I appreciate that."

🌺

Faith couldn't believe how many items Sandy had for sale in her store. She saw three times as much stuff as when they'd visited earlier in the year. "I know you make the peanut brittle you sell," she commented, "but who provides all these wonderful quilts, crafts, and collectibles?"

"I buy a few from out of state, but most are made by local people," Sandy explained. "As I'm sure you can guess, the quilts are made by Amish women here in Webster County. English folks—especially tourists—are willing to pay a good price for a bedcovering made by one of the Plain People."

Faith fingered the edge of a beige quilt with a red and green dahlia pattern. "They are beautiful, aren't they?"

"Yes, they certainly are." Sandy released a gusty sigh. "The other day when I was shopping in Springfield, I found a store that sells baby quilts, and it made me wish all the more that I could have a baby."

Faith wasn't sure how to respond. She knew from what Sandy had said before that she and Hank were unable to have any children of their own. Seeing how much Sandy wanted a baby made Faith appreciate the fact that she had Melinda. "Have you thought any more about the idea of adoption?" she asked.

"I have been thinking about it, but I haven't mentioned it to Hank because I'm sure he'll say no."

"How can you be certain?"

Sandy shrugged. "I'm pretty sure he wouldn't want a child that wasn't his own flesh and blood."

"You'll never know until you ask."

"That's true, and I will think about it some more."

Faith opened her mouth to comment, but Sandy turned the topic of conversation. "I've been wondering about something."

"What's that?"

"How old were you when you left home, and what did your folks have to say about it?"

"I left the day I turned eighteen, and since I hadn't been baptized or joined the church, I knew they wouldn't officially shun me. But earlier when I'd discussed the idea of being an entertainer with my parents, they let it be known that they didn't want me to go. Papa even said if I did, I'd better not come back unless I was willing to give up the English ways and join the church." She groaned. "I took the coward's way out and left a note on the kitchen table, letting them know I had gone."

"Oh?" Sandy's raised eyebrows and pursed

lips let Faith know that she probably thought Faith was horrible for leaving in such a manner. What would she think if she knew Faith was planning to leave again?

"But you're here now," Sandy said. "I never got the chance to ask when you were here the last time, but I'm wondering what happened to bring you home again."

"Didn't Noah tell you?"

"Not really. He only mentioned that you'd been gone a long time and had returned home this summer with your daughter. He also said your husband was killed when he was hit by a car."

Faith nodded. "I tried life on my own for six months after Greg's death, but it was hard to find a babysitter for Melinda. And being on the road full-time isn't the best way to raise a child."

"So you decided to give up being an entertainer and move back home where you knew both you and Melinda would find love and a good home?"

"Uh, something like that."

"Have you joined the church since you returned?"

Faith shook her head. She could hardly tell Hank's wife her plans were to leave Melinda with her grandparents while she went back to the life of an entertainer. Sandy obviously wanted children, and she'd probably see Faith as an unfit mother—someone who could abandon her child as easily as a frog leaps into a pond. "I. . .um. . .haven't felt ready to be baptized and join the church yet."

Sandy motioned to a couple of chairs sitting at one end of the store. "Why don't we take a seat? In another hour or so, this place will be swamped with customers, and I probably won't have the chance to sit down the rest of the day."

Faith followed Sandy across the room, and they seated themselves in the wicker chairs.

"Would you care for a cup of coffee or some hot apple cider?"

"Not just now, thanks."

"Looks like the girls are winding down." Sandy nodded toward Melinda and Susie, who reclined on the floor under one of the taller decorated trees.

"Those kids are like two peas in a pod," Faith said. "I think living here in Webster County has been good for Melinda."

"And you, Faith? Has coming home been good for you?"

"In some ways, I suppose." Faith didn't want to say more. She might let her plans slip; then Sandy would tell Hank, who would in turn let Noah know. Sometime between Christmas and New Year's Day, Faith would tell her folks about her plans to leave, and she didn't want them finding out before.

Sandy smiled. "Noah has spoken of you and

Melinda several times. I think he's grown quite fond of you both."

"Noah's a kind man." Faith stared down at her hands, which she'd folded in her lap to keep from popping her knuckles. "Noah's good with children and even helped Melinda with her studies when she first started school."

"He mentioned that." Sandy touched Faith's arm. "I think Noah would make some lucky woman a fine husband. He'd be a good father, too. Don't you think?"

"I'm sure he would. He just has to find the right woman."

"Maybe he already has."

Faith was about to ask Sandy what she meant, when Melinda and Susie crawled out from under the tree and bounded up to them.

"Mama, Susie says we aren't gonna get to have a tree in the house," Melinda said, her lower lip jutting out. "Is that true?"

Faith nodded. "I've told you before that the Amish don't believe in bringing a tree into the house, but there will be a Christmas program at school, and that will be lots of fun."

"What about presents? Will we still have those?"

"Oh, jah. . .we always exchange presents," Susie said. "Last year I got a new faceless doll and some puzzles."

"We'll have a big family dinner at Grandma and Grandpa's house, too," Faith added. She hoped Melinda wouldn't be too disappointed if she didn't get a lot of gifts.

"Mama always fixes plenty of good food," Susie spoke up.

"Speaking of food, I'm feeling kind of hungry right now," Melinda announced.

Faith wagged her finger. "Where are your manners? You had enough to eat at breakfast for three little girls."

"Aw, but that was a long time ago."

"I think I have just the thing that will make your stomach happy." Sandy stood and extended her hands to both girls. "Come with me, and we'll get some gingerbread cookies and a pitcher of cold apple cider."

The children didn't have to be asked twice, and they skipped off with Sandy to the back of the store.

Faith turned toward the wood-burning stove where Noah and Hank stood. A lock of dark hair fell across Noah's forehead as he propped his foot on the hearth. *Noah may not believe he's good-looking, but I think he's pretty cute.*

Faith drew in a shaky breath as the truth hit her squarely in the chest. No man had ever affected her the way Noah had, and she was tumbling into a well of emotions that could only spell trouble. There was just one way to stop it, and it would have to be done soon.

Chapter 23

Faith couldn't believe how many family members had come to see their scholars put on the Christmas program. The schoolhouse was filled to capacity. As Faith took a seat behind Melinda's desk and waited for the program to begin, her thoughts took her on a trip to the past. She had spent eight years as a student in this same schoolhouse and taken part in many programs. Faith remembered one program in particular, where she'd forgotten what she was supposed to say. She'd made up something silly to keep the audience from knowing she'd forgotten her lines, but afterward, she'd been scolded by her parents for acting childish and not paying attention to the part she'd been given. In that moment, Faith decided that when she was old enough, she would leave home and find a job that would allow her to say and do all the silly things she wanted. Bitterness had taken root in her soul.

Faith was pulled back to the present when Barbara took a seat at a nearby desk and leaned across the aisle. "Is Melinda nervous about being in her first school Christmas program?" she asked.

Faith nodded. "A bit, but I'm sure she'll do fine. Melinda seems to do well with everything she tries. Not like me, that's for sure," she added with a frown.

Barbara's brows puckered. "What are you talking about, Faith? You do lots of things well."

"Name me one."

Barbara held up one finger. "You yodel better than anyone I know." She lifted a second finger. "And you can tell jokes and funny stories so well that it brings tears to my eyes because I'm laughing so hard."

"That may be true, but not everyone appreciates those abilities."

"The women who came to my quilting bee awhile back thought you were funny."

Faith was about to mention that her mother hadn't thought she was so funny, when Melinda's teacher announced that the program was about to begin. It was just as well; Barbara didn't need to hear Faith's negative comment.

A few seconds later, several of the smaller

children, including Melinda and Susie, formed a line and sang two Christmas songs. Faith's mouth dropped open when Melinda started to sway a bit, as though keeping time to the words they were singing. Faith wondered what her parents, who sat a few desks behind, thought of their worldly granddaughter's behavior. Faith caught Melinda's attention and shook her head. She was relieved that the child stopped swaying.

Am I making a mistake leaving Melinda with my folks? Would she be better off on the road with me? Faith gripped the edge of the desk. *No, I want a more stable environment for my little girl. As long as Melinda continues to like it here, she'll stay.*

❧

On Christmas Day, the Stutzmans' house bustled with activity. The entire family had gathered for dinner, including Faith's older brothers, James and Philip, along with their wives, Katie and Margaret, and their four children. Since both families lived up by Jamesport, they'd hired a driver to bring them home. Everyone seemed in good spirits, and the vast array of food being set on the table looked delicious. Even though Faith didn't consider herself much of a baker, she'd made three apple pies using a recipe Noah had given her. She hadn't tasted them yet, but as far as she could tell, they'd turned out fairly well, and she hoped they were as good as they looked.

"It's nice to have you home again," James said as he took a seat beside Faith at the table.

"Jah, I agree," Philip put in.

Faith forced a smile. If her brothers only knew the truth, they wouldn't be smiling at her.

As all heads bowed for silent prayer, Faith found herself thinking about Noah and wondering how his Christmas was going. Noah seemed so content with his life, and he obviously had a close relationship with God. Otherwise, he wouldn't attach scripture verses to the baked goods he gave away, and he wouldn't offer to pray for people as she'd heard him do for Hank Osborn when they'd gone there to look at Christmas trees last month.

"Mama, you can open your eyes now 'cause the prayer's over," Melinda said, nudging Faith with her elbow.

Faith's eyes snapped open. She'd been so preoccupied thinking about Noah that she hadn't heard her father clear his throat, the way he always did when his prayer ended.

"If everything tastes as good as it looks, then I think we're in for a real treat," James said, reaching for the bowl of mashed potatoes.

"Jah." Papa looked over at Mama and smiled. "My Wilma has outdone herself with this meal."

"I wasn't the only one working in the

kitchen," Mama said with a shake of her head. "Our three oldest daughters worked plenty hard helping me, and Faith made several of the pies, which I'm sure will taste delicious."

Faith felt the heat of a blush cascade over her cheeks. She wasn't used to her mother offering such compliments, at least not directed at her. "After eating this big meal, maybe no one will have room for a taste of my pies," she mumbled.

"I'll eat a hunk of pie no matter how full I am." Brian grinned at Faith before helping himself to a piece of turkey from the platter being passed around.

"I believe you will," Papa said with a snicker, "and I'll be right behind you."

Faith began to relax. It felt good to be with her family for Christmas. She had spent too many lonely holidays before she'd met Greg, and after they were married, he'd never been much fun to be with on Christmas or any other day that should have been special. Greg was more interested in watching some sports event on TV or drinking himself into oblivion than he was in spending quality time with Faith. He never complimented Faith on anything—just pointed out all the things she'd done wrong. After Faith left Webster County to return to the stage, maybe she could plan her schedule so she would be free to come home for Christmas and other holidays.

As they continued to eat their meal, Faith found herself sharing a couple of jokes with her family. "You know, the way food prices are going up," she said, "soon it will be cheaper to eat the money."

Much to Faith's surprise, all her siblings laughed, and then, after Faith shared a couple more jokes, James's wife, Katie, jumped in by saying that she'd been on a garlic diet lately.

"How did that work?" Esther asked. "Did you lose any weight?"

Katie shook her head. "No, but I sure lost some friends."

Faith chuckled. She would have to remember that joke for one of her routines. It was surprising to see the way everyone seemed to enjoy all the corny jokes that had been told. Even Mama and Papa wore smiles. *It's probably not because of anything funny I said,* Faith thought regrettably. *More than likely, they're in good spirits because the whole family is together today.*

She glanced around the table at each family member, hoping to memorize their faces and knowing that if her folks didn't allow her to leave Melinda with them, this could very well be the last Christmas they would all spend together.

<hr />

Noah leaned back in his chair and patted his stomach. He'd eaten too much turkey, and now he had no room for the pumpkin or apple pies he had made. He slid his chair away from the table. "As soon as I'm done helping with the dishes, I think I'll go for a buggy ride. Anyone care to join me?"

"Not me." Pop leaned back in his chair and yawned noisily. "I'm going to the living room to rest my eyes for a bit."

"I'm kind of tired, too," Mom said. "After we're done with the dishes, I think I'd better take a nap."

"Jah, okay." Since none of Noah's brothers had been able to join them for dinner today, it was just him and his folks, so Noah figured he'd either have to go alone or simply take a nap, too. If only he felt comfortable with the idea of going over to see Faith today. But it wouldn't be right to barge in unannounced, knowing the Stutzmans had company. Besides, Faith might not want to be with him. She hadn't been all that friendly the last time he'd seen her, and he didn't want to do anything that might push her further away.

Noah reached for his jacket and headed out the door, determining once more that unless Faith had a change of heart about her relationship with God, the two of them could never be more than friends.

A short time later, Noah found himself on the road leading to Osborns' Christmas Tree Farm, and he directed the horse and buggy up the lane leading to Hank and Sandy's two-story house. He didn't see any cars parked out front except for Hank's, so he figured the Osborns probably didn't have company.

Noah tied his horse to the hitching rail near the barn, tromped through the snow, and as he stepped onto the front porch, Amos and Griggs bounded up, wagging their tails. He bent over and gave them both a couple of pats, then lifted his hand to knock, but the door opened before his knuckles connected with the wood.

"I heard your horse whinny," Hank said with a grin. "So I figured you'd be knocking on the door anytime."

Noah chuckled. "Just came by to say merry Christmas to you and Sandy."

"Merry Christmas to you, as well." Hank opened the door wider. "Come on in and have a piece of pumpkin pie and a cup of coffee with us."

"Are you sure? I'm not interrupting anything, am I?"

"No way." Hank motioned Noah inside, and the dogs slipped in, too.

"Sandy and I didn't go see her folks in Florida this year because they went on a cruise for the holidays. And my folks are spending Christmas with my brother in Montana this year, so we're just having a quiet Christmas alone," Hank said. His smile stretched from ear to ear, and Noah had to wonder what was going on. The last time he'd seen Hank and Sandy together, they were barely speaking.

"It's good to see you, Noah," Sandy said. "Merry Christmas." She was grinning pretty good, too.

"Merry Christmas," he responded.

"Drape your coat over a chair and have a seat." Hank motioned to the recliner across from the sofa where Sandy sat.

Noah did as Hank suggested, and Hank sat on the sofa next to his wife.

"Did you get everything you wanted for Christmas this year?" Hank asked, nodding at Noah.

"I guess so," Noah said with a shrug. The truth was, what he wanted most was a permanent relationship with Faith, but he figured that was nigh unto impossible.

The two beagles rested at Noah's feet, and absently, he bent over and began to rub their ears. "How about you and Sandy? Did you both get lots of presents?"

Hank draped his arm over Sandy's shoulder, and she looked at him with such a tender expression that it made Noah squirm. What he wouldn't give for Faith to look at him in that manner.

"Are you going to tell him or shall I?" Sandy asked, patting Hank's knee.

Hank's smile widened as he turned to face

Noah. "Sandy and I are going to adopt a baby."

"Really?"

Sandy nodded. "We had a long talk about it the other day and found out that there had been a misunderstanding."

"Oh?"

Hank nodded. "Yeah. I thought Sandy didn't want to adopt, and she thought the same of me, but once we talked it through, we discovered we both wanted the same thing."

"That's great. Really great." Noah stopped petting the dogs and leaned back in his chair as a vision of Faith flashed into his head. Was it possible that they both wanted the same thing? If he knew that Faith had the least bit of interest in him. . .

Noah gripped the arms of the chair as he came to his senses. Unless Faith got right with the Lord and joined the church, there was no way he could ever ask her to marry him.

Chapter 24

As Faith stood at her bedroom window one evening toward the end of December, she gazed at the carpet of snow below and thought about each family member. Christmas was only a pleasant memory, but Faith knew in the days ahead she would bask in the recollection of the wonderful time she had shared with her family—a family she would soon be telling good-bye. She'd be leaving friends like Noah and Barbara, too. Faith would miss everyone after she was gone—most of all Melinda.

So much for keeping emotional distance from family and friends. Faith grimaced as her thoughts spiraled further. She thought about the jokes she had shared with the family on Christmas Day and how surprised she'd been when they were well received. No matter how enjoyable the holidays had been, she was sure things would soon go back to the way they had been when she was a teenager. It was only a matter of time before her folks started reprimanding her for being too silly or started prodding her to take classes so she could get baptized and join the church. Worse than that, Faith had done something really stupid—she'd allowed herself to fall in love.

She gripped the window ledge so hard her fingers turned numb. *The time has come for me to leave Webster County, and nothing will stop me this time.*

When Faith awoke the following day, her throat felt scratchy. A pounding headache and achy body let her know she wasn't well.

Forcing herself out of bed, she lumbered over to the dresser. The vision that greeted her in the mirror caused her to gasp. Little pink blotches covered her face. She pushed up the sleeves of her flannel nightgown and groaned at the sight. "Oh no, it just can't be."

"What can't be?" Grace Ann asked, sticking her head through the open doorway of Faith's room.

Faith motioned her sister into the room. "Come look at me. I'm covered with little bumps."

Grace Ann's dark eyes grew huge as she

studied Faith. "It looks like you've got the chicken pox."

Faith turned toward the mirror and stuck out her tongue. It was bright red, and so was the back of her throat. "I thought I had the chicken pox when I was a child."

"Maybe not. You'd better check with Mama."

"Has anyone we know had the pox lately?"

Grace Ann nodded. "Philip's daughter, Sarah Jane, but she seemed well enough to travel so they brought her here for Christmas anyway." She shrugged. "Probably thought she was no longer contagious or that we'd all had them."

Faith slipped into her robe. "Guess I'd better go downstairs and have a talk with Mama."

"Want me to send her up? You look kind of peaked, so you might want to crawl back in bed."

The idea of going back to bed did sound appealing, but Faith had never given in to sickness before. All during her marriage to Greg, she'd performed even when she thought she might be coming down with a cold or the flu. She really had to be sick before she took to her bed.

A short time later, with a determined spirit, Faith made her way down the stairs. She found Mama, Grace Ann, and Esther in the kitchen getting breakfast started. The pungent odor of

Mama's strong coffee made Faith's stomach lurch, and she dropped into a seat at the table with a moan.

"Faith, do you want to make the toast this morning, or would you rather be in charge of squeezing oranges for juice?" Mama asked, apparently unaware of Faith's condition.

Faith could only groan in response.

"She isn't feeling well this morning, Mama," Grace Ann said as she stepped in front of Faith and laid a hand on her forehead. "She's got herself a fever, and from the looks of her arms and face, I'd say she's contracted a nasty case of chicken pox."

"Chicken pox?" Esther and Mama said in unison.

Mama hurried over to the table. "Let me have a look-see."

Faith lifted her face for her mother's inspection, and Mama's grimace told her all she needed to know. She had come down with the pox, and that meant she wouldn't be going anywhere for the next couple of weeks. Faith had to wonder if someone was trying to tell her something. If so, would she be willing to listen?

"Didn't I have the pox when I was a girl?"

"You were the only one of my kinner who didn't get it," Mama said. "I figured you must be immune to the disease."

Faith dropped her head to the table. "I can't believe this is happening to me now."

"What do you mean 'now'?" Grace Ann asked.

"Well, I had planned to. . ." Faith's voice trailed off. She was sick and wouldn't be going anywhere until her health returned, so there was no point revealing her plans just yet.

"Whatever plans you've made, they'll have to wait. You'd best get on back to bed," Mama instructed.

"Okay. Could someone please bring me a cup of tea?"

"One of your sisters will be right up," Mama called as Faith exited the room.

A short time later, Faith was snuggled beneath her covers with a cup of mint tea in her hands. If she weren't feeling so sick, it might have been nice to be pampered like this. Under the circumstances, though, Faith would sooner be outside chopping wood than stuck here in bed.

Faith spent the next several days in her room with one of her sisters or Mama waiting on her hand and foot. To Faith's amazement, Melinda didn't get sick. Maybe she was immune to the chicken pox, or maybe she would get them later. Either way, Faith was glad her precious child didn't have to suffer with the intense itching she'd been going through. It was enough to make her downright irritable.

One morning after the girls had left for school, Faith made her way down to the kitchen.

She felt better today and decided it might do her some good to be up awhile. She found her mother sitting at the kitchen table with a cup of tea and an open Bible. Mama looked up when Faith took the seat across from her. "You're up. Does that mean you're feeling better?"

"Some, although I have to keep reminding myself not to scratch the pockmarks." Faith helped herself to the pot of tea sitting in the center of the table. Several clean cups were stacked beside it, so she poured some tea into one and took a sip.

"Sure was a good Christmas we had this year, don't you think?" Mama asked.

Faith nodded. "It was a lot of fun."

"First time in years the whole family has been together."

Faith's breath caught in her throat. Was Mama going to give her a lecture about how she'd run away from home ten years ago and left a hole in the family? Was the pleasant camaraderie they'd shared here of late about to be shattered?

"You're awful quiet," Mama commented.

"Just thinking is all."

"About family?"

Instinctively Faith grasped the fingers on her right hand and popped two knuckles at the same time.

"Wish you wouldn't do that." Mama slowly shook her head. "It's a bad habit, and—"

Faith held up her hands. "I'm not a little girl anymore, and as you can see, my knuckles aren't big because I've popped them for so many years." As soon as Faith saw her mother's downcast eyes and wrinkled forehead, she wished she could take back her biting words. "Sorry. I didn't mean to be so testy."

Mama reached across the table and touched Faith's hand. "I did get after you a lot when you were a kinner, didn't I?"

Faith could only nod, for tears clogged her throat. She opened her mouth to tell Mama of her plans to leave again, but she stopped herself in time. Now was not the time to be telling her plans. She would wait until she was feeling better.

Faith took another sip of tea. "This sure hits the spot."

"Always did enjoy a good cup of tea on a cold winter morning." Mama touched her Bible. "Tea warms the stomach, but God's Word warms the soul."

Not knowing how to respond, Faith only nodded.

"Take this verse, for example," Mama continued. "Psalm 46:10 says, 'Be still, and know that I am God.' If that doesn't warm one's soul, I don't know what will."

Faith let the words sink in. *"Be still."* She'd been very still these past few days during her bout with the chicken pox. *"And know that I am God."*

She closed her eyes. *If You're real, God, then would You please reveal Your will to me?*

A knock on the door drew Faith's thoughts aside. Mama rose to her feet. "Must be someone come a-calling. Your daed and the boys are out in the barn, and they surely wouldn't be knocking, now would they?"

Faith watched the back door as her mother made her way across the room. When Mama opened it, a gust of cold wind blew in, followed by Noah Hertzler carrying a small wicker basket in one hand.

"Noah, what are you doing here?" Faith asked. "Shouldn't you be at work?"

He followed Mama over to the table. "Things are kind of slow at the Christmas tree farm right now, so Hank gave me and the other fellows a few days off. This is for you," he said, placing the basket in front of Faith. "I hope it will make you feel better."

"Aren't you worried about getting the chicken pox?" she asked. "I could still be contagious, you know."

He shook his head. "I had them already—when I was five years old."

"Oh, okay." Faith pulled the piece of cloth back and smiled when she saw a batch of frosted brownies nestled inside the basket. "Chocolate—my weakness. Thank you, Noah."

"You're welcome, and it's good to see you up." Noah pulled out a chair and sat down next to Faith. "The last couple of times I've dropped by, you've been in your room, too sick for visitors."

"Someone in the family has always delivered the goodies you brought me," she said.

Noah chuckled. "Sure glad to hear that. Knowing those brothers of yours, I wouldn't have been surprised to hear if John and Brian had helped themselves to some of the desserts."

"They did try," Mama cut in. She handed Noah a cup of tea. "Why don't you take off your jacket and stay awhile?"

"I think I will." Noah set the cup down on the table, slipped off his jacket, and draped it over the back of the chair.

"If you young people will excuse me, I have some laundry that needs to be done." Mama grabbed a couple of soiled hand towels off the metal rack by the sink and quickly left the room.

Faith had to wonder if her mother had left her alone with Noah on purpose. The comments she'd made lately about how much she liked Noah and how he would make a fine husband for some lucky woman made Faith think Mama and Barbara might be in cahoots.

"How come you didn't attach a scripture verse to any of the desserts you've given me lately?" Faith asked.

His face flamed. "I. . .uh. . .thought maybe I was getting too pushy. Didn't want you to think I was trying to cram the Bible down your throat."

Faith stared at the tablecloth. "Guess I probably have needed a bit of encouraging."

When Noah reached over and placed his hand on top of hers, she felt a warm tingle travel all the way up her arm. Not the kind that felt like fireworks, but a comfortable, cozy feeling. "I'm still praying for you, Faith," he said quietly. "Just thought you should know."

"I appreciate that because I need all the prayers I can get."

"Speaking of prayers. . ." Noah smiled. "I had one answered for me on Christmas Day."

Faith lifted her gaze. "What prayer was that?"

"I stopped to see Hank and Sandy to say merry Christmas, and they told me that they're planning to adopt a baby."

"That's wonderful. They seem to like children, so I'm sure they'll make good parents."

He nodded. "I think so, too."

Faith was happy for Hank and Sandy, but an ache settled over her heart when she thought about her own life. If she never married, she wouldn't have any more children, and Faith knew that once she left home and returned to the world of entertainment, the closeness she and Melinda had now would be diminished. Even so, returning to the world of entertainment was the only way she would ever find what she'd been longing for all these years.

Chapter 25

By the following week, Faith felt much better. The pockmarks had dried up, her sore throat and headache were gone, and her energy was nearly back to normal.

On Saturday morning after the kitchen chores were done, she decided to have that talk with Mama she'd been putting off far too long. Melinda and Susie were in the barn playing. Esther, Grace Ann, and Brian had gone to Seymour with Papa. John was over at his girlfriend's house. This was the perfect chance to speak with Mama alone. When that conversation was out of the way, she would do the hardest part—tell Melinda she was planning to leave.

Faith glanced over at her mother, who sat

in front of the treadle sewing machine in the kitchen. "Mama, before you get too involved with your sewing, I wondered if we could talk awhile."

Mama looked up at Faith. "Is this just a friendly little chitchat, or have you got something serious on your mind?"

"Why do you ask?"

"I figure if it's just going to be some easy banter, I'll keep sewing as we talk."

Faith leaned on the cupboard. "I'm afraid it's serious."

Mama slid her chair back and stood. "Shall we sit at the kitchen table, or would you rather go to the living room?"

"Let's go in there. We'll be less apt to be disturbed should the girls come inside before we're done talking."

Mama nodded, and Faith followed her into the next room. They both sat on the sofa in front of the fireplace. The heat from the flames licking at the logs did nothing to warm Faith. Goose bumps had erupted all over her arms.

"What's wrong, Faith? Are you cold?"

"No, I—"

"Why don't you run upstairs and get a sweater?"

Faith shook her head and rubbed her hands briskly over her arms. "I'll be okay as soon as I say what's on my mind."

"You look so solemn. What's this all about?"

"It—it's about me—and Melinda."

Mama leaned forward, and her glasses slipped down her nose. "What about you?"

"I. . .uh. . .plan to go back to my life as an entertainer, and I hope to be on a bus for Memphis by Monday morning to meet with the agent I've hired." There, it was out. Faith should have felt better, but she didn't. The sorrowful look on Mama's face was nearly her undoing.

"I knew it was too good to be true, you coming home and all." Mama squeezed her eyes shut, and when she opened them again, Faith noticed there were tears.

"I never meant to hurt you, Mama. I hope you know that."

"The only thing I know for sure is that my prodigal daughter finally returned home; only now she's about to leave again." Mama wrapped her arms around her middle, as though she were hugging herself. "No wonder you've put off baptism and joining the church. You've been planning this all along, haven't you?"

Faith nodded solemnly. "I would have told you sooner, but things kept getting in the way of my leaving."

Mama stood and moved toward the fireplace. "Why'd you come home if you were planning to leave?"

"I—I wanted to—"

"You were down on your luck and needed a

place to stay for a while, isn't that it?"

"No, it's not."

"You allowed us to get close to Melinda, and now you're taking her away?"

Faith jumped up and hurried to her mother's side. "I'd like Melinda to stay here if that's okay with you and Papa. She needs a home where she'll be well cared for and loved. It's not good for a child to be raised by a single parent who lives out of a suitcase and has no place to call home."

Mama turned to face Faith. The tears that had gathered in her eyes moments ago were now rolling down her cheeks. "Melinda can stay if that's your wish. But I'd like you to think long and hard about something before you go."

"What's that?"

"If Melinda needs a good home where she'll be loved and cared for, then what about her mamm? What's she needing these days?"

Faith nearly choked on the tears clogging her throat. She was afraid if she said one more word she would break down and sob. She had made her decision and felt certain it was the best thing for both her and Melinda.

"Oh, and one more thing. . ."

"What's that, Mama?"

"If you leave again, then you're not welcome to come home."

"But what about Melinda? I'll need to be with her for holidays and special occasions."

Mama shook her head vigorously. "If you go and Melinda stays, it wouldn't be good for her to have you showing up whenever you have a whim. It would only confuse the girl. Might make her want to go back to the English world with you."

Faith's mouth dropped open. She couldn't believe Mama was putting stipulations on leaving Melinda with them. The thought of never seeing her daughter again was almost too much to bear. Faith needed to think more about this. She had to spend some time alone and figure out what to do.

Giving no thought to the cold, she dashed out the front door and into the chilly morning air.

A few minutes later, a blast of warm air greeted her as she entered the barn. Papa had obviously stoked up the stove before he and the others left for Seymour.

Figuring Melinda and Susie were probably on the other side of the barn, Faith headed in that direction. She came to a halt when she heard her daughter's sweet voice singing and yodeling.

Surprised by the sound, Faith tiptoed across the wooden floor until she spotted Melinda. The child knelt in the hay with three black-and-white kittens curled in her lap. Susie sat off to one side, holding two other kittens.

"Oddle—lay—oddle—lay—oddle—lay—

dee—tee—my mama was an old cowhand, and she taught me how to yodel before I could stand. Yo—le—tee—yo—le—tee—hi—ho!"

Faith sucked in her breath. She had no idea Melinda could yodel or that she knew the cute little song Faith had sung so many times onstage. Apparently the child had been listening whenever Faith practiced. Melinda actually had some of the yodeling skills mastered quite well.

When Melinda finished her song, she looked over at Susie and smiled. "When I grow up, I'm gonna be just like my mamm. I'll travel around the country, singing, telling jokes, and yodeling. Oh—lee—dee—tee—tee—oh!"

Faith's heart sank all the way to her toes. She'd never dreamed Melinda was entertaining such thoughts. She'd been so sure the child was settling in here and would grow up happy and content to be Amish.

The way you were? a little voice in her head asked. Faith wanted better things for her daughter than to spend the rest of her life traipsing all over the countryside, hoping to succeed in the world of music or comedy and seeking after riches and fame.

Feeling as though she'd been struck by a bolt of lightning, Faith realized those were the very things she had spent ten years of her life trying to accomplish. She wasn't rich. She wasn't famous. Had any of it brought her true happiness? Traveling from town to town, performing at one theater after another was a lonely existence. At least for Faith it had been. Being married to Greg hadn't given Faith the fulfillment she'd been searching for, either. Their tumultuous marriage had only furthered her frustrations.

I brought it on myself by marrying an unbeliever. Faith remembered what the Bible said about being unequally yoked with unbelievers. Of course, she hadn't exactly been living the life of a believer during her entertaining years.

She blinked back the tears threatening to spill over. *It's just as Mama said—the very thing I've been wanting for Melinda is exactly what I need. How could I have been so blind? I don't need fame or fortune. I've been selfish, always wanting my own way. My truest desire is fellowship with good friends, the love of a caring family, and a close relationship with God.*

Faith knew without a shadow of a doubt that if Melinda was ever to settle completely into the Amish way of life, she must see by her mother's example that it was a good life. Faith would need to stay in Webster County. It was either that or say good-bye to Melinda and spend the rest of her life wishing she had stayed.

But do I have enough faith in God to live by His rules? Staying Amish would never work unless she strengthened her faith. She must rely wholly on the Lord to meet her needs. No amount of money or recognition could fill the void in a person's heart the way Jesus' love did. The scripture verses Noah had shared over the last few months had told her that much.

It's time to come home, Faith.

She leaned against the wooden beam closest to her and closed her eyes. *Heavenly Father, I need Your help. I know now that I want to remain here with my people, and I want to draw closer to You. Forgive my sins, and please give me wisdom in raising my daughter so she will want to serve You and not seek after the things in this world.*

When Faith opened her eyes, Melinda and Susie were gone. They'd apparently left the barn, seeking out new pleasures found only on a farm. The kittens were with their mother again, just as Faith's child would be with her in the days ahead.

Faith left the barn and found the girls playing in the snow. On impulse, she scooped up a handful of the powdery stuff and gave it a toss. It hit the mark and landed squarely on Melinda's arm.

The child squealed with laughter and retaliated. Her aim wasn't as good as Faith's, and the snowball ended up on Faith's foot. She laughed and grabbed another clump of snow. For the next half hour, she, Melinda, and Susie frolicked in the snow, laughing, making snow angels, and yodeling. Faith hadn't had this much fun since she was a young child.

When it got too cold, Faith suggested they go inside for a cup of hot chocolate and some of the frosted brownies Noah had brought over. The children were quick to agree, and soon they were all seated at the kitchen table.

Melinda took a bite of brownie and smacked her lips. "Noah sure does bake good, don't ya think?"

"Jah, he does."

"I really like him, don't you, Mama?"

Faith nodded.

"I think I'd like to have Noah for my new *daadi*."

"When and if the Lord wants you to have a new daddy, He will let us know."

Melinda's forehead wrinkled. "I'm wondering if my daadi went away so Noah could come."

"Oh Melinda, you shouldn't be talking that way."

"Why not?"

"Jah, Faith. Why not?" Susie chimed in.

A vision of Noah's face popped into Faith's mind. She did care for him, but was that enough? Could she trust him not to hurt her the way Greg had? Did Noah care about her in any way other than friendship? There were so many unanswered questions.

For a while, Faith had thought Noah might have some romantic interest in her, but here of late, he'd pulled back. She figured he must have some reservations about becoming involved with a woman who didn't share his strong faith in God. Or maybe it was their age difference that bothered him.

Faith shook her head, trying to clear away the troubling thoughts. From what she'd come to know about Noah, she doubted he would see the few years between them as a problem. It was probably her lack of faith that concerned him the most. As tears clogged her throat, she reached over and pulled Melinda into her arms.

"What's wrong, Mama? How come you're crying?"

"Mine are the good kind of tears. Tears of joy."

"What are you so happy about?" Susie questioned.

Faith hugged both little girls. "I'm thankful to God for giving me you two. I'm also happy to be back here in Webster County, and this is where I plan to stay." She turned toward the living room. "Now I must speak to Grandma Stutzman. She needs to know what I've decided."

Chapter 26

As Wilma sat in her favorite chair, rocking back and forth with her eyes closed, she thought about her conversation with Faith and grieved over the thought of her oldest daughter leaving home again. Wasn't it bad enough that Faith had left home once? Did she have to put her family through that horrible pain again? And what of Melinda? How did Faith think her daughter would understand her own mother leaving her with grandparents she barely knew while she went out into the world to seek her fortune and fame?

Father in heaven, she silently prayed, *please show me what I might say or do to persuade Faith to stay. I know I'm not the perfect mother, but I love my daughter and can't bear to think of her going away again.*

A chill shot through Wilma's body as she realized for the first time what her part had been in driving Faith away. If she'd only been more accepting when Faith wanted to tell silly jokes and yodel, the girl might never have left home in the first place.

I need to apologize—make things right between us. Even if Faith does leave home again, I can't let her go with bad feelings between us.

Wilma's eyes snapped open when she heard the floorboards creak, and she blinked a couple of times when she saw Faith standing near the front door. "What are you doing here?" she croaked. "I thought you'd gone outside to tell Melinda that you'll be leaving soon."

"I—I did see Melinda."

"How'd she take the news? Does she want to stay here with us or go away with you?"

"Melinda will be staying here."

A sense of relief flooded Wilma's soul. At least they wouldn't be losing their granddaughter. "I'm glad she won't be leaving. I've come to care a great deal for that child," she said, choking back the tears clogging her throat. "And I want you to know that—" Wilma's voice caught on a sob. She needed to tell Faith what was on her mind, but she couldn't seem to get the words out.

Faith took a seat on one end of the sofa as she shook her head. "I didn't tell Melinda my plans because I've changed my mind. I won't be leaving Webster County, after all."

Wilma's mouth dropped open. "You won't?"

"No, I've decided that my place is here—with Melinda and my family."

Wilma let Faith's words sink in. Finally, she stood and rushed to the sofa, where she dropped to her knees and hugged her daughter tightly. Tears of joy burst forth and dribbled onto her cheeks. "Oh, thank the Lord. This is such an answer to prayer."

Faith nodded and leaned her head on Wilma's shoulder, as her own tears wet Wilma's dress.

"I should've been more understanding. Maybe if I'd taken time to enjoy your humor and had looked for the good in you, things would have gone better," Wilma murmured.

Tears rolled down Faith's cheeks, and she shuddered. "You might feel bad for driving me away, but Papa sure doesn't. In all the time I've been home, he's never once said he was glad I came back or that he hoped I would stay." She shook her head. "I'm sure he would never take any of the blame for me leaving, but to be honest, I know it's as much my fault as it was yours and Papa's."

"What do you mean?" Mama asked.

"It was selfish of me to want my own way and desire recognition for talents." Faith sniffed deeply. "I'm sorry for all I put you and Papa through when I left home."

Wilma stroked Faith's back as they held each other and wept.

"Your mamm and I are both at fault for you leaving."

Faith's head came up as Menno stepped into the room and placed his hand on her shoulder. "Papa," she murmured. "I—I didn't know you'd come in. I'm so sorry for everything I put you and Mama through. Can you ever forgive me?"

He nodded slowly. "I owe you an apology, too, daughter. I should have been more accepting of your jokes and even your frog-croaking yodeling."

Faith laughed, hiccupped, and then started to cry again.

"I promise you that I'm going to be more accepting from now on," Menno said as he pulled Faith to her feet and gave her a hug.

"And I'll try not to act silly at inopportune times," she said between sniffs.

Wilma reached for a tissue from the box on the table near the sofa and handed it to Faith. "So Melinda doesn't know you were planning to leave?"

Faith shook her head. "I saw no reason to tell her since I'll be staying."

"You're right. You're right. There's no reason for her to know. It might upset her even though you're not leaving after all," Menno said.

"Jah, I agree." Faith nodded. "God has shown me that my place is here."

The next day during church, Noah couldn't help noticing Faith, who sat across the room on the women's side. Something about her expectant expression made him wonder what was going on with her. She sat up straighter than usual and seemed to be listening to everything Bishop Martin said. Every once in a while, she blew her nose or dabbed the corners of her eyes with her handkerchief. Noah couldn't wait for the service to end so he could talk to her.

When church was over, tables were set up in the barn for the men and boys to eat their meal. Noah was disappointed when Faith wasn't one of the servers at his table, but he hoped he would get the chance to speak with her after he ate.

He hurried through the meal and was about to head for the house, when his father showed up saying Mom had taken ill.

"Sorry to hear that," Noah said. "Is her blood sugar out of whack?"

Pop shrugged. "I'm not sure. She's feeling weak and shaky, so it could just be the flu, but I think it would be best if we went home now."

Since Noah had ridden to church with his folks that morning, he felt he had no choice but to leave when they did. "Okay, Pop," he said with a nod. "I'll get the horse hitched to our buggy right away."

As Noah headed toward the corral, he spotted Faith talking to Barbara Zook on the front porch. He started that way, thinking he would at least say hello, but halted when he heard Barbara say, "What's that big smile all about, Faith?"

"I'm smiling because I'm so happy," Faith replied.

"Happy about what?"

"Well, I've been planning to leave Webster County for some time—ever since I brought Melinda here, and—"

Faith's voice was drowned out when Barbara's two boys dashed up, hollering that they wanted to play ball but the older boys wouldn't let them join the game.

"Noah, have you got the horse yet?" Pop called out. "Your mamm's feeling really light-headed."

"I'm coming, Pop." With a heavy heart, Noah moved on to the corral. He'd feared the day would come when Faith would leave Webster County, and he had been a fool to allow himself to fall in love with her. If only he could do something to make her stay. He didn't understand why God hadn't answered his prayers concerning Faith, but he knew it wasn't for him to question God's ways.

"I'm sorry for the interruption," Barbara said to Faith once she'd gotten her boys calmed down and sent them inside to get a piece of cake. "Now what was that you were saying?"

"I've been planning to leave Webster County ever since I brought Melinda here."

Barbara's heart began to pound. "You're going to leave again?"

"Oh no. I had planned to go back on the road and leave Melinda with my folks so she would be raised in a stable home and not have to be hauled around the country while I entertained." Faith shook her head. "But I changed my mind—or I should say that God changed it for me."

"What happened?" Barbara questioned. "Why did you change your mind?"

"I heard Melinda talking to Susie about growing up to be an entertainer someday, and I realized that I didn't want that for my girl. I knew in my heart, and have known it for some time, that what I really wanted was here all the time—my family and friends."

"Oh Faith, I'm so glad to hear that." Barbara wrapped her arms around Faith and gave her a squeeze. "Jah, I truly am."

Faith touched her chest. "I've changed, Barbara. God's changed me from the inside out, and for the first time, being in church today seemed so right to me. I've finally come to realize how much I need my family—and most of all, how much I need God."

Chapter 27

Since his mother's bout with the flu had gone on for several days and had affected her blood sugar, Noah had gone straight home after work to cook, clean, and help his father with some of the outside chores. But Mom was doing better today, and since it was Saturday and Noah didn't have to work at the tree farm, he decided to head over to the Stutzmans' and have a talk with Faith while Mom took an afternoon nap. Pop was visiting his friend Vernon, the buggy maker, so it would be the perfect time for Noah to slip away. He'd been praying about things and had decided that, before Faith left Webster County, he needed to be honest with her about the way he felt. He just hoped he wasn't too late.

As Noah hitched his horse to one of their open buggies and climbed into the driver's seat, he prayed for the right words to say to Faith and for God's will to be done.

Noah directed the horse down the driveway and drew in a deep breath. It was a fine winter afternoon, and even though the air was frosty and several inches of snow covered the ground, the sky was blue and clear.

Noah glanced at the cake sitting on the seat beside him. He remembered the conversation he'd heard Faith and Barbara having after church last Sunday and hoped with all his heart that he would find Faith at home and that they would be given the chance to talk in private. The words he had in his heart were for her ears alone.

❦

Faith couldn't believe she and Melinda had the whole house to themselves. Her folks had gone to Seymour for the day, and they'd taken Grace Ann, Esther, and Susie with them. John and Brian were over at their friend Andy's house, so it was a good opportunity for Faith to work on her baking skills.

She'd thought Melinda might enjoy helping her make a lemon sponge cake, but the child had acted sleepy after eating their noon meal and had gone to the living room to take a nap on the sofa.

"It's probably just as well," Faith murmured as she got out the ingredients. Melinda had stayed up later than usual last night, and Faith figured a nap would do the child more good than playing in dusty flour and lemon juice.

If the cake turned out well, Faith planned to give it to Noah. He had given her so many special treats over the last few months; it was the least she could do to reciprocate. He'd been kind in other ways, too—helping out when it was needed and sharing God's Word with her on several occasions.

Faith was sure those scripture verses had taken root in her soul, but it wasn't until the day she'd discovered Melinda yodeling in the barn that she'd really given her heart to Jesus.

As Faith mixed the cake, she smiled at the remembrance of telling her folks she had changed her mind about leaving and how they'd responded. Everything was better at home now, but she still had some unfinished business with Noah.

Faith halted her thoughts and focused on putting the cake together, but when it was ready to bake, she discovered that the oven wasn't hot enough. During the summer months, the Stutzmans used their propane-operated stove, but in the wintertime, Mama insisted on the wood-burning stove because it gave off more heat that circulated throughout much of the house.

Faith slipped the cake pan onto the oven rack and opened the firebox door. Then she grabbed two pieces of wood from the wood box and tossed them in. One of the burning logs inside the stove rolled out and landed on the floor.

Faith gasped as she watched the braided throw rug ignite and flames shoot out in every direction. She'd never dealt with a situation like this and wasn't sure what to do. She ran to the sink, filled a jug with water, and flung it on the burning rug. Then she opened the back door and kicked the rug with the hunk of wood outside. By this time, the room was filled with smoke.

"Melinda!" Faith shouted. She rushed into the living room, scooped Melinda off the sofa, and bounded out the door into the frosty afternoon air.

By this time, Melinda was wide awake. "Mama, what's going on? Why are we outside with no coats?"

Faith seated her daughter on a bench at the picnic table and drew in a deep breath to steady her nerves.

"I caught the rug in the kitchen on fire, and I need to get the smoke out of the room. You stay here, and I'll be right back."

"Mama, where are you going?"

"Just stay put!"

When Noah pulled into the Stutzmans' driveway, his heart gave a lurch. Melinda sat at the picnic table with her arms wrapped tightly around her middle. What was Faith thinking, letting her daughter play out in the cold with no coat?

He grabbed the lemon sponge cake, hopped down from the buggy, and was heading for Melinda when he noticed a chunk of smoldering wood and what looked like the remains of a throw rug lying in the snow several feet from the house.

Melinda jumped up and raced over to Noah. "It's good you're here. I'm worried about Mama."

Noah's heart began to pound, and then he saw it—smoke drifting out the back door of the Stutzmans' home. "Where is everyone, Melinda? Where's the rest of your family?"

"Everyone except for me and Mama are gone today." The child pointed toward the house, her lower lip quivering like a leaf blowing in the breeze. "Mama's in there."

The reality of what the smoldering log and burned throw rug meant caused Noah to shudder. "Stay here, Melinda." He handed her the cake. "I'm going inside to help your mamm."

Noah took the steps two at a time, and when he bounded into the smoke-filled kitchen, he was thankful he saw no flames. "Faith! Where are you?"

Through the haze of smoke, Noah noticed a moving shadow, and he reached for it. What he got was a wet towel slapped against his arm. "Hey! What's going on?"

"Noah, is that you?" Faith stepped through the stifling haze, waving the towel in front of her.

Relieved to see that Faith was all right and with barely a thought for what he was doing, Noah grabbed her around the waist. "Are you okay? What happened in here?"

Faith coughed several times. "I was trying to bake, and the oven wasn't hot enough. When I opened the firebox, a log rolled out and caught the rug on fire." She leaned on him as though she needed support.

Noah's heart clenched at the thought of what could have happened if Faith hadn't thought quickly enough. The whole house might have burned to the ground, the way Pop's barn had when it was struck by lightning.

"Melinda told me that you're the only ones at home today," he said, stroking Faith's trembling shoulders.

She coughed again and pulled slowly away, leaving him with a sense of disappointment. "That's right, and I was trying to bake you a lemon sponge cake." Her voice quavered, and she gasped. "Oh no! My cake! It must be burned to a crisp."

She jerked the oven door open and withdrew the cake. Even in the smoky room, Noah could see it was ruined.

Faith groaned and set the blackened dessert on the counter. "I can't believe what a mess I've made of things. It seems I can never do anything right."

"It's okay," he said. "It's the thought that counts. Besides, I brought you a lemon sponge cake I made this morning. I left it outside with Melinda." Now it was Noah's turn to cough. Between the firebox being left open and the burned cake, the smoke was dense, and he was worried about Faith breathing in the fumes. "We need to get this room cleared out. Let's open some windows and head outside."

Soon they had the doors and windows open, and Noah took Melinda and Faith to the barn, where it was warmer. He noticed Faith's eyes brimming with tears and wondered if it was from the acrid smoke or because she was upset over the frightening incident. *Probably a little of both,* he decided.

Relief flooded his soul as he stared down at Faith, sitting beside her daughter on a bale of straw with a horse blanket draped over their shoulders. His chest rose and fell in a deep sigh as he fought the temptation to kiss her.

❦

From the look of desire Faith saw in Noah's dark eyes, she was fairly certain he wanted to kiss her. She leaned forward slightly, inviting him to do so, but to her disappointment, he moved away. Had she misread his intentions? This was the man she had come to love. She could hardly bear the thought that he might not love her in return.

"Mama, I'm warmed up now. Can I play with the kittens?" Melinda asked, pulling Faith's thoughts aside.

Faith nodded. "Jah, sure, go ahead."

Melinda scampered off toward the pile of hay across the room where a mother cat and five fluffy kittens were sleeping.

Faith looked up at Noah and rubbed her hands briskly over her arms as she tried to calm her racing heart. "I could have burned the house down today, but the Lord was watching out for me—for all of us really."

"I believe you're right about that, but I'm surprised to hear you say so."

"I'm not an unbeliever, Noah," she murmured. "I recently asked God to forgive my sins, and I believe He will strengthen my faith as time goes on."

A slow smile spread across Noah's face. "Really, Faith?"

She nodded.

"That's *wunderbaar*." His smile faded.

"What's wrong?"

"I heard you were planning to leave Webster County, and the reason I came here was to try and talk you out of going."

"I'm not leaving," she said with a catch in her voice.

"But I heard you tell Barbara you were."

She nodded soberly. "I was, until God changed my mind."

"I've suspected for some time that you were thinking about going, but I was afraid if I said too much or pushed too hard it might drive you further from God—and me."

Faith dropped her gaze to the floor. "From the beginning, I'd planned to leave Melinda with my folks and head back on the road again."

"You were gonna leave me here?"

Faith spun around at the sound of her daughter's voice. She hadn't realized Melinda had returned. What had she been thinking? She hadn't wanted Melinda to know.

She swept the child into her arms. "I'm so sorry. I thought it would be best for you, but God kept causing things to happen so I'd have to stay put."

Melinda sniffed deeply. "You're not leaving then?"

"No, I'm certainly not. My place is here with you."

"And you won't be telling jokes and yodeling no more?"

Before Faith had a chance to answer, Noah cut in. "I think it would be fine if your mamm told funny stories and jokes right here with her family, don't you?"

Melinda nodded and swiped at the tears rolling down her cheeks. "Will you still be able to yodel, Mama? I love it when you do, and I want to yodel, too."

Faith smiled through her tears. "Most folks in our community don't see yodeling as wrong, but I probably won't do it when Grandpa Stutzman's around. He says it bothers his ears."

Noah chuckled and motioned to Faith. "Well, he's not here now, so why don't you do a little yodeling for your own private audience?"

Faith squeezed Melinda's hand. "How about if you help me yodel?"

Melinda leaned her head back and opened her mouth. "Oh—lee—dee-ee—oh—lee—dee—tee!"

Noah did his best to join them, but he finally gave up. Suddenly, his expression turned serious, and Faith wondered if something was wrong.

"What is it, Noah?"

He leaned over and looked deeply into her eyes. "I love you, Faith Andrews, and if you think you could learn to love me, I'd like the chance to court you."

Melinda jumped up and down. "Yippee! I knew it!"

Faith swallowed and squeezed her eyes shut. "Oh Noah, I don't have to *learn* to love you, for I already do. Thanks to God's love and to Him showing me what's really important, I know I can have the best of both worlds—the love of a wonderful man; my family and friends; and most of all, a closeness to my heavenly Father that I've never had before."

Epilogue

Two years later

Faith brushed Noah's arm with her elbow as she squeezed past him to get to the stove. Two more lemon sponge cakes were ready to take from the oven. These would be given to Barbara and David Zook in honor of their son, Zachary, who had been born the week before.

"I can't believe we've been doing this for almost two years," Noah said as he nuzzled Faith's neck with the tip of his nose.

Faith glanced down at the floor, where their one-year-old son, Isaiah, was being entertained by his big sister, Melinda. "God has been good and blessed our marriage," she said.

"That's so true."

"What scripture verse have you decided to use?"

"I was thinking maybe Luke 16:10: 'He that is faithful in that which is least is faithful also in much.'"

"Sounds like a good one." Faith grabbed a pen and paper off the counter. "I think I'll add a couple of funny quips on one side, and you can put the Bible verse on the other."

Noah nodded. "We make a good team, *fraa*. I'm sure glad you decided to marry me."

Faith wrapped her arms around Noah's neck and kissed his cheek. A few tears slipped under her lashes and splashed onto Noah's blue cotton shirt. "I thank the Lord for bringing me back here to Webster County. Home is where my heart is. Home is where I belong."

NOAH'S LEMON SPONGE CAKE

Ingredients:
- 1 cup sifted cake flour
- 1 teaspoon baking powder
- ½ teaspoon salt
- ½ cup cold water
- 2 teaspoons grated lemon rind
- 2 egg yolks, beaten
- ¾ cup plus 2 tablespoons sugar
- 2 eggs whites, beaten
- 1 teaspoon lemon juice

Preheat oven to 350°. Sift the flour, baking powder, and salt together four times. In a separate bowl, add the water and lemon rind to the egg yolks and beat them until they are lemon-colored. Add ¾ cup of sugar a little at a time, beating after each addition. Then add the sifted ingredients, slowly stirring to blend them in. In a separate bowl, beat the eggs whites until they form peaks, then add the lemon juice and 2 tablespoons of sugar, beating until they are well blended. Fold this mixture into the rest of the batter, and pour into an ungreased tube pan. Bake for 1 hour. Remove from oven. Turn pan upside down with tube over the neck of a funnel or bottle. Cool thoroughly; remove from pan.

ABOUT THE AUTHOR

New York Times bestselling author, Wanda E. Brunstetter became fascinated with the Amish way of life when she first visited her husband's Mennonite relatives living in Pennsylvania. Wanda and her husband, Richard, live in Washington State but take every opportunity to visit Amish settlements throughout the States, where they have many Amish friends.

Let's Keep In Touch!

Want to know what Wanda's up to and be the first to hear about new releases, specials, the latest news, and more? Like Wanda on Facebook!

 Visit facebook.com/WandaBrunstetterFans